TANYA ANNE CROSBY

LYON'S GIFT

An Avon Romantic Treasure

AVON BOOKS NEW YORK

This is a work of fiction. Names, characters, places, and incidents either are the product of the author's imagination or are used fictitiously. Any resemblance to actual events, locales, organizations, or persons, living or dead, is entirely coincidental and beyond the intent of either the author or the publisher.

AVON BOOKS
A division of
The Hearst Corporation
1350 Avenue of the Americas
New York, New York 10019

Copyright © 1997 by Tanya Anne Crosby
Inside cover author photo by Clay Heatley
Published by arrangement with the author
Visit our website at http://AvonBooks.com
Library of Congress Catalog Card Number: 96-95163
ISBN: 0-380-78571-4

First Avon Books Printing: June 1997

AVON TRADEMARK REG. U.S. PAT. OFF. AND IN OTHER COUNTRIES, MARCA REGISTRADA, HECHO EN U.S.A.

Printed in the U.S.A.

RAI 10 9 8 7 6 5 4 3 2 1

LYON'S PRIDE

Piers de Montgomerie, known as "Lyon" for his fierceness in combat, accepts the challenge of the Scottish king, agreeing to quell a troublesome highland feud and to accept the disputed lands as payment. But his battle skills are no match for the flashing eyes and barbed tongue of "Mad" Meghan Brodie— the spirited wench he now holds hostage, who fires his blood with her heart-stirring beauty.

LYON'S GIFT

Distrustful of men and feigning madness, in truth Meghan is cunning as a fox—and far too loyal to her clan to be swayed by her arrogant captor's honeyed words and virile charms. She will make the Lyon pay dearly for the "gift" he has so brazenly stolen— even as her own traitorous heart begs her to surrender gladly to the one great love that can heal an injured land.

Prologue

The forest had always been their sanctuary.

Meghan and her grandmother had spent many a morn in the dimness of the woodland, gathering herbs for her grandmother's potions. Just now they were searching for sweetbriar upon MacLean land, and Meghan was on her hands and knees, crawling across the ground at the forest's edge, painstakingly inspecting the foliage.

They were not supposed to be here, she knew, as old man MacLean was like to be angry to discover them once more upon his land. Last time he had accused her grandminnie of poaching, though there had not been a whit of evidence in their sack. All they had borne away with them that day was weeds and little more. He did not know her grandmother at all if he thought she would do such a thing; her grandminnie would not eat an animal's meat if she chanced to look the creature beforehand in the eyes.

1

"Ye dinna ha' tae look sae carefully, Meghan!" her grandminnie told her. " 'Tis no' sae wee a plant, child—more a shrub!"

"Yes, I knoo, Grandminnie, and ye told me tae look for the pink flowers, too. I'm looking, but I dinna see them anywhere!"

"Och, lass! That is because ye're crawling on yer belly like a bluidy viper! Get yerself up before ye grind the dirt intae yer sweet knees!"

Meghan peered back at her grandmother over her shoulder, watching her an instant. The old woman was hunched over, scanning the plants, murmuring to herself as she scrutinized each one. Every so oft she would bend to pluck a sample and then crush it between her fingers.

"Be careful wi' the thorns," her grandminnie said absently as she inspected a small branch of some plant.

"I will!" Meghan said, wishing her grandminnie wouldn't treat her like a bairn. She was all of eight summers after all, and not nearly so little anymore.

Her grandmother, oblivious to her complaint, began to sing and dance.

> *"Wretched mon, why art thou proud,*
> *That art of earth made?*
> *Hide no' behind yer shroud!*
> *But fore thou came naked!"*

Meghan giggled at the sight of her, dancing so lively, and felt warmed by her joy.

"Ta ta dum, da dum, da dum," her grandmother hummed.

Meghan made to rise, except that in that instant, she spotted a face peering out at her from behind a wide oak. She gave a startled blink, but made not a sound as the face was just about the size of her own, and the eyes were wide and full with fright. They were visible just an instant, and then they were gone, vanished behind the tree.

Her grandmother carried on.

> *"When thy soul ha' journeyed oot,*
> *Thy body wi' the earth covered o'er!*
> *That body that was sae haughty and loud*
> *Of all men is hated!*
> *Ta dum dee dum, dee dum!*

"Meghan!" she called out suddenly.

"Aye," Meghan answered, turning to peer over her shoulder to see if her grandminnie had noticed the face as well.

"Dinna ye ever let a handsome smile turn yer head and woo yer heart, d' ye hear me, lass?"

"Aye, Grandminnie," she replied.

"Ye knoo that Adam took that apple upon his own, d' ye no'? Bluidy knave blamed it upon Eve only because he didna ha' the nuts tae take the burden upon his own!"

Meghan had heard this tale more times than she could count.

"It serves him right that Eve shoved that apple down his cowardly throat and that he bears it still!"

"Aye," Meghan answered absently, and crawled closer to the tree, her heart pounding within her breast. The face did not peek around again, even when she'd reached the trunk, and she was sorely afraid that they'd scared her off. Holding her breath, she craned her head around the trunk, and gasped at the sight of a wide pair of eyes as green as her own staring back.

"Oh!" Meghan exclaimed. "Ye are there! I feared ye'd run awa'!"

The little girl said nothing, merely stared at Meghan and cast nervous glances over Meghan's shoulder at her grandminnie carrying on so behind her. Meghan turned and appraised her grandmother an instant, seeing her through another's eyes, and frowned. Her grandmother suddenly fell to the ground upon her knees, cackling in delight at some discovery she made there, and Meghan winced at the sight she presented.

"She'llna hurt ye, I promise," she swore, turning back to the little girl. "She's no' really mad, she's just my grandminnie."

The little girl's face was frozen in an expression of doubt and her eyes shifted once more to Meghan's grandminnie.

"Och, Meghan!" her grandminnie said, "I believe I ha' discovered something here!"

The little girl's eyes widened in sudden fear.

"Dinna worry," Meghan said, understanding her alarm. "I willna tell her ye are here." Meghan smiled at the little girl and then called out, "What, Grandminnie?"

"Touch-me-nots!" her grandmother declared.

Meghan loved the delight with which her grandmother embraced all things great and small.

"What is it guid for?" Meghan asked her, trying to keep her attention from turning to their unexpected guest.

"No' a bluidy thing!" her grandmother said and cackled. "Have ye ever seen such a thing, Meghan?"

"Nay, mum," Meghan answered, glancing again at her grandmother who was now lying upon her belly on the bracken of the woodland floor. And she would have Meghan get up off her knees? Meghan rolled her eyes.

"Ye touch the bluidy little buggers and the pods burst wi' wee seeds!" Meghan watched her poke her finger at a few, and then listened to her laugh uproariously at the outcome.

"I am Meghan," she said, turning back to the little girl. "What is yer name?"

"Alison," the little girl answered quietly, still staring at the cackling old woman.

"We are looking for sweetbriar," Meghan told her.

"For what?" Alison whispered.

Meghan shrugged. "I dunno," she whispered back. "My grandminnie, she makes these potions." And then she winced at how her disclosure sounded.

"Tae turn people intae toads?" the little girl asked with no small measure of concern.

"Och! Nay!" Meghan said. "Grandminnie Fia wouldna do such a thing! I ha' never once seen her turn anyone intae a toad," she swore. "Though I ha' heard her call my brother Leith a frog."

The little girl tilted her head, looking as though she wanted to believe Meghan. "She wouldna?"

" 'Course no'!"

The two of them sat peering at each other a long instant, and Meghan wondered if she dared ask.

"Do ye wanna be my friend?" she whispered to the little girl. "I ha' never had a friend sae little as ye!"

The little girl suddenly seemed to forget her grandmother and her fear. "I am no' sae much more little than ye! Ye are no' sae verra big!"

Meghan grinned. "Nah," she agreed. "But I ha' never had a friend 'cept for my grandminnie."

"Meghan!" her grandmother said. "D' ye hear them, child?"

"Hear who?" Meghan asked, and Alison retreated behind the tree once more.

"The woodland sprites! I think they are

speakin' tae me, lass, but I canna be certain. Di' ye nae hear them?"

"I heard naught!" Meghan called back, and peered around the tree again. "She will no' hurt ye, Alison. I swear it upon our friendship."

"I didna say we would be friends!" Alison hurried to say. "My da willna let me play aboot the auld wi—yer grandminnie," she amended.

Meghan's face fell, her hopes dashed.

"But I can sneak awa'," Alison offered a little hesitantly. "If ye will too?"

Meghan thought about it less than an instant, hungry as she was for a friend her own age. "I will," she promised. "Sae then we are friends?"

"Aye," Alison said, and smiled.

"Are ye certain ye dinna hear them, Meghan?" her grandmother asked, cocking her head to listen. "I knoo I do! Listen noo."

"I'm listening, Grandminnie!" Meghan said, and turned again to her newfound friend. "I must gae and help her noo, as she needs me, but shall we play in the meadow this noon?"

"Aye," Alison agreed, and smiled again. "I shall meet ye there by the cairn."

"Verra well, then."

"But come alone," Alison urged her.

"O' course I shall," Meghan promised. "Ye will love my grandminnie when ye knoo her, but until ye wish tae meet her I will come alone."

Alison nodded.

"Gae then," Meghan urged her, "before she comes tae find me."

Alison nodded again, and didn't tarry any longer. She cast a glance at Meghan's grandmother and then leapt up and hurried away.

Meghan watched her go, and felt as great a burst of joy at her own discovery as her grandmother certainly had with hers. And then she turned toward the old woman to see what she had uncovered.

She crawled to where her grandmother lay, and sprawled beside her upon the ground. The two of them completely forgot about searching for herbs as they played with the little yellow flowers and green pods, poking at them and watching them explode, giggling together there upon the forest floor.

It was very, very nice to have such a sweet grandminnie, Meghan thought. But it was a special, special day for she had also made herself a friend.

Chapter 1

"Twenty-seven!" Baldwin announced, marching into the room where Piers sat poring over his survey.

It was a lesson Piers had taken from old King William: one could scarcely rule a land unless one knew what one held to rule. He'd followed William the Conqueror's example, and the first thing he'd done upon receiving this fief was to survey his holdings, meager though they might be. And it was a good thing, as it seemed his stock was dwindling quickly. He might never have known until they'd been seriously depleted.

Thieving, conniving Scots.

"Twenty-seven!" he exclaimed. Christ, but he didn't know whether to be angry or amused. At last count—only yesternight—the sheep had numbered thirty-four. "When did those whoresons have the occasion to rob me once more? I thought I told you to set a man to guard the beasts!"

"The Scots?"

"Them, too, cunning bastards! But I meant the bloody sheep, Baldwin! The bloody rotten sheep! I thought I told you to set a guard for them!"

Baldwin's ears reddened. "Well . . ." His face twisted into an abashed grimace. "I *did* set a man to guard them, you see," he said. "Though it seems I set a wolf to guard the sheep's pen."

"Wolf?" Piers lifted both brows. He couldn't wait to hear this one.

Baldwin winced. "I appointed Cameron," he revealed, looking shamefaced. "He was already keeping watch over his own, you see, and I—"

"Cameron!" Piers exploded. "The arse who refused to leave his parcel and hut?" He tossed down his quill in disgust. "Damn it all, Baldwin! Whatever were you thinking to put a thieving Scot to guard against his kinsmen!"

"I thought—"

"That he would give his loyalty to an Englishman over his own countrymen?"

Baldwin frowned. "He *did* remain when the rest abandoned us," he pointed out.

"Only because he's a stubborn old coot who refused to abandon his land *to a bloody Sassenach. His* words, do you recall? His behavior was certainly not born out of any sense of loyalty!"

"Aye, but it's not what you think," Baldwin said. "He merely fell asleep, is all."

Piers sighed and slumped within his chair, smacking his head in exasperation against the high back of his seat. He rolled his eyes, then stared up at the ceiling, noting its rotten condition for the first time.

He frowned.

Damn, but how had he missed that before now? His chamber was directly above. He was going to have to fix that bloody ceiling soon, lest he plummet through the floor onto the table before him and find himself fare for the band of misfit Scots who had remained with him.

"My lord?"

Piers turned his attention from the rotting floorboards and eyed his longtime friend with a mixture of bemusement and displeasure. It seemed to him that Baldwin had taken to behaving less like a friend and more like an underling, and though this new manner wasn't entirely without its merits, he was nevertheless uncomfortable with Baldwin's unexpected attention to the proprieties. He much preferred the drunken companionability he and his men had shared in the years before his enfeoffment.

Christ, but he'd never expected to find himself lord—or laird, for that matter—and he'd certainly never aspired to it. It seemed wholly unnatural to him now to be fussed over as though he were some grease-lipped lord casting dinner bones to his dogs. He was a commander first and foremost. It had been his skill at arms that had won him this little piece of Highland hell, and he didn't see the bloody need to change what had served him so well so long. His men worked well beside him because they were foremost his fellows. He didn't want, or need, a bunch of knock-kneed lackeys running about according him undue honors.

"Sire?" Baldwin's tone clearly revealed his uncertainty over Piers's mood. "What is it you'd have me do?"

"You might first cease to call me *my lord*," Piers suggested, his tone unmistakably provoked. "And sire, as well, as neither am I your bloody father!"

Baldwin lifted his head in surprise. "What is it you'd have me call you . . . if not 'my lord'?"

Piers thought the answer rather obvious. "What is it you called me before?"

Baldwin cocked his head a little uncertainly. "Lyon?"

Piers responded with a droll grin. He'd been given the name by his men after a particularly bloody battle: they'd said he'd appeared to them coming off the battlefield, with his long, gilt mane of hair and bloodied face, like a lion fresh after its kill. It wasn't an honor he was particularly proud of, but he'd gotten used to the name after all.

Baldwin's brows lifted. "You wish me to call you Lyon?"

"I prefer it to *my lord*."

Baldwin's lips curved into a smile. "If 'tis your wish..."

"It is," Piers assured him. "I'm no bloody different merely because I now have a parcel of land to piss upon and call my own. Why should we resort to ceremony after all these years? I didn't like the damned name before and you hounded me with it even so! Why not still?"

Baldwin nodded, his grin spreading from ear to ear. " 'Tis relieved I am to hear you say so."

"Are you now?" Piers was relieved as well at having settled the matter once and for all. Now wasn't the time for maudlin expressions, as he still had these bare-arsed Scots to deal with.

And yet... strangely enough, though the Brodies had all but robbed him blind, it was a simple enough task to temper his anger against the thieving curs. Why was that? he wondered.

Truth to tell, accustomed as he had become to the intrigues of court and the stealth of warfare, this matter of feuding seemed more like sport.

In fact, Piers could scarcely help but admire these Scots. They fought their battles fiercely, and by some strange code of honor that somehow appealed to him. They spat upon your boot; you drew your sword; they stole your goat; you stole their sheep; and so on and so on—though bloodshed seemed proscribed— and all of it done openly, as though thieving your good neighbor were the most natural and honorable thing to do. Thus far, not so much as a single beast had been harmed, though Piers had not enjoyed a moment's peace since first he'd stepped foot upon these Highlands.

It was more than apparent that a bond of blood was as binding as a Scotsman's honor would allow—that they defended kith and kin unto their dying breath.

It was also apparent that an outlander would always be just that . . . an outlander.

Well, Piers was perfectly accustomed to that. He didn't need their bloody approval.

David of Scotia might, but he sure as hell didn't.

He had grown up an outlander, didn't they know.

His father was a king and his mother a whore.

And while his mother had slept in a different bed many a night, Piers had slipped away and curled beneath a pew within the chapel to close his eyes and dream of all the things he wanted in life.

And he had wanted so much!

He had wanted to go away and study in one of those places he'd only heard speak of . . . He'd wanted to read until his eyes went blind . . . He'd wanted to learn things, and do things, and see things.

He'd wanted to know why the sky was so blue and the grass so green. He'd wanted to know what stars were made of, and why they burned so brightly. And he'd wanted to know why his veins were blue while his blood was red. He'd wanted so much more than a bed on a cold, hard floor and to stand alone behind invisible doors . . . watching other children at play.

What should he have cared if the other children were outside playing and laughing? Thanks to his mother, he'd been able to study with the Archbishop of Canterbury and that had been no trifling thing. He'd had every reason to be grateful and no reason at all to yearn for something so negligible as dirty knees or silly games.

"Damn it all!" he exclaimed, lifting up his pen and rapping the quill's end upon the wooden table. "We're going to show these bloody Scots we can feud with the best of them!"

And savor it every bit as much.

That's what it was going to take to win their alliance, he surmised.

Or not.

Either way, he would relish the sport.

Though at first he'd been taken unawares by their unanticipated raids, some part of him reveled in this honest form of warfare, where one's enemy stood up to be numbered, and one's friends openly declared they'd as soon pluck out your eyes did it profit them.

There was something particularly heartening in that.

Aye, he was perfectly pleased to play their games.

"These bare-arsed savages'll not run us off this land!" he vowed, then: "Damn you for a witless arse!" he reprimanded Baldwin, though he knew his eyes didn't quite conceal the smile he hid. "I should take the price of those beasts out of your hide, you realize?"

Color returned to the tips of Baldwin's ears. "I wouldn't fault you for it if you did, Lyon," he answered soberly, though neither did his smile vanish altogether either. "What would you have me do?"

"What else?" Piers replied, grinning. "We steal the buggers back—and a few more for good measure!"

Baldwin smirked. "If I didn't know better," he said, "I'd think you were enjoying this, Lyon."

Lyon lifted a brow. "And you would probably be right," he returned, rising from his seat and taking his sword from where he'd placed it upon the table before him. He slid it into his scabbard and winked good-naturedly at Baldwin. "Now, let us go teach these Scots how to do it right!"

Chapter 2

It was a raven, no mistaking it.

Its blue-black wings pummeled the air in obvious distress though it made not a sound as it flailed about the rafters searching for escape. Within the silence of the chapel its flight for freedom—like a soul fighting to be free—was a cry that stirred Meghan Brodie's heart.

She had cast open the shutters to the bright summer day and the poor bird had flown within as though it had been anticipating her appearance at the window. It had startled her, certainly, but Meghan wasn't the least bit superstitious, else she might have considered it an evil omen.

Certainly, her grandmother, Fia, would have claimed it to be so.

The last time she recalled a bird flying into their home—and it had been a sparrow then, not even a wicked raven as was this—her dear grandmother had taken great pains to make it fly out the same way it had flown in, so that it

17

might take with it whatever curse it had brought. Else, old Fia had explained, the sparrow would die and the one who'd let it in would remain cursed for all eternity. In her quest to set it free, Fia had blocked off every window and every door except for the one the bird had flown in through, and then had stood speaking to the creature for hours, until she'd managed to coax it into her hand with bread crumbs. And then with blessings she had cast it out the door.

Meghan hadn't believed a word of it, of course. She'd thought her grandminnie incredibly silly, while her brothers had simply thought her raving mad—as everyone else had. Superstition was, in her opinion, merely a way of explaining away circumstances one could not fully comprehend. Nothing more. When it came to such notions she was truly quite unromantic. Her mind couldn't quite embrace the mystical, though her grandmother's tales had certainly been useful for frightening wee grandchildren into good behavior.

The memory brought a wistful smile to her lips.

Her mother had never meant to frighten Meghan, of course—and her brothers were entirely fearless—but her grandmother was another matter entirely.

All that Meghan remembered of her dear mother was her sad, grieving face; she'd lived only until Meghan's third summer. Her da she remembered not at all, as he'd died when Meghan was but a bairn.

But her grandminnie, the old lovable lunatic, had walked the halls of Meghan's home until Meghan's sixteenth winter, all the while talking to faeries and wraiths—at least that's what Fia had claimed. Meghan suspected she'd merely been too chagrined to admit she liked to talk to herself, as Meghan was wont to do— och, but she made no apologies for it! She liked her own company and that of animals so much more than she did that of people.

People, Meghan often thought, were entirely too fickle in their attentions, and never seemed to look beyond the mask of her face. It made her uncomfortable, and truth to tell, she must not see the same person in the looking glass, for she couldn't conceive what it was about her face that made men daft in her presence and women loathe her at merely a glance.

It seemed to Meghan that nobody cared one whit for the person within.

Both Meghan's mother and grandmother had been blessed with loveliness, but Meghan hadn't inherited their delicate beauty at all. Her cheekbones were much too prominent, her lips much too full, and her auburn hair a riotous mess of curls that refused to remain bound. At least she hadn't the tendency to freckle, though the sun colored her skin much too dark in the summer.

Her most distinguishing feature, she

thought, was her eyes: they were the deep cool shade of a forest glen. She had her da's eyes, she'd been told. Betimes they appeared nigh black, though they were truly a pure, deep, woodland green. It was the same eye color her brothers shared, all but for Colin, whose eyes were the pale shade of a cloudless summer sky.

She lifted her gaze once more to inspect the chapel's ceiling as the raven began to caw. Its blue-black wings beat the rafters in growing distress, and Meghan frowned. The chapel had once been naught more than the ruins of an old stone temple built by the ancients. Its ceiling had stood wide open to the heavens for most of her life, but her brother Gavin had recently erected a sloping wooden shelter, and the new wood was sturdy and true, reinforced by beams that were braced along the stone walls. No amount of thrashing, not even from stalwart Mother Nature, was going to raise it. The poor raven had nary a chance.

She stood there wondering how best to get the bird out.

What might Fia have done? Her sweet, mad grandminnie had had a way with creatures that far exceeded what paltry influence Meghan thought she had.

Though Meghan had been raised by her three brothers, she'd spent the greater part of her childhood with her grandminnie, either searching for herbs to make potions, or listening to tales of good faeries who peeked out from behind trees in the woodlands. Och, but loony as the old woman had been, Meghan missed her fiercely.

Though Meghan knew her brothers loved her well and truly, it was a burdensome thing to be the only woman in a household of men.

Not to mention lonely.

If it weren't for Alison, the MacLean's daughter, her very best friend, Meghan didn't know what she'd have done.

Leith, her eldest brother, was laird of their clan. He was sweet and good to her, even if he was entirely too overbearing and protective. With all his rules, he kept her from life just as surely as though he were a wall she could not pass. What he didn't seem to realize—thank God—was that she had her own little tunnel burrowed beneath those bulwarks, and the defiant thought brought a tiny smile to her lips. What he didn't know, she decided, couldn't possibly hurt him.

Her brother Colin, on the other hand, was much too unconcerned with aught but women and drink. Blessed as he was with good looks, Meghan only wished he didn't give the pursuit of his own pleasures such import above all else.

Poor, sweet Alison hadn't a chance with him!

Then there was her dear brother Gavin, the only brother younger than herself. Gavin held another view entirely from both Leith and Colin. He was the one who disregarded the mind and physical beauty altogether, thinking it a sin to worship the temple of the spirit and a complete waste of one's time—a woman's, at least—to ponder life's mysteries. Alas, that was something Meghan was surely wont to do. Her youngest brother encouraged her incessantly to seek to purify her soul, lest she end like their mother and grandmother before her—mad and alone.

Och, but she rather relished the thought of being alone, didn't he realize? And if people thought her mad . . . well, then . . . She shrugged. They'd simply think her mad and leave her be, now wouldn't they? And that was well and good, as far as Meghan was concerned.

She only wished Gavin would live a little more and leave off with the preaching, for his own sake, certainly not for hers. Meghan had absolutely no qualms about boxing his ears when he carried on so. She loved each of her brothers dearly—as she knew they did her—and she'd do anything for them, anything at all, except listen to Gavin's accursed sermons!

Christ only knew, they were almost as harrowing as the poor raven's unrelenting cawing!

Sweet Mary, she had no notion what to do to help the accursed bird! She stood, hands at her hips, before the open window, frowning after it as it flew amuck about the rafters and finally lit upon one of the support beams.

There it remained, and she could swear it stared expectantly down at her.

By the blessed rood! Whatever did it expect her to do?

"Och noo, but I canna help ye all the way up there, dinna ye know, ye silly creature!" Although she knew it was an absurd thing to do, she extended her hand to the agitated bird, and demanded, "Come down here noo!"

The raven merely flapped its wings, and cawed at her.

She crooked a finger at it. "Dinna ye speak tae me sae rudely," she told the bird. "I canna help ye if ye willna let me!"

The raven quieted and cocked its head. It peered down at her curiously, but didn't move.

Had she expected it to? It was ludicrous to be nettled by the bird's lack of response, but she was.

"I'd wager ye'd come down for Fia! Foolish auld bird!" she scolded it. "Stay, then, if ye—"

"What are ye doing, Meghan lass?" a voice interrupted at her back.

Meghan shrieked in alarm, casting up her hands. She turned to face Colin. "Och, but ye scared me, ye ill-bred oaf!"

Her brother merely grinned at her, and cocked his head, in much the same manner the bird had.

"Did no one ever teach ye guid manners?" she muttered, narrowing her eyes at him.

"Ye knoo the answer tae that, Meghan, love," he told her. "I learned my guid manners from the same place ye did." He winked at her and chuckled. "Only it seems tae me ye learned a few more lessons from daft auld Fia than I. What d' ye think ye're doing, talking tae the witless bird? Ye dinna think it understands, do ye?"

Meghan's cheeks flamed. She peered up at the bird, and then lifted her chin as she faced her brother, her hands going to her hips. "O' course not! I was only tryin' tae help the silly thing! It flew in through the bluidy window," she explained, undaunted by Colin's amused expression. "And he canna seem tae find his way back oot."

Her brother smiled benevolently at her. "Meggie, dearlin', ye've a guid heart, lass, but ye're wastin' yer sweet breath. That bird doesna comprehend a word ye're speaking and ye'd do better tae smack yer bonnie head against a wall for all the guid ye're doing."

"I suppose ye're right," Meghan conceded, frowning up at the bird. "Ungrateful creature," she muttered.

Colin's lips curved into a roguish grin. "O' course I'm right."

"Och, but I hate it when ye are, ye wicked gloating knave!"

He lifted a brow at her. "That's another thing ye learned from auld Fia, lass, and I'm here tae tell ye, 'tis a foul thing tae hear ye speakin' like

a mon. I'll warrant ye'll never be finding yerself a mate wi' that rotten tongue ye bear."

"Guid, then, ye silly oaf! What would I be
wantin' wi' a mon, when I've my hands full
wi' the three o' ye already?"

Colin's smile turned ribald and Meghan
lifted a brow at him in censure. He was the
only one of her three brothers who would
speak so frankly to her of matters betwixt men
and women. She ofttimes appreciated it, but
then again, neither Gavin nor Leith was so
overly preoccupied with such things, and she
wished Colin were not either.

"I could think of a few things," he told her
plainly, "but if I told ye I'd ha' tae box yer ears
for hearing them, Meghan. And then I'd ha' tae
kill the bluidy fool who fell prey tae yer curiosity."

"Nay, ye wouldna!" Meghan said with absolute certainty, her cheeks burning with chagrin. "You wouldna ha' tae kill anyone, brother
o' mine, because there isna a mon under God's
heaven that I'd care tae burden myself wi' long
enough tae appease any curiosity!"

"Well," Colin countered, shaking his head as
though she were no more than a wee misbe-
having child, "as I said ... ye'll never ha' tae
worry over such things, anyhoo—no' wi' that
vicious tongue." He peered up at the squawk-
ing bird, his cheeks turning suddenly pink as

he revealed, "At any rate . . . I only came tae tell ye something . . ."

Meghan's brows lifted. "Something?"

"Aye. Alison awaits ye on the meadow," he blurted.

"Alison?" Meghan's brows lifted higher in surprise, and then she narrowed her eyes at him, scrutinizing his expression. "Ye saw her?"

He nodded, his hands going to his hips. "I did, Meghan, and dinna look at me sae. I didna say a bluidy thing tae the wench!"

Meghan narrowed her eyes at him. "That is precisely the trouble," she said. "How could it possibly hurt ye tae sit and visit wi' her for a wee bit, Colin? She likes ye sae verra much—though for the life o' me I canna see why!"

"Why thank ye verra much!" he said, looking offended.

"Ye're no' verra nice tae her."

Colin's face twisted into a grimace, and his cheeks turned, if possible, a deeper shade of red. "Och!" he protested. "She's sweet enough, Meghan, if only she didna ha' those eyes!"

"There is naught wrong wi' Alison's eyes," Meghan said. "They are merely crossed. They are much the same as Leith's or mine."

"Aye, but it makes me uncomfortable tae even look at her."

"Arggghhh!" Meghan said, shaking her head in utter disgust. "Tae think I share the same blood wi' ye, Colin Mac Brodie. I canna believe ye would be sae cold and cruel tae a poor lass merely because her face doesna suit ye!"

"Cruel!" His fist went to his breast.

"If ye would only speak wi' her a time, ye would see how verra sweet her heart is," Meghan beseeched him, "and how verra smart she is! Alison would make any mon a fine wife! Ye should only feel fortunate tae ha' such devotion as that she gives ye—even undeserving as ye are!"

"Och, noo!" he objected, meeting her eyes with his sad soulful ones. "Dinna be sae fierce wi' me, Meghan." His gaze lowered unhappily. "I wouldna hurt the poor lass," he swore. "I merely dinna wish tae wed her is all, and dinna see the point in misleading her. I wasna mean tae her."

"Nay?" Meghan asked him, eyeing him shrewdly. "Swear it upon yer verra manhood, Colin! May it fall off and rot like a bluidy worm in the ground if ye've made her weep again."

He cast her a pained glance, grimacing. "Och, Meghan! Ye're bluidy cruel tae be sure!"

"Swear it!" she demanded of her brother.

"All right! I swear it! I swear it," he declared. "Though I canna be certain she wasna weepin'," he amended quickly.

"Colin!"

He held up both his hands in protest. "I didna do anything, Meg, but she came and found me wi' Suisan. I canna be blamed for that!"

His hand went to his groin in a protective gesture—unconsciously, Meghan knew—and she suppressed a grin. He did have a point, she was forced to admit. He couldn't be faulted for that.

And it would truly serve no one at all—most of all not Alison—for Colin to lead her astray. Alison was not like Meghan, after all; her feelings were entirely too tender.

"Can ye no' see that I canna be false tae her?" Colin asked her, his brows lifting in supplication. "It wouldna be right!"

Meghan frowned. "Aye," she yielded, though grudgingly. "I do, ye miserable wretch. I only wish—"

"I ken what ye're wishin', Meggie. And ye're a guid-hearted lass, tae be sure—but och! I dinna want a wife, anyhoo!"

Meghan understood that better than any.

"And did I crave one," he added honestly, "the MacLean's daughter isna the one for me." He made a gesture at his breast that made Meghan blush. "I'm wantin' more from a lass," he informed her. "No' merely a bonnie face, but *more* if ye knoo what I mean?" He lifted his brows.

"Acck!" Meghan shrieked in protest. "I dinna wish tae hear such things!"

"Well," he continued, lecturing her, "ye should knoo that a pretty face isna all a lass needs in order tae win herself a mon. She must have a pleasin' body, as well."

Meghan narrowed her eyes at her brother.

He nodded. "And ready laughter."

"And I'm supposin' she must knoo how tae cook and mend and wash and—"

"And make healthy bairns," Colin agreed with another nod.

"Arggh!" Meghan shrieked once more, and leapt upon him in a fit of outrage, pummeling his chest.

Colin yelped in protest.

"Ye're incorrigible, Colin Mac Brodie!" She smacked his arm, and made to go around him. "Ye're a bluidy mon!" she declared, as though it were the worst thing he could possibly be. "And I'll no' be listening tae ye any longer!"

"An' ye're a bloodthirsty woman!" he returned. "God's truth! We'll be havin' tae *pay* a mon tae take yer blasted arse from off our hands!"

"Nay, ye willna!" Meghan assured him, swinging about to face him as she reached the chapel door. "Ye willna, because I'llna be a wife tae any mon! Ye're stuck wi' me, the lot o' ye, don't ye knoo!" And with that she pivoted about and made to open the chapel door.

"And thank God for that!" Colin swore at her back.

She swung about to face him once more. "What did ye say?"

"I said God help the bluidy lot of us, Meghan Brodie!"

She eyed him doubtfully. "God help ye is right!" she agreed, and turned once more.

She jerked the door open.

From the rafters above, the raven let out a terrible shriek of protest, and Meghan halted in her step. Frowning, she turned slowly to look at Colin.

"What?" he asked her, reacting to the harassed expression upon her face. "What is it I've done noo?"

Meghan shook her head as she gazed up into the rafters. "No' a bluidy damned thing. Rotten bird!" she exclaimed, and with a harried sigh, started at once toward the chapel's single window.

At the window, she threw the shutters wide and peered down in exasperation. It wasn't that far a drop to the ground, but it annoyed her that she should feel compelled to adhere to some silly bit of superstition only because her grandminnie would have done so. She tossed a leg over the sill, all the while vexed with herself for succumbing.

"Meghan lass?" Colin asked at her back, his tone bewildered. "What the devil are ye doing?"

Meghan turned to look at her brother and snapped, "What does it appear I am doing, ye daff mon? I'm climbing oot the bluidy window is what I'm doing, canna ye see!"

"Och, Meghan! I see that ye're climbin' oot the bluidy window, but *why* is it ye're climbin' oot the bluidy window?"

"Because I bluidy well feel like climbin' oot the bluidy rotten window, Colin!" Meghan answered peevishly. She cast him an annoyed glance. "Doesna everybody noo and again?"

He answered with an exasperated shake of his head. Meghan ignored him.

"Ye're going tae be as mad as auld Fia one o' these days," he announced with certainty.

Meghan thought it might very well be true. Only a mad old Brodie would feel compelled to climb down a bloody window in order to revoke a nonexistent curse. Rotten bird!

Colin came to the window and peered down at her while she hung by her fingers from the sill. Meghan glowered up at him as she tried to locate the ground with her toes. He merely stared at her, unaffected by her threatening look, and watched.

A knowing grin unfurled across his face. "Um, Meghan," he said, as she dropped to the ground, "if I recall aright, ye were supposed tae make the bird fly oot the same way he flew in, not gae oot that way yerself."

"Ouch!" she exclaimed as her foot twisted in the drop to the ground. She bent to massage her ankle, and peered up at her brother, nettled that he felt compelled to point out that minor detail just now—or that he should even remember, for that matter—and worse, that she should feel compelled to heed such a silly ritual at all.

"I tried," Meghan explained quite reasonably. "But he wouldna listen tae me, so I did the next best thing." She slapped her hands together, ridding them of grime from the windowsill, and straightened. "Anyhoo," she informed him baldly, casting a wily smile up at him, "superstition is naught but silly nonsense! And I dinna believe a word o' Fia's ravings."

"Nay?" he asked her, chuckling. "Silly wench."

"Nay," she answered pertly, and turned to go, limping.

"Och, Meghan! Gae on wi' ye then, before I change my mind and make ye stay," he announced. "Leith would peel the skin from my arse if he knew that I'd let ye leave, wi' all the trouble we've brewing wi' that idiot Sassenach."

"Tell him ye tried tae keep me, but couldna."

"I'll tell him, instead, that I never saw ye, Meghan," he shouted after her. "If I wanted tae stop ye, he knows verra well I could!"

"Only if ye sat upon me," she called back. "But I wouldna suggest it," she apprised him, "unless ye're sure and certain ye're never wantin' tae conceive yourself a bairn!"

"Impertinent wench!" her brother shouted after her. And then: "Be careful, Meghan! See Alison, then hie thee back at once!"

"Dinna fret, Colin! I shall be well and fine," she assured him, turning to wave him away from the chapel window. "Gae on noo, and get that bird oot for me!" she demanded.

"She awaits ye by the old cairn in the meadow just beyond the forest," Colin told her.

"Dinna worry! I'll hurry back!" She limped backward toward the woodlands, shading her eyes from the brightness of the noonday sun. She grinned impishly. "And I'll be sure tae gi' Alison yer love when I see her," she teased him.

"Do that, brat," he apprised her, crooking a finger at her in warning, "and I'll take a bluidy switch to yer arse when ye return!"

Meghan laughed. "Dinna ye even try, Colin Mac Brodie," she countered. "Dinna ye even try!"

And with that, she turned her back to him and hobbled into the cool shade of the forest.

Chapter 3

⟨⟐⟑⟐⟩

God save her rotten soul . . . she just didn't think she could do it.

Alison, youngest daughter of Dougal Mac-Lean, sat fretting upon a weather-beaten boulder, the noon sun glaring down into her face. She sat unblinking as she contemplated the dilemma at hand: however was she supposed to face her best friend and explain that it was her own guile that had instigated the feud betwixt David's Englishman Lyon and Meghan's own sweet brothers?

Whatever could she say to make amends?

I'm sorry, Meghan, but I didna wish tae wed the awful brute, sae I stole his goat and blamed it upon yer kinsmen.

The very thought of such a confession made her miserable.

The truth was that she hadn't meant to blame it upon Meghan's kinsmen at all; it had merely worked out that way. Her plan had simply gone awry. She nibbled anxiously at her thumbnail. Terribly, terribly awry. Her shoulders slumped dejectedly. Horridly awry. She'd intended, in fact, to initiate the feud betwixt her own kinfolk and Montgomerie, not the Brodies and Montgomerie, except that the blasted evidence had strayed upon Brodie land and the Montgomerie brothers had discovered their rotten little goat in the wrong hands!

She regretted her fouled plan wholeheartedly, of course, though she knew it was entirely too late for mere regrets. What was done was done, and it was up to her to make amends. Somehow, she had to set things aright.

The rope within her hand jerked, recalling her attention to the gift she'd brought for Meghan and her brothers—her own pet lamb, paltry compensation though it might be for the loss of an entire flock. She tugged the wee lammie within arm's reach and patted its newly sheared coat as she considered her options.

She *could* go to her father and reveal to him what she'd done, but he would blister her rear and make her marry the loathsome Englishman anyway.

Or . . .

She *could* confess to the loathsome Englishman, wed him as she was supposed to do, and then die of a broken heart—if he didn't chance to murder her first for her duplicity.

Or . . .

She *could* continue to await Meghan here

upon the meadow, tell her the truth, beg her forgiveness, and then help her in rectifying the situation.

Meghan always seemed to know what to do.

Why, oh, why couldn't she be more like Meghan? Meghan was pretty and kind and brave and intelligent. She was all the things Alison wished she could be, and more.

Beauty alone was not enough recommendation, she knew. Her eldest sister, Mairi, had been beautiful beyond words, but not so very intelligent, and certainly not so very kind. Mairi's beauty hadn't gotten her anywhere but dead. And though her father had blamed Iain MacKinnon for Mairi's death, Alison knew very well that her sister had always had a tendency toward melancholia.

Her sister hadn't loved her husband; she had chosen to kill herself rather than share her life with him. As dour as Mairi had always been, the prospect of living with a man she couldn't possibly ever love must have proven such a terrible burden for her to have committed such an atrocious sin as self-murder. It made Alison heartsick to think her sister had been so very unhappy.

And the last thing she wished to do was to end like Mairi. Nay, she couldn't wed with Piers Montgomerie—she just couldn't! She didn't love him. Alison had been so very relieved when her father had refused Lagan MacKinnon's offer of marriage. As flattered as she had been that a man such as Lagan would take interest in a girl as plain as herself, her heart was pledged to another. And if she couldn't bear the thought of wedding Lagan, less could she bear the thought of wedding some English vulture.

The faintest smile curved her lips at the thought of Colin Mac Brodie.

His very name made her quiver.

And his face made her sigh at the mere sight of it—och, but it was the sort of face that tied a girl's tongue into knots and made her heart leap like an exultant dancer within her breast.

And his voice . . . it was the voice of an angel . . . soothing like warm honeyed mead. It made her belly flutter and her breast burn with longing. Oh, what she wouldn't give to hear him whisper in her ear.

Resting her chin upon her hand and her elbows upon her knees, she thought about his eyes . . . clearest blue, they were . . . like the reflection of a bright-blue summer sky upon a glass pond.

Aye, Colin Mac Brodie was a beautiful, beautiful man . . .

But he didn't even know she existed.

Her wistful smile faded.

She'd come upon him here this morn in the arms of another woman, the two of them stealing kisses and laughing. And oh, how it had made Alison's heart ache to watch them together!

How she wished it could have been her!

But alas, it was not.

She sighed heavily, knowing very well that Colin had a great fondness for women; it was obvious in the fact that he was with a new one every time she saw him. Usually, it didn't bother Alison so much, because she hoped he would take his fill of them all, and wished with all her might he would someday see her as someone more than simply *Meggie's little friend*. But this morn it had been different. Alison hadn't yet been able to dispel the heaviness from her heart over seeing him. It had taken all her resolve to approach him and ask after Meghan with the two of them laughing and carrying on so.

Perhaps it had been harder than ever because she knew Colin was like to loathe her when he discovered what she'd done—och, but she couldn't bear that!

She stared at the lamb, wishing there were more she could give . . . more she could do . . . There must be something . . .

The Brodies still had possession of the original goat she'd stolen from Montgomerie, but she could scarcely count that a boon . . . because that rotten little beast had prompted Montgomerie to steal two of the Brodies' sheep before the spring shearing.

To which the Brodies had responded by thieving his cow.

To which Montgomerie had responded by thieving a horse.

To which the Brodies had responded by taking four more goats.

And then Montgomerie had taken two more cows. Alison sighed wearily at the thought of so much stubborn male pride.

The Brodies had then stolen seven of Montgomerie's sheep—and Montgomerie had responded by thieving them all back, and then some! In fact, he'd left them with none at all! And this one poor lambkins wasn't nearly enough to compensate for the loss of so many.

Good lord! Whatever did she think she could possibly say to the Brodies to set things aright? God's truth, there was nothing at all!

She could confess to Meghan, aye! But what could Meghan do? Nothing, and then her dear friend would surely feel compelled to tell her brothers—Colin included. After all, how could they possibly think to put an end to a feud without having someone else to blame for it?

And that someone would be Alison, of course.

And then her father would discover her perfidy and take a strap to her bottom.

And the English Lyon would feast upon whatever remained of her thereafter!

And worst of all, Colin would know. And he'd cast her hateful glances rather than look right through her as he did now. While she could scarcely bear his present disinterest toward her, the thought of his enmity was tragic!

She nibbled contemplatively at her thumbnail as she deliberated the possible consequences of coming forward.

Whatever should she do?

Stay and confess to Meghan?

Or go?

Her sense of obligation vied with her fear.

What to do . . . what to do . . .

Och, but she should simply let these silly men carry on their feud. To fight amongst themselves was what they loved to do, after all.

Though what, prithee, would be its conclusion? She'd heard of these things outlasting even the memory of their origin. Foolish men!

Would the Lyon feud with honor? she worried.

Or would he resort to bloodshed? Sweet lord, but she hoped not! She had to believe not!

She should speak up and put an end to the escalations once and for all, she knew. All she had to do was step forward and take responsibility.

Right?

She tapped a nail against her teeth, considering . . . What precisely would confessing accomplish? As she'd very likely still have to wed the Englishman, after all—and truth to tell, the Montgomerie-Brodie feud had reached a level to which her simple confession of stealing a single Montgomerie goat was like to make no difference at all.

Too much had passed between them already, she reasoned.

So, then . . . all Alison could *truly* hope to accomplish with her confession was to make everyone angry with her—and nay! That simply wouldn't do at all!

Springing up from her think-place upon the boulder, she hurriedly tethered the lamb to a nearby bush.

Of a sudden, she didn't even wish to wait for Meghan, because Meghan would know intuitively that something was wrong. And if she asked, if she merely glanced at Alison with that canny way she possessed, Alison would be forced to confess all. She would never be able to keep anything from Meghan, she knew—and truth be told, she didn't wish to confess anything at all!

The only thing worse than having Colin Brodie angry with her, she determined, was to have *everyone* angry with her.

Abandoning her gift for Meghan to find, she hurried away from the meadow as fast as she was able.

There was no sign of Alison when Meghan entered the clearing—merely a tiny lamb tied to a bush near the old cairn, where her brother said Alison would be awaiting her.

Her brows drew together into a frown as she contemplated the bleating little creature. Either her dear friend had left in a terrible rush, abandoning her charge, or this was some cruel joke of Colin's in order to make clear his feelings toward Alison MacLean.

She didn't think Colin could be so cruel. It had to be that Alison had hied away for some reason. But . . . unless Alison were in danger . . . why would she leave without taking her sweet little lamb?

Meghan's gaze scanned the meadow for some clue as to her friend's sudden disappearance, but there was no sign of disturbance at all: the hillside meadow seemed as serene as ever. The posies swayed with the breeze, like little dancing people with painted faces, whilst in the distance the birds chirped merrily from the lush green treetops of the forest.

All was as it should be.

Shrugging, Meghan made her way to the little lamb, intending to set it free. She stroked it gently while she untethered it and then wrapped the lead rope about her wrist.

"Poor wee lammie," she commiserated with it. "How could anyone abandon such a sweet little thing as yerself?"

The lamb bleated shyly and peered up at her with bright trusting eyes, and Meghan smiled as she drew upon the lead rope, prompting it to follow.

"Let's gae noo!" she urged it. "Ye're comin' home wi' me. Findings, keepings!" she announced. Och, but why would anyone bind an animal so and then leave it? she wondered.

"Poor wee lost lammie," she said, coaxing it to follow. Unless the owner planned to come back for it later?

She scanned the meadow once more, still finding nothing. Shrugging, she started away. The lamb hesitated, and then followed, and Meghan smiled down at it.

Well, it was her lamb now, she determined. They certainly could use the livestock after having been so thoroughly raided by David's English lackey. And this *was* Brodie land, after all! It made little sense that someone would leave their animal bound here, whether they were returning for it or not.

And furthermore, they didn't deserve the poor beast if they could so cruelly leave it to thirst beneath the hot sun.

Unless . . . She faltered in her step. Perhaps it did belong to Alison and she'd had to abandon it suddenly—though what Alison would be doing with a single lamb this far from MacLean land, Meghan certainly didn't know. Her brow furrowed.

It left her to wonder whether Alison might truly be in danger.

The tiny hairs at the back of her nape prickled suddenly.

Perhaps she shouldn't leave so hastily?

She halted again, and the little lamb stopped, too. Meghan peered down at the wee thing, frowning, and then once more glanced around her.

Naught at all.

What if Alison were in danger? What if she left and forsook the opportunity to help her dear friend?

And yet what could Meghan possibly do alone?

She suddenly wasn't certain what to do.

"What do ye think, wee lammie?" she asked. "Do we stay or do we gae?"

The lamb bleated and stared up at her, its expression blank.

"Ye dunno, ye say?"

She unwrapped the lead rope from her wrist and stared pensively at the frayed end, brushing it absently with her thumb.

There certainly weren't any signs of a struggle in the meadow, as best she could tell, and Alison was nowhere to be found. The best thing she could do, she decided, was to get her brothers to order a search. And truth to tell, she was beginning to feel a bit uneasy . . .

As though someone were out there . . . watching . . .

"Well," she concluded, frowning, "I dunno either, but I'm supposin' I should take ye home." She cast an anxious glance over her shoulder, and told the wee lamb, "Come along then." And she led it toward the forest path from whence she'd come.

It wasn't the safest way home, but it was certainly the shortest, and since she'd only just come that way and had encountered nothing amiss, she decided it was the best route to take. She didn't particularly care to take the long way home with the sun bearing down upon the meadow. The poor lamb was enervated already.

The shaded forest path, though it meandered in and out of Brodie and Montgomerie land— the latter being filled with thieving, conniving Sassenachs—was well worn by Brodie feet and little-traveled by anyone else. It sat at the far, far edge of Montgomerie land—land that had once belonged to the MacLeans until King David of Scotia had *requested* it from Alison's father.

The thought made Meghan glower.

As she understood it, Alison's father had agreed to give it, only so long as Alison wedded the lumpish, greasy English bugger—well, Meghan didn't know if he was lumpish or greasy, precisely, because she'd never set eyes upon the man, but she certainly knew he was greedy! Alison, poor lass, was of a different mind entirely, as she didn't wish to wed with Montgomerie at all—and Meghan could scarcely blame her!

It seemed to Meghan that the rotten Sassenach had no sooner set foot upon Scot soil than he was already ravaging and pillaging his good neighbors—greedy, misbegotten cur that he was! And in truth, she might not hold him in such contempt, for she was no stranger to feuding and raiding, but he'd thieved from her own kinsmen and without provocation no less!

Well, her brothers were sworn to set him to rights, and if Meghan knew them at all, they wouldn't stop until they did. Meghan only hoped it would end without bloodshed. These were not Scotsmen they were dealing with, and she was afraid her sweet brothers had forgotten that simple fact.

"Englishmen ha' no honor!" she told the little lamb as they entered the shade of the forest. "Nor ha' they any hearts at all!"

The lamb walked silently at her side, though its stride seemed uncertain.

"Their mothers eat them when they are wee bairns, ye see," she explained, feeling quite wicked. "That is why they ha' none."

The lamb peered up at her, as though in disbelief, and then its gaze shied away.

" 'Tis God's truth I'm telling ye!" she persisted. "And they're trying tae bring Scotia tae her knees. If ye ask me," she told the lamb in no uncertain terms, "I think David is a fool for trusting those he calls friends! Pah!" she exclaimed, as though the lamb cared one whit what her opinion was—though why should it care when no one else seemed to think she had a brain to think with either? "Rotten Sassenachs dunno the meaning o' the word friendship!" she muttered crossly to herself.

Chapter 4

⟨━━⟩⟨ᗧᑦ⟩⟨━━⟩

Lyon was determined to keep his borders well defended.

After his last raid, he wasn't taking chances. Those damned Brodies were as devious as London thieves, and just as bold, raiding in the broadest light of day. This last round had been his victory, and he was damned well going to keep it that way.

He swore to God they must sprout limbs and leaves, playing like bloody trees to his face, and then when he turned his back they scurried away like rats with their stolen cheese.

Damn, but they were good.

Only, *he* intended to be better.

They were now appraising his land to determine the best course of defense.

"Well now!" Baldwin exclaimed, sliding back down the flank of his steed after another failed attempt to mount. "Do you see what I see, Lyon?" He shielded his embarrassment behind a mask of interest and stepped away from

47

his horse in order to better see through the lush woodland foliage.

Lyon had spied the approaching woman long before Baldwin had turned his attention from his struggles, and her presence did, in fact, engage him, but his concern for his friend overrode his curiosity for an instant. "I do indeed," he answered. "But you realize, my friend, that these bare-arsed Scots might have easily overtaken you just now?"

Baldwin's ears turned red.

"I have given you leave to ride free of your armor," Lyon told him, "and I think it best under the circumstances. These Scots do not battle as we do; they fight free of the restraints of armor. What good will your mail do you if your movements are so sluggish that they've a blade to your throat before you can chance even to mount?"

Baldwin set his jaw stubbornly. "It took me years to earn this armor, Lyon," he said, facing Piers with determination.

Lyon understood what the small defiance cost him, for Baldwin was ever dutiful, ever faithful. He would badger Lyon on occasion, as any longtime companion might, but when it came to matters of war, he obeyed Lyon's every word.

"I shall practice swiftness, but do not ask me to cast away my honors," Baldwin begged.

"As you will it."

Baldwin smiled. "I shall exercise more," he

answered. "You have my word."

"I've little doubt that you will," Lyon said, and offered a reluctant smile in return.

"Thank you, Lyon," Baldwin said. And with that settled between them, he once again peered out through the covert, watching the woman make her way toward them down the narrow lane. "I wonder who she is," he remarked as she came into clearer view.

"I'm certain I've no idea," Lyon answered, bending low over his mount to peer beneath the overhanging limbs. With his height, he was afforded a clearer view, but the forest was overgrown with vegetation. "Though she's coming from our direction, it seems."

"Our direction?" Baldwin turned to face him. "From our land, do you mean?"

Lyon didn't answer; his attention was completely engaged now by the young woman.

His first impression of her was of willowy limbs and shimmering hair: she was tall and thin, with a lithe, slim form that swayed with feminine self-assurance as she walked. And that hair—a wanton mass of coppery ringlets— ignited like the biblical burning bush as she passed through a nimbus of light from above.

And then she neared enough for him to see her face, and his breath caught.

Christ, but she was an angel incarnate!

That face . . . it was the face he'd imagined belonged to Helen of Troy . . . or to the Aphrodite of legend.

Her delicate features were nothing less than perfection—her nose not tiny and upturned, like that of a child's, but straight and lovely.

And her eyes . . . He could scarcely see their color at this distance, but they were almond-shaped and exotic like those of the Saracen women he'd encountered in his travels.

And her mouth . . . it was full and sensual . . . A mouth that demanded to be kissed . . . A mouth formed by Eros himself . . . A mouth made to be pleasured . . . and to pleasure in return.

It stirred the imagination, hardened his loins.

Christ and bedamned, as jaded as he'd become, his body's response to the woman surprised him—pleasantly, as it had been much too long since something so simple as a glance at beauty had roused his lust—a misfortune of his upbringing, no doubt.

Growing up as *the whore's son* had definitely had its downfalls. It was a label that had found him feeding his high-minded peers a mouthful of his fist more oft than not. And yet, he'd certainly relished some of the inherent benefits, shameless libertine that he was.

Like mother, like son, they'd claimed.

And so he was.

And he hadn't had the right to take offense. It was certainly true enough; he loved women, as his mother had loved men. And there didn't seem to be any point in denying the obvious. At least he knew that much about himself. It was the reason he'd not pursued the life of a celibate, for while the pursuit of knowledge and reason had been his mind's greatest desire, his body was innately weak to the pleasures of the flesh.

And yet it had been a long time since he'd taken simple pleasure in a woman.

That he lamented.

Though not as much as he regretted the course his life had taken—resorting to brute force for gain. It defeated his personal philosophy despite that it had been the way of his life since the moment of his birth. He'd gained naught, accomplished naught, save through the might of his arm.

That he'd clung to his erudite ideals so long was a matter of stubborn pride. Though his conventions negated his convictions, he still believed that the mind was more powerful a tool than the body—knowledge more effectual than mere brute strength. Though his body might fail him, his mind would see him through. But if the mind failed . . . well, then . . . What good was a body of any sort?

Though—God's truth—a body such as the one *she* possessed was certainly rewarding no matter what the state of her mind.

He took a deep breath, and cast a glance at Baldwin to find that his friend and confidant was as entranced by the woman as he had been, and he frowned at the discovery. Why did that provoke him? Not immensely, but enough that he could scarcely deny it.

Baldwin whistled low. "She's exquisite!"

Lyon said nothing, merely watched the woman's approach with growing interest.

It was only belatedly that he realized she wasn't precisely alone.

"Lyon," Baldwin began, his attention to detail scarcely more timely than Lyon's own, "she has a bloody lamb with her. What do you suppose she's doing with a lamb?"

Lyon's frown deepened as he watched the animal tangle its lead rope about the woman's legs.

"And she's coming from our direction," Baldwin felt compelled to say.

Lyon reconsidered that particular fact as woman and animal made their way nearer.

"What do you suppose it means?"

It was rather self-evident, Lyon thought.

Then again, much that was apparent was also misleading.

The lamb lagged behind, and the woman slowed to allow it to catch up. It meandered about to her other side, tangling the lead rope further about her long, lean limbs.

She didn't seem to notice.

"And she's talking to herself," Baldwin added. "Do you hear?"

"Nay," Lyon replied with a narrow-eyed glance down at Baldwin's back. He refrained from pointing out that he could scarcely even think over Baldwin's prattle. How could he possibly hear the wench?

"Do you think she's daft?" Baldwin persisted.

It was certainly a possibility, though Lyon hoped not. He hoped she was as quick-witted as she was beautiful. Anything less would dull his interest, he feared, and he didn't particularly wish it to be dulled this time.

"Baldwin," Lyon whispered.

Baldwin peered up at him, murmuring in return, "What, Lyon?"

"Shut up."

Baldwin smiled sheepishly and ducked his head once more beneath the branches to spy at the woman.

"Well!" the woman exclaimed, near enough to be heard now, her brogue soft and lyrical. She peered down at the bewildered-looking beast. "If Lyon Montgomerie knoos what's best . . ."

"Lyon," Baldwin began, "she's—"

"Shhh," Lyon commanded him, not wanting to miss a word of her discourse with the animal.

". . . he'll thrust that venerable sword o' his between his puny legs," she haughtily informed the beast, "and hie himself back tae his bluidy England! We dinna need another rotten Sassenach aboot tae plague us!"

Lyon raised his brows at her declaration.

Baldwin turned to him, grinning. "Puny?"

he said low. "I wonder just which venerable sword she's referring to?" His shoulders shook with ill-suppressed laughter.

Lyon glowered down at his back.

Christ, he'd been called many a thing in his time, but never puny. Even as a lad, lanky though he might have been, none but one would have dared call him such a thing to his face.

And then never again.

Impudent wench.

He'd like to show *her* puny!

Damned if the mere thought didn't quicken his loins, and the response took him once more by surprise.

Provoked him, as well . . . Damn it all, why should he feel annoyed over her disparaging remark, and then feel compelled to prove himself like some bare-arsed lad with his first chin hair?

"Do you think she stole the lamb from us?"

"Why would she steal a single lamb?" Lyon replied, and found himself wondering whether she was wife or daughter—or mayhap both. Women of her beauty rarely went unspoken for.

She was nearly upon them now, and Baldwin whispered lower, "Do these Scots need a bloody reason to steal?"

Lyon responded with a wry twist of his lips. The truth was that they didn't seem to. He certainly hadn't instigated the raids between them.

"Lyon!" the woman spat, successfully recapturing their attention. "Pah!" She cast a downward glance at the lamb ambling beside her. "He's no bluidy lion!" she exclaimed. "Only a cowardly milksop skulking aboot in the dark o' the night!"

Coward?

"Milksop?" Baldwin echoed, and his shoulders once again began to quake.

Lyon ignored the bastard.

"Why, he canna even face them—hah! Lion! *Worm* is more the like!"

Lyon scowled. Face who? The Brodies? Damn them all to hell. He couldn't imagine who else she might be speaking of, but he hadn't noticed that they'd made any particular efforts to face him, either!

"Steal from my brothers, will he!"

Brothers.

His brows lifted with comprehension. Baldwin turned to look at him then and nodded. She had a reason after all, it seemed, bootless though her raid might have been.

Though she'd nearly passed them by now, Lyon restrained himself still, contemplating his best course of action. She was merely a woman, and hardly a threat, but he didn't think he should simply allow her to walk away with his livestock. Then again, what retribution could he possibly deliver against a woman? It was from her brothers he desired satisfaction.

Damn, but if she were in truth their sister, why didn't he know of her? He'd made it a point to learn all that he could about his new neighbors.

Then again, he reminded himself, other than the fact that the MacLeans had a long-standing feud with the nearby MacKinnons, these were said to be peace-loving clans, and that certainly hadn't turned out to be so.

"Well," she continued, sounding particularly vengeful now, "he shall knoo soon enough what it means tae deal wi' Brodies!"

Would he now? Bloody hell! He suddenly didn't feel so charitable. And he'd heard quite enough, besides.

Without warning, he spurred his mount, startling Baldwin.

"Where the devil are you going, Lyon?"

"To put an end to this feud once and for all!"

Never mind that only moments ago he'd reveled in it.

Meghan was so immersed in her discussion with the lamb that she heard the voices too late.

Without warning, the foliage parted and the path before her was suddenly barred by a most fearsome sight. She froze in mid-stride and shrieked.

For an instant, she couldn't speak, so stunned was she by the horseman's sudden ap-

pearance. She could merely stare at the devil.
By Jacob's bloody stone, she swore silently, no
man had ever stood so tall in his stirrups! As
it was, she had to crane her neck up at a painful angle in order to see his face. And sweet
Mary, Joseph, and Jesus! What a face it was! In
truth, he looked more like an angel than a devil.

Though swarthy, his skin appeared to be as
soft as the skin of her arse. And his flaxen hair
was the richest of gold, though she couldn't tell
its length for it was bound at the back of his
neck. His cheekbones were high and well-
hewn, but it was his eyes that held her transfixed: uncanny blue, they bore into her very
soul. He wore blue, but a blue so dark it was
almost black—blue tunic, blue breeches, black
boots. The tunic upon his chest was embla-
zoned with a blood-red lion rearing back upon
its beastly little legs—no mail as the English
were wont to wear, but he certainly had no
need of mail to look invulnerable.

God's truth, were her legs not so entangled
within the rope she held so firmly within her
fist, she would have turned and fled.

She swallowed convulsively, and stammered, "Who . . . who are ye?"

"Who are *you*? The question might be better
asked," he countered, his tone furious. "And
what the bloody hell are you doing upon my
land?"

Meghan gulped back a welling of panic. "*Yer*

land?'' she asked, trying to sound as calm as she might while her heart seemed bent upon pummeling its way out from her breast.

He leaned forward over the horse's withers, and enunciated slowly and more clearly, lest she mistake him, *"My land."*

Meghan swallowed the knot of apprehension that appeared in her throat. It was Montgomerie himself. Henry's Lyon in the flesh—King David's accursed Sassenach mercenary baron!

Sweet Jesu, it suddenly occurred to her—had he left her a trap with the lamb?

Nay, why would he do such a thing? she reasoned. He had nothing to gain.

Och, because he was a greedy, deceiving Englishman. That was why!

"What business have you upon my land, wench? And what are you doing with that lamb?"

Meghan tried to remain composed, but fidgeted under his scrutiny. Her heart hammering fiercely, she searched about for some means of escape, and her heart lurched as she spied a second man emerging from the thicket. This man was dark-haired and burly, with eyes that assessed her quite rudely. Her panic increased tenfold.

"Well," she said, fumbling for an answer, "I—I was walkin', ye see . . ."

"Walking?" he repeated.

"Aye, walkin'," Meghan lied, blinking. "I—I was taking a blessed walk."

"A blessed walk?"

The other man laughed. "Is that like taking a holy shit?" he asked, and chortled at his own childish humor.

Meghan cast him a withering glance.

"So you were taking a walk?" Montgomerie inquired much too pleasantly, but with an unmistakable note of suspicion in his voice.

"I believe 'tis what I said," she snapped, becoming vexed with his annoying echo of her answers. Nor did she bloody well appreciate his tone any more than she did his companion's humor. He spoke as though he thought her an idiot or a liar, neither of which was acceptable to Meghan.

"Did you really?" he asked, with that same unmistakable air of suspicion.

"Och! Do ye no' ha' eyes tae see wi'?" she asked him, losing her temper, jerking up the lead rope to display the evidence. But jerking up the lead rope turned out to be the wrong thing to do. Tangled as it was between her limbs, she tripped herself and promptly fell upon her rear.

"Bluidy rotten rope!" she railed, tossing it down in a fit of fury. "See what ye did!" she hissed at the animal knowing even so it wasn't the poor lammie's fault. And still she couldn't quite help herself. Taking comfort in the fact that the poor beast couldn't possibly comprehend what she was spouting in anger, she railed, "Och, but I should ha' left ye there upon the meadow!"

It was all Montgomerie's fault, she assured herself, and glowered up at him, her cheeks burning with chagrin and no small amount of ire.

"So you found the lamb upon the meadow?" Montgomerie persisted, mocking her still with his tone.

"Will ye stop, please!"

"Stop what?" he asked, arching a brow, as though he thought her completely witless. Meghan bristled.

Och, but his gaze unsettled her. Those blue eyes focused upon her too intensely. "Repeating everything I say, ye ill-bred oaf! I'm no bluidy half-wit! Nor am I deaf!"

"Not mute either—more's the pity," his friend answered blithely.

"Nay!" Meghan agreed, her face heating with indignation, "no' mute, either, ye contemptible boor!" That he'd professed no more than her brothers had long since lamented was of little consequence. He was an ill-bred churl to have said such an insulting thing to her!

Montgomerie smiled darkly. "Now that we've established as much . . . tell me, do you make it a habit to walk and talk with animals?" he asked her.

Meghan blinked, a thought suddenly occurring to her. Sweet Mary, had he overheard her talking to herself? Did he realize who she was?

She bit down upon her lip, and fretted. That's what she got for being so like her grandmin-nie—walking about talking to herself like a bloody loon!

He nodded in her direction. "Give her a hand, Baldwin," he commanded his compan-ion.

"No thank ye!" Meghan declared at once, "I already ha' two!" She glared up at Baldwin. "Keep yerself awa' from me, ye boot-licking toad!"

"Impertinent wench!" Baldwin proclaimed, and came after her anyway. "I'll show you who's more the fool!" he told her.

Meghan scrambled to her feet. "I may be a fool, but I vow I will shriek until yer ears bleed if ye lay a Sassenach hand upon me!" He con-tinued to advance upon her. "Dinna ye touch me, ye . . . ye . . ." She couldn't think of a ter-rible enough epithet to call him. "English cadger!"

Montgomerie had the audacity to chuckle. "Leave her be," he said to his lackey, and the man halted at once.

Scowling fiercely at both of them, Meghan brushed the dirt from her hands, and made ready to flee if the opportunity arose.

"Damn it all, Lyon!" Baldwin protested. "I'll warrant the wench is in need of a good spank-ing, and I'm in the mood to give her one!"

Meghan gasped. "Dinna ye even think it!"

"I'll warrant the same," Montgomerie

agreed, ignoring her protest. "Though I think I'll save that particular pleasure for myself." His eyes fairly gleamed at the prospect, and Meghan bristled.

"Och!" she exclaimed, and clenched her fists at her sides. Who the devil did they think they were? These bloody Sassenachs—discussing her as though they had a right to! If they thought themselves unaccountable for their actions simply because they were David's champions, they were in for a rude awakening, as King David was not well favored in the Highlands. Whatever fear she'd been harboring dissipated in the face of her outrage.

"Greedy rotten bastard!" Baldwin said, breaking into a wide grin. He cast his hands into the air. "She's all yours, *sire*!"

Montgomerie frowned and cast him a warning glare.

"I am *no'* his!" she informed them both at once.

The arrogance of men! How dare they discuss her as though she were a wayward child in need of a good strapping! Not even her brothers treated her so disrespectfully. "I belong tae no mon!" she assured them.

Montgomerie's brows lifted as he turned once more to face her, and Meghan had the sudden impression that for once, she ought to have held her bloody tongue. Something in the way he regarded her made her grimace at her choice of words.

Chapter 5

"**H**ave you no husband?" Lyon asked with no small measure of surprise.

She took a step backward, her delicate brows drawing together into a lovely frown, and hissed like a bloody viper, "Whyever should ye be concerned wi' such a thing, Sassenach?"

Lyon tried not to laugh at her sudden show of wariness. Not even when he'd appeared so suddenly to block her path had she regarded him so suspiciously—anxiously, aye, indignantly, certainly, even a bit fearfully, but not so guardedly.

"Mere curiosity," he answered truthfully, and watched her expression with keen interest.

"Aye, well," she replied with a narrow-eyed glance and an admonishing nod, "ye knoo what they say aboot curiosity!"

"Nay," Lyon replied, unable to keep himself from baiting her, wicked as his mood was. "I'm afraid I don't, wench. Tell me . . . what is it they say?"

He grinned when she glowered at him, but that only seemed to vex her all the more. "Och! I dinna ha' any idea what they say!" she snapped. "Who bluidy cares anyhoo! But 'tis no' guid, I can tell ye that!"

Lyon chuckled. He couldn't seem to help it; her fit of temper amused him. She was strong-willed like his mother, aye, but with one intriguing exception. His mother had expressed herself with words alone, softly spoken but deadly in earnest. The harridan before him spoke with every inch of her lovely body: her eyes, her face, her hands, her very stance bespoke her every emotion. She was as easily read as was Mother Nature in her change of seasons, and as irrepressible and vivid in her expressions as a burst of spring wildflowers.

Christ, but she was a beautiful little termagant.

And she had no husband.

The thought niggled its way into his consideration.

A vision of luscious red hair against pale sheets accosted him, and the image tightened his loins. Damn, but it had been a long time.

Much too long.

Damn it all. Suddenly, he didn't wish to fight anymore; his fun was spoiled. How could he battle against her bastard brothers when he coveted their lovely sister in his bed? He'd much rather be wooing her . . . making love to her . . . kissing those delectable lips . . .

The problem was ... how was he supposed to get her brothers to leave off now that they'd come so far in this feuding? He wasn't naive enough to think it would cease simply because he suddenly wished it so.

Unless he married the wench.

His gaze settled upon the long-legged harridan standing before him. With arms akimbo she stood watching him warily, her beautiful face a testament to God's mastery. Christ, but even scowling she was exquisite. It made him yearn to coax a smile from those sweet lips. He could do it, he was certain.

How many pouty mouths had he cajoled into smiles? More than he could count.

She had no husband.

The thought reared once more, and he suddenly knew what he wanted to do.

David had given him a piece of Scot soil in hopes that his skill at arms would provide unity and peace for Scotland, but Lyon had a far more useful talent to apply toward David's cause.

'Twould be a sin to leave his experience to waste.

He grinned.

She took a step backward, seizing her skirt in her hand as though she would flee. "Why are ye looking at me sae strangely?"

"Because," he answered simply, grinning at her, "I believe I have the perfect solution." He turned to Baldwin, nodding in her direction, commanding him without words to seize her. Baldwin lifted his brows, understanding at once, and he smirked at the girl.

Lyon felt a sudden unreasonable stab of protectiveness toward her.

She took another step backward, seeming to sense the exchange between them. He and Baldwin had been together so long words were seldom necessary between them.

"Solution?" she asked him, cocking her head adorably. "What sort o' solution? What are ye speaking of, Sassenach?"

Lyon didn't answer at once, and she continued to move backward, instinctively placing the lamb between herself and any imminent threat.

Damned if it was going to do her any good, because Lyon was suddenly determined as hell. Knowing her gaze was focused primarily upon him, he spurred his mount to the left of her, blocking escape in that direction. He hoped Baldwin had his wits about him just now, because he'd need to be quick to catch her unawares. The woman was shrewd; he recognized the canny gleam flickering within her green eyes. Careful not to glance in Baldwin's direction—the last thing he wished was to remind the wench of Baldwin's presence—he drove her toward Baldwin. He didn't give her time to think, because she'd doubtless realize his intent. He feigned an advance to the left, forcing her toward Baldwin—only Baldwin

was no longer there. Baldwin had dropped
back to remove himself from her field of vision.
Lyon waited to spy Baldwin's face behind her
now, not daring to give her time to look about,
and then charged after her. She turned instinctively and fled into Baldwin's waiting arms.

She shrieked in outrage.

"Insolent wench!" Baldwin exclaimed.
"Who's more the fool now, heh?" he taunted
her, and began to drag her toward the bushes
behind which he'd tethered his mount.

"Nay! She rides with me," Lyon announced.

Baldwin made the mistake of turning to
question him. "Are you certain, Lyon? She's a
wild one."

Lyon didn't have time to respond.

"I'll bluidy well no' ride wi' either o' ye!"
she said vehemently, and to Lyon's surprise
and Baldwin's misfortune, twisted like a snake
within his friend's arms, catching his wrist
firmly between her teeth. She bit down. Hard.
Lyon could almost hear the crunch of Baldwin's bones and he cringed, but was too awed
by her mettle to do aught but watch the scuffle.

Baldwin howled in pain, and spat a few of
his favorite expletives, but she didn't let go.

"Wench!" he yelped, sounding distressed
now. "Take her, Lyon! Arggghhh! Take her!
Aaaeeeeyyahhh!"

Christ, if he didn't stop her, Lyon decided,
she was going to kill the poor bastard!

She reached back to seize a handful of Baldwin's hair when he didn't at once release her, and then suddenly seemed to change her mind and reached beneath his mail to catch the unfortunate Baldwin between the legs.

Lyon's eyes widened in alarm, but not wider than Baldwin's.

Cunning vixen.

Baldwin's yelp betrayed shock first, then pain. He went pale as parchment. His wild-eyed gaze met Lyon's. "Please!" he managed to squeal. "Pleeeeeeeze!"

Lyon shook himself from his stupor and spurred himself to Baldwin's rescue, plucking the wench's writhing form up from Baldwin's limp grasp. It was more than apparent as he lifted her who had hold of whom, and Lyon couldn't smother a chuckle of disbelief.

The vicious little wench!

Poor Baldwin staggered as she released him.

"How dare ye treat me sae!" she railed at Lyon, kicking as he lifted her. She seemed entirely unconcerned over the thud of Baldwin's burly body as he fell limply onto the forest floor.

"Christ, wench! You've killed him!"

Deciding that he couldn't afford to attend Baldwin until his own private matters were safely guarded, Lyon scooted backward and settled her before him upon his mount. As a matter of self-preservation, he forced her arms to her sides and lifted his thighs over her legs, allowing his weight to pinion her.

Baldwin groaned, but didn't stir.

"Let me gae, rotten Sassenach! He's no' dead, can ye no' hear! Serves him bluidy well right!"

Lyon was certainly relieved to see it was true, but he wasn't stupid enough to release her.

Peering up with glazed eyes, Baldwin announced, "She's riding with you!"

Lyon answered with a chuckle.

"She's a bloody menace!" Baldwin squealed, his voice yet to return to normal.

Damned if Lyon didn't agree. He grinned down at his old friend, holding the wench more firmly when she twisted furiously before him, and said, "I noticed."

His grin widened when Baldwin scowled up at him.

Meghan watched the both of them incredulously.

How dare they simply sit there conversing so blithely—as though he weren't cleaving her arm in twain with the force of his grip!

"Ye'll let me gae if ye ken what's guid for ye!" she interjected.

Montgomerie loosened his grip, though he didn't release her. He slipped one arm firmly about her waist and leaned to speak low into her ear. The warmth of his breath made her cheek tingle, sent a quiver down her spine. "Mayhap I don't know what's good for me, wench?" he suggested, his voice much too whispery to be soothing.

Meghan reared back and slapped his face for taking such liberties, and resisted the urge to yelp when she managed to push his face against her own in turn.

"Bloody hell!" he said and glared down at her, looking more startled by her slap than angered.

Meghan was startled by her reaction as well, if the truth be known, but she certainly wasn't going to show it. She rubbed her cheek in dismay. Och, but her temper was surely going to be the death of her one of these days! She peered at him with narrowed eyes. "Trust me when I tell ye that it hurt me more than it did ye, Sassenach!"

"The bloody woman's insane!" Baldwin declared, staring openmouthed from the ground below.

"Hurt *you* more?" Lyon repeated, sounding bemused. He raised a hand to his face, stroking where she'd slapped him. "That's precisely what my mother used to claim when she would rap me upon my head." Even as Meghan watched, her handprint manifested itself upon his cheek. Guilt pricked at her, but she ignored it. There was no way she was going to feel remorseful for defending herself against these mercenaries! "Somehow," he went on, "I cannot think so."

"O' course it hurt me more," Meghan persisted. "I managed tae strike myself as well, dinna ye see?"

His brows twitched. "What a pity," he said, his mouth quirking, and Meghan was no longer certain whether he was angry or amused.

Surely not amused?

"I say we let her go!" Baldwin announced. "For her own sake," he explained. "If you don't strangle the insolence out of her, Lyon, I bloody well will!"

"Nay, you'll not," Lyon proclaimed in deadly earnest. "You'll accord her the respect due your mistress."

"What!" The outcry came at once from both Meghan and Baldwin together. Their gazes collided, and then each turned to stare in disbelief at Lyon. He smiled at her, and she knew he must be mocking her. "What did you say?" she and Baldwin asked again in unison, and then turned again to glare at one another.

"Will you stop!" Baldwin hissed. "I've no need of an echo!"

"I ha' a right tae speak, ye graceless oaf!" Meghan answered, wholly undone now. Surely she hadn't heard aright! She narrowed her eyes at Baldwin. "By the by," she added, "I think I should tell ye that ye look like a quivering fish flopping aboot in that silly mail shirt. Why dinna ye worry yerself aboot gettin' up, and mind yer own affairs while ye're aboot it!"

His ears turned bright-red, Meghan noticed,

and she smiled with satisfaction. He turned to Lyon. "She's bloody mad, I tell you! No woman I've ever known speaks to a man so disrespectfully, Lyon! She's no lady!"

Meghan would have cast herself at him to slap his face had Lyon not restrained her. "Mayhap because ye bluidy Sassenachs dunno a real lady when ye see one! Ye like yer women bloodless as cadavers wi' all that paint upon their milksop faces! And spineless as slithering slimy worms!"

"God's teeth! She's not only mad, but she's bloodthirsty," Baldwin declared, "and a thieving Scot, as well!"

Meghan gritted her teeth. Och, but she was going to murder the rotten Sassenach. "Why, ye . . . !" She tried to kick out at him, but couldn't move her legs with Montgomerie's blasted ten-stone thigh draped over her limbs. "I'm no bluidy thief! Ye're the bluidy thieves! Ye're the ones who've robbed everything but the teeth from my brothers' mouths!"

He had nothing to say in his own defense, Meghan noticed. Instead he turned to Montgomerie.

"What in God's name are you thinking, Lyon?" he asked.

Montgomerie had remained entirely too silent during their furious exchange, Meghan realized suddenly, and turned to face him, only to find him grinning at her.

"I'm thinking the two of you are going to

need keepers, is what I'm thinking," he said, his blue eyes twinkling with mirth.

Meghan blinked at their brilliance.

Och, but up close, his eyes were bluer, even, than her brother Colin's, and as luminous as sapphires.

"Ye canna be serious?" she asked him.

"Why not?" he answered, grinning still.

Meghan couldn't begin to conceive of what he could possibly find so amusing just now. "Ye canna simply wed wi' someone against their will," she apprised him as calmly as she was able. He was making sport of her now, she realized.

"Of course I can," he argued. " 'Tis quite commonly done."

Meghan stared at him in utter disbelief.

" 'Tis the perfect solution, as I've told you."

"Tae what?" Meghan answered, aghast, only to find herself with an echo once more.

Baldwin, the idiot, was still lying upon the ground, staring up at his lord as though he thought him gone utterly mad. "Solution to what?"

"To end the feuding, of course," Montgomerie replied. "I grow tired of sparring with children."

Meghan screwed up her face in disbelief as she turned toward him. "Och! But ye canna believe that forcing me tae wed wi' ye will end the feuding, ye daff mon! My brothers would sooner see me a widow!"

"You *want* to end the feud, Lyon?" Baldwin asked, sounding nonplussed by the notion. "But I thought—"

"I've changed my mind!" Montgomerie replied. "Get your arse up, Baldwin!"

"Ye've changed yer mind?" Meghan repeated, a sudden apprehension rearing.

She peered from one man to the other, not liking what it was she was hearing.

"What do ye mean ye've changed yer mind?" She narrowed her gaze upon him.

"Nothing less, nothing more," he answered much too easily. "Simply that ... I've changed my mind, wench."

Meghan went wholly still before him.

The bloody wretch!

"Ye mean tae tell me ye only noo ha' suddenly decided ye no longer wish tae feud wi' my brothers?"

"Something like that."

"Why?" Meghan demanded at once.

He had the decency at least to appear a little chagrined by her question.

He might have said she looked like a cow, and she wouldn't have taken such offense! He could have told her she was mad as a loon, and she might have bloody well agreed! He should have admitted to aught but this, because Meghan was suddenly insanely furious!

She inhaled a breath, and said when her temper was restrained enough to speak, "Let me be certain I ha' this aright, Sassenach!"

He tightened his hold upon her waist, seeming to sense her rising fury, but answered calmly. "Certainly."

"Ye didna mind the feud before?"

"Not particularly."

"Though noo ye do?"

"Aye."

"And ye wish tae end it. Why?" Meghan demanded once more.

He cocked his head, offering a waggish smile. "For the good of Scotia," he answered evenly.

"I see," said Meghan, gritting her teeth, restraining herself, though barely. "And when did it occur tae ye tae be sae blessed noble?" She narrowed her gaze at him, casting daggers with her eyes.

His brows lifted. "Sudden inspiration, shall we say?"

Meghan lost her composure at that. She twisted wrathfully within his embrace, trying to little avail to free herself. If he wouldn't let her go, she was going to see both of them toppled off his mount to the ground! "My sweet grandminnie said ye were all wolves, and ye are! Ravenous, gluttonous wolves!" she raged, maddened at feeling so helpless against his greater strength and unwelcomed good humor. "I'll no' wed wi' ye, ye thieving, conniving, lascivious, shallow-brained oaf of a man!" Och, but he would not budge. "What are ye made o' anyhoo! Stone?"

No matter how hard she tried to free herself, he was faster, stronger.

And he had the audacity to laugh!

"I dinna see what is sae blessed funny!" Meghan snapped.

He continued to laugh, restraining her with too-little effort, and Meghan, in her frustration, lunged at him, trying to find purchase for her teeth on his too-beautiful cheek, the knave!

He jerked away, laughing all the harder.

Chapter 6

"**I** think you've gone as mad as the wench!" Baldwin exclaimed, leaping up and out of the fray.

"She's mad as a fox, I wager!" Montgomerie declared, laughing still.

Mad as a fox.

Meghan ceased her struggles of a sudden, hearing her grandminnie's voice as though it were a murmur in her ears.

"They think I'm mad," she'd oft said. *"I knoo they think I'm mad, Meggie dearlin'—and I am! I am! Mad as a fox!"* And she'd wink and cackle in amusement. And then more seriously she'd say, with a crook of her long slender finger, *"Ye be the same, Meghan, and wi' that face o' yers ye'll possess the world in the wee palm o' yer precious hand."*

Fia had certainly had a way with people, as well as with animals. Mad as they'd all thought her, she'd always seemed a step ahead of them, bending everyone to her will. What would Fia do now? she wondered. What would she say? How would she deliver herself from a situation such as this?

The little lamb bleated in that instant.

Meghan turned to see that the poor creature had retreated against the brush and was watching them warily. They had yet to accuse her outright of stealing the animal, which told her in truth that they weren't entirely certain she had.

She peered back at Montgomerie, gauging his expression. He was watching her curiously, waiting.

Mad as a fox . . . Ye be the same, she heard Fia say to her.

The little lamb bleated once more . . . and suddenly Meghan knew what to do.

She cast another glance at the lamb, trying not to smirk. So Baldwin thought her mad, did he? Well, it certainly wouldn't serve her to confirm that notion because he wouldn't believe her then, but Meghan could certainly *prove* him right . . . if she tried.

She had *mad auld Fia's* example to follow, after all.

It wasn't easy to smother her grin, but she did, thinking that surely Montgomerie wouldn't wish to wed with her . . . if he truly thought her mad.

She turned to face the wee lammie, and asked, "What did ye say?"

"Not a bloody thing, wench," Montgomerie

answered, sounding suddenly bemused.

She cast him a glare. "I wasna talkin' tae ye!" she snapped and turned again to the lamb.

The glade went utterly silent. It seemed even the wind stilled in the treetops. She felt Montgomerie's gaze upon her nape—Baldwin's, as well. Sweet Mary, but she prayed she could pull this off.

She waited for the lamb to bleat once more, and then replied, as though she were in actual conversation with the creature, "I canna, Fia! I simply canna! And ye canna make me!"

Oblivious to her spurious indignation, the little lamb cried out once more.

Meghan slumped her shoulders. "Nay," she answered, hoping she sounded perfectly disheartened, but respectful, "ye never ha'."

She lowered her head in a moment of contemplative silence, and the little lamb bleated once more.

Both men were suddenly very quiet, Meghan noticed, and it was all she could do to strangle the laughter that welled within her.

She straightened, wholly aware of the grip that slackened upon her arms. She thought he might be a little bewildered.

"Well," she said, sounding utterly resolved as she faced the lamb once more, "if ye really think sae, I will. But I willna like it."

"Is she talking to that bloody animal?" Baldwin asked, sounding quite appalled.

Montgomerie didn't reply.

Please talk back, she pleaded with the sweet little creature. *Say something . . . say something . . . anything . . .*

The lamb bleated.

God bless ye! she silently lauded the animal.

"I'll do my best, Fia," she responded, then peered back at Lyon Montgomerie. "Verra well!" she said, sounding exasperated. "I'll do it!"

Meghan could have sworn she'd caught him with his mouth agape, but he recovered quickly enough. "What?" he asked her, his expression clearly unsettled, though collected. "What is it you will do?"

Meghan rolled her eyes. "Why, I'll wed wi' ye o' course, ye silly dolt! What else?"

He blinked, and Meghan felt almost smug over the look of surprise that appeared in his stark blue eyes.

"You will?" Baldwin asked, sounding non-plussed as well.

"Aye! I'll wed wi' him—though I willna like it!" she assured them both.

Montgomerie narrowed his eyes at her. "And why the sudden change of heart?"

Meghan lifted a brow. "Who says I've had a change o' heart, Sassenach?"

"Very well then, why the change of mind?"

"Because she's mad, I tell you!" Baldwin persisted. "Can you not see that, Lyon?"

Meghan smiled inwardly. Now was the perfect opportunity, she thought, to introduce them to "Fia." It was all she could do to keep the laughter from her voice as she informed them both, "Why, because Fia says sae, o' course!"

Montgomery frowned at her. "Fia?"

She gave him her most guileless look in response. "My grandminnie!" she explained, and smiled fondly at the animal, waving at it as though it might wave back. "She never leads me astray. Grandminnie always knoos best!"

His face screwed up with what Meghan could only interpret as disbelief, and she had to bite the inside of her lip to keep from giggling.

He blinked. "You *are* speaking of the lamb?"

Meghan returned a frown, pretending ignorance, and prayed she'd not spoil the effect by laughing out loud. "What lamb?" she asked him.

He didn't answer at once. "That lamb," he said finally, pointing to the beast in question.

Meghan gave him a glower of the sort she usually reserved for Colin. "That's nae lamb, ye knave!" she declared, pretending to be insulted. "That's my grandminnie!"

He scowled. "You cannot be serious?"

"O' course I am!" Meghan assured him, trying not to laugh at the outrageous lie.

"Of course she is!" Baldwin maintained. "Do you not recall that she was talking to the beast when we discovered her?"

The lamb bleated. Perfect timing, Meghan thought.

"Och! Nay! I dinna think I can do it, Fia!" Meghan exclaimed, effecting a tone of defiance.

"Christ!" Montgomerie exploded. "You cannot believe I would fall for such a ludicrous tale? That's a bloody rotten lamb you're talking to!"

Meghan didn't have to pretend outrage now. His very tone vexed her. "I dunno what ye're speakin' of, Sassenach, but dinna ye dare speak sae rudely o' my grandminnie!"

"You cannot be serious?" he said once more.

"I can, and I am!"

Lyon studied her face for some indication of her lie.

Her expression revealed only her umbrage.

She was a bloody stinking good actress, he decided.

"You would have me believe..." He pointed at the lamb once more just to be certain there was no mistake. "... that dumb beast is your grandmother?"

"I would ha' ye believe naught a'tall, Sassenach! I dinna care what ye think! I'd ha' ye let me gae! And I take it back!" She tried to shrug free of him again. "I willna wed a mon who is sae rude!"

The little lamb bleated.

She turned to the beast, and said vehemently, "Ye dinna ken what ye're askin' o' me, Fia! I willna wed this brute! Not for Scotland,

not for my brothers, not for peace, nor anythin'
else a'tall!''

Lyon blinked in the face of her ridiculous ti-
rade.

She couldn't be serious.

She certainly looked serious.

She was talking to the beast as though it
could comprehend what she was saying. And
the animal turned away, looking for all the
world disgusted with her reply. If Lyon didn't
know better, he might have imagined the two
were actually communicating.

He frowned as he looked from one to the
other.

What the devil was he thinking? They
couldn't possibly be conversing. It was incon-
ceivable.

Unless she truly *was* mad?

Something about the way she peered up at
him then, the shrewd sparkle in those beautiful
deep-green eyes, gave him pause. She watched
him expectantly, and seemed to be searching
his expression. And it struck him of a sudden
. . . she wasn't talking to the bloody animal at
all. She was contriving. Cunning wench. She
was using Baldwin's insult to her gain.

Well, it wasn't going to work, because he
was suddenly resolved to his plan. He wanted
peace and was willing to sacrifice for it—particularly so when the sacrifice would make
such a lovely bedfellow.

"Very well!" Lyon exclaimed. "The more the

merrier. We shall simply bring Grandminnie along, too!"

It was her turn to blink in stupefaction, and Lyon could but grin at her startled expression. "We will?"

"Aye!" he said exuberantly. "Please accept my sincerest apologies for having insulted your lovely grandminnie. She does indeed know best," he declared.

She narrowed her eyes, and gave him a look of apprehension that made him smile. "She does?"

He winked at her. "Of course she does. I can tell she's a very wise woman, besides."

"Ye can?"

"Aye! And only consider the good we shall accomplish, you and I, if we follow your sweet grandminnie's counsel."

"We shall?" Meghan blinked. Somehow, this plan had gone terribly awry.

"If you can but forgive my churlishness," he continued, "and agree to be my bride . . . you and I shall put an end to this feud once and for all. Only think of it. No more fighting."

Meghan lifted a brow. She doubted that; men were born to fight. She frowned. Rot and curse him, he didn't have to present it quite so nobly.

And yet, he spoke true enough. The feuding would indeed be over, her brothers would be safe—and she would be doing Alison a favor besides.

Still, she wasn't quite willing to give up her

yarn. "Fia can come too?" she asked him with lifted brows.

He nodded. "I give you my word," he answered much too soberly. "I shall do my utmost to make your grandminnie welcome in my home."

Meghan's brows collided. "Ye will?"

He didn't have to be so blessed accommodating! It wasn't so easy to dislike him this way.

Nor was it easy to think when he smiled at her so engagingly.

His blue eyes flickered with amusement.

At her expense?

She thought so, but was unwilling to sound the retreat as yet. Stubborn she might be, but there was much to be said for sheer determination.

"And what o' my brothers?" Meghan persisted.

"We shall invite them to the wedding, of course," he answered blithely.

Meghan winced at the very notion. She could scarcely imagine her brothers so conciliatory. "They would dine upon yer eyes and feast upon yer tongue!" she advised him with absolute certainty. "Even were I tae agree tae such a thing, my brothers would never concede."

"We shall see," he said, and then instructed Baldwin to retrieve his mount. Baldwin did as he was told without another word. "And don't forget *Grandminnie*," Montgomerie called after him. Baldwin gave him a harried glance, but turned and went after the lamb. If Meghan hadn't been so distressed, she might have had to laugh at Baldwin, clad in his silver mail, chasing after a bald little lamb.

"Ye canna simply take me!" she protested, when it seemed he was serious. "No' withoot giving me the chance tae speak tae my brothers! They will never agree tae this!"

"Then we shall find a way to convince them," he told her, and spurred his mount, drawing her firmly against him.

"Never!" Meghan vowed, and shoved away from him. "Never!"

Chapter 7

Lyon merely smiled.

"Ye can force me tae stand at the altar, ye knoo, but ye canna make me say the vows!"

"We shall see."

"Never," she swore again.

That was what they all said: *Never.*

Only Lyon knew better. He hadn't met a woman yet he couldn't woo with pretty words and a few stolen kisses. Women were fickle creatures with pudding hearts and insatiable vanities; they said *Never* all the while their hands reached out to draw his lips to their lovely, greedy mouths.

That was his experience.

Not even his mother had been so different: all the while she'd claimed her independence of men, she'd been a slave to her excessive pride. And she was, in truth, a beautiful woman—even now in her later years. At two score and two years, his mother still commanded her choice of men. They gave her jew-

els and fine cloth and anything her heart
desired . . . until she grew tired of them and
discarded them for another. They even
mourned her when she was gone. Lyon could
easily count upon his two hands—and then
some—the men whose hearts his mother had
stolen.

And yet his mother was not hard-hearted.
She was kind and generous and good-natured
to a fault. And if she never returned her lovers'
affections, she treated them well enough. Nay,
his mother was simply . . . free and easy.

Or rather, her price was extravagant and she
was quite discriminating, but she lived her life
without concern for aught but the present.
Lyon admired her for that. It was something of
a mystery to him that most people either remained so entrenched within the past, or lived
entirely for the morrow, that so few remembered to live for the moment.

And he was as guilty as any.

Well, not today . . . not *this* moment. He was
following his greatest impulse just now, and
damn the consequences! It had been much too
long since he'd followed his blood knowledge.

His mother had cosseted him in his early
years, encouraging him to follow his heart's
desires. She'd sacrificed to see him well edu-
cated. She'd made compromises for his sake
when she would never have done the same for
herself. Lyon's greatest regret was that he had
forsaken his own institutions. He'd relied all of

his life upon his size and brawn to survive amongst peers who'd viewed him as little more than a castoff, a poor relation. Though never acknowledged by his father, he'd grown up amidst the elite of Henry's court. And it hadn't been long before he'd discovered that might and sword brought respect in his cast-off world. And with little hope of ever earning his own fief or pursuing his own life, he'd resigned himself much too early to a mercenary way.

He'd given in.

He'd compromised his convictions.

And for what? A fistful of jewels and a bloody name.

And an even bloodier sword.

Women had come and gone from his life in that time, but he'd regarded them as little more than passing fancies—a mutual perception, he was well aware—for he'd had nothing to offer them, nothing to give of himself. From the time he'd been a lad, he'd known he was destined to be alone. As a boy he'd stood apart from his peers, an observer, his hours spent in learning with the clergy. When he became a man, others trod lightly in his presence. It was the most he could have expected. *Respect.* Even if they didn't quite see him as an equal, they'd respected him at least.

And that had been enough.

"What do you wish to be when you grow up?" David of Scotia had once asked him in gratitude for Lyon's defending him.

Piers had thought about it an instant and had shrugged and answered simply, *"It matters not as long as I am happy."* And had truly meant it.

"That's all you want?" David had asked in surprise, cocking his head and staring at Piers as though he were a two-headed calf. *"Well,"* he'd announced importantly, *"I wish to be king! And when I am king,"* he'd promised, *"I shall give all my friends whatever they wish for! If you wish for happiness, Piers of Montgomerie, I shall find it for you and then wrap it up in golden fleece and hand it to you upon a silver plate. What do you think about that?"*

Piers had thought it a generous if pompous gesture, but decided he had best find happiness for himself, as the ninth son of a king—any king—was like never to sit upon any throne at all, but the one in his own garderobe. He hadn't said so, however. He'd simply smiled his appreciation at his friend.

Well, David of Scotia had won his throne, after all, and he'd given Lyon the next best thing. He'd favored Lyon with land: good rich Scot's soil, upon which he could build his own legacy. And suddenly, he was free to dream and plan.

The woman sitting before him was a new beginning.

An alliance with her brothers would bear him roots upon this land.

He wanted that. Wanted her.

It wasn't merely that she was beautiful,

though she was. Wildly so—with her luscious red hair and cool green eyes, a man could lose himself in those eyes. Aye, but she was more . . . she was the first brick in his foundation.

"You are quiet," he said at her back. She stiffened before him, and her reaction made him smile. She might not particularly like him, but she certainly wasn't indifferent toward him, and that knowledge pleased him. Love and hate were not so disparate emotions that one could not be manipulated into the other. They, at least, were extremes of emotion, while indifference was another matter altogether; it was the lack.

"And how would ye ha' me sit before ye?" she snapped, not bothering to peer back at him. "Ye're a contemptible Sassenach boor who's taking me against my will!"

Nay, he thought, she definitely wasn't indifferent toward him, and that pleased him immensely.

Challenged him, even.

Her animosity was like a gauntlet tossed at his feet. He couldn't walk away. Nor did he wish to, as he sensed the prize was unparalleled.

Nor had he lost a match as yet, and that knowledge gave him satisfaction as it never had before. He didn't fight unfairly, but neither did he give any mercy. He fought to win.

If it was the last thing he accomplished, he was going to tame the little harridan sitting before him. He'd once been told his tongue wove words of gold. No woman was immune to praise.

He gently lifted a strand of her hair in his hand. She didn't seem to feel it . . . or perhaps she simply allowed it.

Soft.

His fingers reveled in the texture, silky and thick. He brought the strand to his nostrils and inhaled its scent. He knit his brows. "Lovely," he told her. "Quite lovely. But the scent eludes me."

She didn't thank him for the compliment, nor did she seem to take the bait.

"I like it," he continued.

"I see that," she answered, quite flippantly. "I can tell by the way ye've buried yer nose in it, Sassenach. Enjoying yerself?"

Lyon couldn't help but chuckle. Smart-arsed wench. He moved closer, drawn to the softness of her tresses like a lodestone to metal. "Mmmmm," he murmured, "it rather seems I am."

"Do ye mind no' doing that?" she asked him, sounding vexed now, shrugging away. " 'Tis a rinse made from marrow, if ye must knoo. That's what ye smell. I use it ofttimes after washing my hair, else I canna comb it. It's one o' my grandminnie's recipes. And it seems tae ha' that same effect upon all animals—dogs in particular!"

He had to crush the urge to laugh. Was she

calling him a dog? Certainly an animal, at the very least.

"Does it now?" he answered.

"Aye!" she declared, turning and jerking her hair from his grasp. "It does!" She turned her back to him once more, leaning away from him, so as not to touch him.

Lyon grinned. She certainly was not going to be an easy victory, that was plain to see. But then . . . something worth having was certainly worth fighting for.

He'd raised his sword enough times for lesser things.

And he was certainly going to enjoy the battle. It thrilled him as nothing had in a very long time.

Perhaps she would appreciate a more direct approach? "I beg to differ, wench," he said softly at her nape. " 'Tis *you* who has that effect upon me, not your bloody hair rinse."

He felt her shiver, and was satisfied.

Amazing how her simple reaction to his words could warm his loins and heat his blood, when it had begun to take so much to stir him at all in the past years. It elated him.

He'd become rather jaded in his tastes. But she was different somehow. Even her barbs seemed to enchant him.

He bent nearer, savoring the sweet scent of her flesh. "Tell me, wench . . . Shall I call you 'wench'? Or do you have a name of preference?"

She turned and glowered at him. "O' course I've a name, Sassenach, but ye can call me *wench* if it pleases ye."

"You'll not tell me?" He gave her his most wounded look.

She merely smirked, unmoved. "Seems no'."

He lifted his brows. "I *could* ask your grand-minnie," he proposed, certain she wouldn't carry on the charade any longer as it was a lost cause. He planned to have her, will she nill she.

"Gae on, then," she answered, mocking him in return. "She'll no' tell ye, unless I give her leave tae, Sassenach, and I shallna give her leave," she assured him.

Stubborn Scot.

"Somehow," Lyon replied sardonically, "I guessed she'd not."

"That's because *Fia*," she stressed, "respects the wishes of others. *Unlike some people I've encountered*," she told him quite pointedly.

Lyon ignored the barb, determined to woo and win her. "Pity you won't say . . ."

"Isn't it though?" she answered blithely.

"Aye . . . a beautiful woman could only bear a beautiful name."

She turned to cast him a wicked glare. "I should warn ye, Sassenach, I'm no' some empty-headed wench that flattery can fill my head sae easily. Ye'll no' sway me wi' pretty words!"

Cunning vixen, but he didn't believe it. All women loved adulation.

"Idiocy," she assured him, "doesna course through Brodie blood!"

"But madness does?"

Meghan opened her mouth to speak, and then closed it again, uncertain how to reply to that particular remark.

He was baiting her, she realized by the tone of his voice. It was quite clear he did not believe her little tale. But all was not lost.

It *had* been said that madness cursed Brodie blood.

It wasn't true, of course. It was just that no one understood her mother or her grandmother. The truth was that her mother had simply been aggrieved by lost love, while old Fia had been a bit eccentric . . . and yet the rumor had been spread . . . and Meghan could possibly use it now to her benefit. But she must be careful in answering . . . if she truly wished Montgomerie to believe her little fabrication. And she certainly did.

Surely he would let her go if he truly thought her insane? No man could willingly wed a woman who was mad.

Could he?

How now to plant the seed without being so obvious in her intentions?

And suddenly it came to her.

No need to sweeten her tone, as it would merely stir his suspicion. "Do ye always believe everything ye hear?" she asked him, her tone as snappish as she could manage. Ire was as good a defense as any against the sound of his voice. God help her, the tone of it sent shivers down her spine . . . The feel of his breath against her nape sent gooseflesh racing across her skin.

He was silent an instant, and then answered, "What precisely is it I am to have heard?"

Meghan smiled to herself, pleased he should fall so easily into her snare. "Well, it is no' true!"

"What is not?" His confusion was manifest in his tone.

"They've no idea o' what they are speakin' of!" Meghan assured him, well aware that she was confusing him all the more and thinking she was enjoying this entirely too much. Och! Since when had she enjoyed telling a lie so bloody much? What devil had gotten into her? And why did this suddenly seem more a challenge of wits than a clever machination to save herself from an unwanted marriage?

"You're confusing me, wench," he announced quite frankly.

Meghan tried to sound perfectly innocent. "I am?"

"You are," he replied, sounding much too distracted to be precisely angry. "What the bloody hell are you talking about?"

"There is no curse on Brodie blood!" she swore. " 'Tis all a bluidy rotten lie!"

"I never said there was, wench," he answered, sounding befuddled now.

"Oh!" Meghan exclaimed, and hushed herself, waiting.

He said nothing more, and she pretended an interest in the woodlands as they passed through them.

It had been a long time since she'd ventured this way. The MacLeans had owned this adjoining land and she and Alison had explored it all at some point or another. She and her grandminnie had as well, though old man MacLean had never taken quite so kindly to Fia's foraging. Meghan vividly remembered the verbal warfare the two frequently engaged in—MacLean calling her a crazy old hag, and Fia calling him a mean, selfish, fat old arse.

The memory made her smile.

Lord, how she missed her sweet grandminnie! Fia had never cowered before anyone in her life—most certainly not to Meghan's brothers, nor to old man MacLean. Not Leith, not Colin, or Gavin had ever understood their grandmother in the least.

Meghan secretly wished she could be her.

"What curse?" Lyon asked suddenly.

Meghan bit the inside of her lip. "Oh . . . never mind," she answered evasively. She peered back to gauge his expression, then pretended an interest in Baldwin's whereabouts. "I wonder if my grandminnie will fare well enough wi' that daft mon o' yers," she fretted.

"I'm certain she'll be just fine!"

"She has terrible gout," Meghan elaborated.

"Does she?" he asked tersely. He sounded quite skeptical.

"Oh, aye!" Meghan exclaimed. "It pains her terribly."

"Does it?" he answered.

"Aye," Meghan said.

"I have to wonder," he said, "just why it is you would lead your grandminnie about with a rope."

Meghan thought about that merely an instant before replying pertly, "She's half-blind, o' course."

"So she has the gout and is blind, as well . . . Anything else?"

Meghan bit the inside of her lip, trying not to smile at their ridiculous discourse. "Well, she's a little bit deaf sometimes, sae ye ha' tae scream, or she willna answer."

"You don't say?" he replied acerbically. "Anything else?"

"Let me think," she said. And then, "Nay . . . nay . . . I think no'."

"Are you certain?"

"Oh, I think sae," Meghan said, and smiled to herself. "Unless ye consider chin hairs an affliction?"

"Chin hairs?"

Meghan could hear the incredulity in his tone. She sincerely hoped she was driving him as mad as she hoped he thought *she* was.

"Aye," she said. "Fia certainly thinks they are."

Chapter 8

The woman was incorrigible.

She was enjoying herself, Lyon was certain.

And she'd managed to pique his curiosity despite the fact that he knew she was baiting him. "What curse?" he asked once more.

She peered coyly back at him. "Och, noo! Surely ye dinna believe in curses, Sassenach? No' the mighty Lyon!"

Vixen.

He could tell by the sparkle in her eyes that she was mocking him. And quite well, besides.

Well, two could certainly play at this game . . .

"You are correct, of course," he relented. "Never mind, wench, I've no longer any desire to know."

She went still before him, quiet too for an instant, and Lyon smiled.

"Ye dinna?"

"Nay."

"Well, 'tis naught more than silly babble at any rate," she said after another moment's contemplative silence.

"I'm certain," he agreed, and suppressed a grin.

They came from the forest into the bright afternoon sun. Lyon could make out the pounding of hammers and the clamor of voices in the distance, and the sound made him feel a sense of pride unlike any he'd ever experienced. This was his land, his home: his men were at work rebuilding, and there was something incredibly rousing about bringing this particular woman into his domain. Something about the occasion made him sit straighter in the saddle . . . compelled him to suck in a breath.

The scent of wild heather permeated the air . . . laced now with a more elusive and intriguing scent. His gaze returned to the woman sitting before him, and his loins tightened familiarly. Aye, something about her inspired him in a way he hadn't been inspired in much too long.

She made him feel alive.

Bloody hell, who was he fooling?

She made him feel.

All of his senses were heightened.

He leaned closer, unable to keep himself from it, compelled to move nearer, inhaling the sweet scent of her beautiful hair once more. Marrow, was it? The mere thought made him smile. Saucy wench. Nay . . . what he scented was the faintest trace of rosemary . . . and sunshine.

There was nothing ostentatious about the woman sitting before him, nothing embellished. She was earthy and honest, and while there was nothing naive about her, she had an air of innocence that was decidedly refreshing. Unlike the women he'd known in his life, her eyes did not speak of seduction all the while her lashes fluttered with affected innocence.

But she seduced him nevertheless.

She sighed audibly and Lyon felt the breath leave his own lungs. How was it that she affected him so keenly?

What was it about her that made him so attuned to every breath she took and every word she uttered?

"I shouldna ha' said anything," she lamented.

On the contrary, he thought, he relished hearing her voice. Somehow it was the embodiment of both woman and child at once—her tone both sweet and provocative. It bewitched him, made him yearn both to coddle and to devour her all at once.

She sighed again, and he smiled to himself, knowing it was torturing her not to be able to elaborate, and decided to put her out of her misery once and for all. "Though now that you have," he prompted, smiling, "you'll expound?"

"Weel!" She relented at once. "If ye insist!"

Lyon's grin widened.

"Och, but if I tell ye, ye mustna believe it!" she instructed quite firmly. "Swear it!"

"How can I promise such a thing, wench, when I've no idea how your disclosure will strike me? Tell me your tale and I shall tell you quite frankly whether I believe it or nay."

She seemed to consider that an instant. "Fair enough," she replied. " 'Tis wholly untrue, o' course, and unfairly said, but they claim we Brodie women are cursed."

He sensed where she was leading with this, and it was all he could do to keep from laughing. "How so, wench?"

"Weel," she continued, " 'tis rumored that madness runs in Brodie blood—but 'tis no' true!" she was quick to add.

Lyon had no doubt.

"And quite unkind tae say! Dinna ye think sae?"

"I've not heard such a thing," he admitted. He wondered if she could possibly be speaking the truth, and decided not, as she was clearly enjoying this far too much.

"You hadna?" She sounded so bloody disappointed that he had to reconsider. "Oh," she said.

Christ, but she was a bloody good liar. Lyon tried not to laugh, though his shoulders shook with mirth. He couldn't answer at once, and was relieved when she continued of her own accord.

"The truth is that my mother was hardly mad," she went on, "merely a bit . . . emotional. And my grandminnie . . . she was only eccentric."

Lyon's brows lifted. "*Was?*" he asked her, catching her slip of the tongue, and unable to keep himself from baiting her in return. "She *was* eccentric? And what is she now?"

She peered back at him, her brows drawn together into a frown. She didn't seem to catch his meaning for an instant, and then: "Is!" she amended at once. "Is, o' course!"

This time he couldn't contain his chuckle. " 'Tis good to know," he said, laughing softly, "as I wouldn't wish to bring a madwoman into my home."

"Oh?" she answered, and managed to instill a note of hope in the single word.

Lyon waited for her to suddenly spout some confession of her own madness, but he waited for naught. She was much too shrewd for that.

"I wonder what is keeping them!" she said a little worriedly.

Stubborn wench.

He couldn't believe she would persist in this absurd charade. He supposed she was hoping he would change his mind, but she was hoping in vain, because the longer he considered it, the more convinced he was that he was doing the right thing. It truly was the perfect solution for all concerned.

She turned to search the path behind him,

and Lyon was at once intrigued by the flush high upon her cheeks. Not only was he going to wed her, he vowed, but he was going to wed her of her own accord.

Arrogant though it might be, he was perfectly confident in his . . . *powers of persuasion*.

And he was feeling quite merciless just now, quite the Lyon circling his prey.

She brought out something primordial in him—something more than mere lust. The need to possess was overwhelming.

"They'll be along," he assured her, and had to restrain himself from leaning forward and brushing his mouth across the warmth of her cheek. He imagined the feel of it against his lips . . . of his tongue against her burning skin . . . and it sent a jolt of pure sensation through him.

Christ, but she seemed to have little notion of the tempest that raged within him. If only she realized, he was certain she'd be kicking and screaming just now, instead of employing such sophistry against him. He swallowed with some difficulty as his mouth was becoming quite dry, and said, " 'Tis more than likely Baldwin may have—"

"There they are!" she exclaimed. "And 'tis aboot time!"

Lyon turned to find Baldwin emerging from the woodlands some ways behind them, dragging the little lamb in tow.

She shrieked suddenly, startling the hell out of him.

He had to reach out and snatch her back before she was able to leap from his mount.

He jerked the reins, halting at once.

"Are you truly insane, wench?"

Meghan didn't have to pretend outrage for her grandmother's sake.

Her temper erupted at the sight of Baldwin dragging the lamb behind him.

How dare he treat the poor creature so cruelly! She wanted to leap at Baldwin and snatch the hair from his head. Mounted upon his horse, he held the lead rope in hand, and was dragging the poor creature behind him, not bothering to slow when the confused animal resisted in fright. He was all but strangling the poor sweet baby! "How dare he!" she exploded.

"How dare who what?" Lyon snarled, scowling at her.

She didn't bloody care if he was angry with her just now. "Stop him!" she shrieked in outrage. "Let me down! How dare he treat her sae unkindly!" Meghan glared up at him. "Tell him tae lift her onto his mount, Sassenach, or I'll no' gae wi' ye!"

"The lamb?"

Meghan cast him daggers with her eyes. "Fia," she countered. "Her name is Fia! Tell him tae let her ride, or I'll no' gae wi' ye!"

His jaw clenched, and he seemed vexed that she persisted.

Meghan didn't care.

"Does it seem you have a choice?" he had the nerve to ask her.

How dare he think she did not! "This isna England, Sassenach," she answered, unshaken by his implication. "Aye, I *do* ha' choices, and ye shall find yerself cold in yer bed one morn if ye dinna think sae!"

His brows lifted. "Do you threaten me, wench? Shall I need bind your hands behind your back each night?"

Despite the implied warning, his face revealed little more than impatience, and Meghan clenched her teeth.

"Take it as ye will," she countered. "But I stand my ground. Tell him tae let her ride!"

His eyes slitted, gleaming oddly, and Meghan's belly lurched.

Mayhap it was a mistake for her not to fear him?

He was Henry's infamous *Lyon*, after all, champion of the highest bidder—reputed to have spilled the blood of Englishman, Frenchman, Scotsman, and Saracen alike.

And yet she didn't seem to fear him at all.

In truth . . . he made her feel . . . curiously excited. Particularly now when they were face to face, so close . . . clashing wills.

She was acutely aware that his fingers remained closed about her arm, restraining her, lest she leap from his mount.

"I wonder if you might enjoy that?" he asked suddenly, grinning a little wickedly. "Being bound to my bed."

Meghan refused to cower before him. "Tell him tae let her ride," she persisted, ignoring his taunt. "Or—"

"Or what?" He tightened his hold slightly upon her arm, not enough to injure, though enough to remind her of his superior strength.

Meghan thought about it an instant, well aware that they were near his manor, and that Baldwin approached them still.

"Ye say ye wish tae wed me for the sake o' peace? Isna that right?"

"Aye, wench, 'tis what I said."

"Wouldn't it be a pity for everyone tae see ye carry me in against my will—kicking and screaming? I wonder what my brothers would do did they discover ye'd treated me sae brutishly?"

He was grinning still, but Meghan vowed not for long. "More threats, wench?"

"Mayhap," Meghan admitted.

He lifted one brow and cocked his head at her. "So, then, let me understand . . . Are you saying you'll agree to wed . . . if I simply make Baldwin carry the beast within his arms?"

Meghan shrugged. "Perhaps, perhaps no' . . . Ye'll simply ha' tae wait and see, will ye no'?"

His smile widened, revealing gleaming

white teeth, and Meghan felt her heart quicken within her breast.

And yet she wasn't about to relinquish her one advantage: the question of her will.

She returned his smile, hoping she appeared as merciless as he. And then she opened her mouth and began to scream.

"Christ!" he exclaimed, and slapped a hand over her mouth in an attempt to muffle her.

Meghan didn't bother to struggle, merely continued to scream at the top of her lungs, ceasing only when she needed a breath. He released her when she stopped abruptly, and she gulped in another breath and launched into an ear-piercing screech.

"All right, damn it all!" he relented. "Cease, wench! Cease, already! Baldwin, put her bloody grandmother on your gaddamned horse!" he ordered.

Meghan stopped screaming and smiled with satisfaction.

Baldwin's eyes widened. "But I cannot mount with—"

"Do it!" Lyon demanded of him.

"Thank ye," Meghan said sweetly, and tried not to laugh at the flustered expression upon Baldwin's face. "Fia will appreciate it, I assure yae," she went on. "Ye see, she has the—"

"Gout, I know!" Lyon answered. "Smart-arsed wench!"

Meghan fluttered her lashes at him, giving him her most ingenuous look.

Chapter 9

~~~~oOOo~~~~

Alison had fled the meadow in panic, and had sequestered herself within her bower for at least an hour's time before realizing she didn't like herself very much for what she'd done.

Meghan Brodie had been her very best friend since the day Meghan had discovered her spying upon her and her grandminnie in the woods that day as they'd set about collecting weeds and leaves for one of Fia's potions. From her father, Alison had heard naught but horrid things about the old woman, and Alison had been watching like a coward from behind a big fat oak. Curiosity had kept her rooted to the spot. Meghan hadn't exposed her to her grandminnie; instead she'd crawled over to Alison's tree upon her hands and knees and had peered around it at Alison, and said in such a dulcet tone, *"She'llna hurt ye, I promise. She's no' really mad, she's just my grandminnie."* And she'd said it with so much love and such hope that Alison would believe her that Alison had at once felt contrite for every tale she'd ever listened to about the old woman—even though she hadn't started a one, merely believed them all.

And now she sat in Meghan's brothers' hall, waiting while they searched the surrounding area for her. It was dusk now. Outside, the lavender skies darkened ominously. And with every passing moment the Brodie brothers were away, Alison's unease intensified.

What was taking them so long?

She was beginning to have the most terrible, terrible feeling about it all. Something had gone awry, and once again it was all her fault! Her shoulders slumped dejectedly, but she straightened at once when Meghan's eldest brother, Leith, entered the room.

"Did ye find her?" Alison asked anxiously, and then she spied the expression upon his face and her hopes fell.

"Nay," he answered, frowning. "But Colin and Gavin are still searching, lass." He approached the table where Alison sat, and perched himself upon it, his expression tense but his demeanor composed and deliberate. He crossed his arms, and seemed to be considering the situation. With his tall, lean frame, he seemed no more than a boy, but in his face, Alison could see the wisdom of his years . . . and more.

She had never spoken much with Leith, for she'd always been cowed by his sober inten-

sity. It had always been difficult to tell whether
he approved or disapproved of her friendship
with Meghan. Though Alison couldn't think of
a reason he should disapprove, neither had he
ever been entirely friendly to her—cordial certainly, but never warm. Today, however, she
appreciated his staid demeanor, for while he
didn't seem particularly pleased with the circumstances, neither did he seem to blame her.

Of course, she hadn't precisely revealed
everything as yet, and she feared now she was
going to have to. She wished with all her might
that she didn't have to confess under such circumstances, and then reproached herself for
being such a selfish dolt that she would consider her own well-being over that of
Meghan's.

Where could Meghan possibly have gone off
to?

It wasn't like her to simply wander away.

Well . . . perhaps it was, but not for long. Besides, they were usually together, she and Alison.

Gavin entered the hall, looking graver still.
Leith peered up at him, but Gavin shook his
head. "Naught!" he announced.

"Did ye search the chapel?" Leith asked.
"Colin said she was there this morn, fretting
over some bird."

Gavin continued to shake his head. He
peered down thoughtfully at the floor, looking
troubled.

Alison listened to their conversation with growing trepidation and no small measure of guilt.

" 'Twas the first and again the last place I looked," Gavin disclosed. "She's no' there, Leith."

"Damn!" Leith said. "Where the devil could she be?" There was a note of panic in his voice now.

"I've said before that if she spent more time at prayer, and less at—"

Leith raised his hand, silencing him. "Cease, Gavin!" he demanded. "I canna hear this noo!"

Gavin seemed determined to make his point. "Noo is when ye must, Leith. If ye dinna hear it noo, when will ye?"

"This has naught tae do wi' yer perceived notions of her irreverence, Gavin."

Colin entered, saying, "Meghan has a right tae believe whatever she will." His expression was angry. He didn't acknowledge Alison, but he rarely did straightaway.

"It has everything tae do wi' it!" Gavin persisted, causing Colin's anger to ignite.

Alison had never seen him so furious.

"Shut yer mouth, Gavin, unless ye can open it tae help instead o' making things worse wi' your damned sermonizing. Ye're gettin' on my bluidy nerves!"

Gavin glared at Colin. "Why, ye—" His body tensed.

Alison held her breath at the sight of the

brothers sparring. She'd never seen them so at odds before. They were usually the most mild-tempered men, and she had always envied Meghan's easy relationship with them.

"Why me, what?" Colin fired back, standing with his fists clenched at his sides. "Say it like a mon, Gavin, or dinna begin tae say it a'tall!"

"Shut yer bluidy mouths, both o' ye!" Leith commanded.

Gavin and Colin obeyed at once, though both of them were physically bigger than their eldest brother. Leith was tall, certainly, but Gavin, though he was youngest, was taller yet. And Colin, though he was of goodly height, was by far the most muscular.

"This is no time tae be locking horns. This is aboot Meghan, remember?" He cast a pointed glance at Colin.

Colin's jaw tautened, but he nodded.

"Gavin?" Leith prompted.

Gavin nodded as well.

"We are all concerned here," Leith added. "It will no' help us tae battle each other."

"I should never ha' let her gae," Colin said. "Damn, but I knew no' tae let her! I had this feeling, Leith!"

"This is no' the time for that, Colin," Leith said. "I would ha' forbade her myself, but ye and I knoo perfectly well that Meghan would ha' done whatever she pleased."

"That's exactly the point I was getting at," Gavin interjected.

"Make it another time, Gavin," Leith commanded him. "No' noo, I said."

Colin's eyes met Alison's suddenly, and they were full of emotion—though not precisely what she'd hoped for. It was clear to her that he blamed her mostly.

And what would he think of her when she told them everything?

"I shouldna ha' told her that Alison awaited her upon the meadow," he lamented. "I shouldna ha'!"

Alison lowered her head. " 'Tis my fault, I knoo," she offered.

"Nay, lass," Leith assured her. "It is no'. Colin is simply angry wi' himself."

As much as it pained her to confess, she knew she must now. "Aye," Alison insisted. "It is." She met Leith's gaze, not daring to face Gavin or Colin. Somehow, it was easier to do this if she pretended those two were not listening.

"Nay, lass," Leith persisted, shaking his head.

"Aye, but it is!" Alison asserted, straightening her spine. "Because I stole the goat!" she disclosed.

Leith's brows collided. His expression clearly revealed his confusion. He uncrossed his arms. "What the devil are ye speaking of, lass? What goat? What has a bluidy goat tae do wi' Meggie's disappearance?"

Alison's lower lip began to tremble, but she

faced him squarely. "Montgomerie's goat," she explained.

"What are ye saying?"

"*The* goat?" Leith asked, clearly stunned by her proclamation.

Alison nodded.

"*The* goat?" Colin asked as well, his tone one of disbelief.

"Aye," Alison replied, keeping her gaze fixed on Leith.

"*The goat?*" Colin repeated, his temper obviously rising. Alison cringed, though she didn't dare look at him, for fear of what she would see in his eyes.

"*Montgomerie's goat?*" Gavin asked her, as though to be certain they were all hearing correctly. Alison turned to face him and nodded, still avoiding Colin's gaze.

"What would make ye gae and do a thing like that, lass?" Leith sounded dumbfounded.

"Christ!" Gavin exclaimed, and both Leith and Colin looked at him in surprise.

Alison couldn't help it; tears pricked at her eyes, as she'd never heard him once, not ever, take the lord's name in vain.

"Explain," Leith said, turning once more to face her.

Alison's eyes welled with tears. "I didna intend for Montgomerie tae blame ye. I only meant tae keep from wedding him, ye see."

"By stealing his goat?"

Alison faced him then, and wished at once

that she had not. His expression was undeniably full of disgust.

And fury.

"I just didna want—"

"Ye should be pleased tae wed any mon a'tall!" he told her cruelly, shouting now.

Alison flinched at the tone of his voice. "I didna mean tae . . . I only thought that if he and my da would be at odds . . . I didna mean for him tae believe—"

"I dinna want ye, Alison MacLean. I dinna knoo how tae make it plainer than that!" Colin told her.

Tears spilled over Alison's lashes and streamed down her cheeks. "But I only didna wish tae wed wi' him!" she explained once more, pleading with Colin to understand. He *had* to understand how she felt about him. "I canna love him, dinna ye see!"

His eyes glittered with anger. "If anything happens tae my sister because o' yer foolish little-girl notions, I willna forgive ye," he said, and the contempt in his tone, more than his words even, cut like a blade to her heart. "I willna forgive ye, Alison MacLean."

Alison gasped for breath; she couldn't seem to catch one.

"Enough!" Leith demanded.

"Leave her be, Colin," Gavin entreated. "She didna mean tae."

"I'll leave her be all right!" Colin announced. "I'm goin' oot again tae look for my sister. The two o' ye can stay and play nursemaid if it pleases ye!" And with that, he pivoted upon his heel and stalked angrily from the hall. Alison kept her eyes on his back until he was gone from the door. All the while, tears streamed from her eyes.

She loved him madly and he hated her truly.

Leith came about the table to where she sat. Alison watched his approach with hazy vision. She peered at Gavin and saw the pity in his gaze. She couldn't bear it, and, leaning forward, rested her head upon the table and cried even harder.

She felt Leith's hand upon her back, soothing her. "Colin doesna mean it," he swore.

"I'm goin' tae look for Meghan as well," Gavin said. "Mayhap she merely lost track o' the hours."

"Gae on," Leith agreed as he knelt beside Alison. "Be certain tae check the shortcut from the meadow. I knoo she favors it though I've asked her no' tae take it."

Alison was acutely aware of Gavin's footsteps as he left them, but she continued to sob, unable to face even Leith in her shame.

Leith continued to soothe her. "Noo, noo," he said tenderly. "I knoo ye didna mean tae, Alison."

He leaned awkwardly toward her, and Alison, desperate as she was, turned into his arms, grateful that he was here to reassure her. Colin hated her! Gavin pitied her! And her very best friend was in trouble—and it was all her fault, she just knew it!

"We shall find her," Leith assured her, and Alison wanted so desperately to believe him. She clutched at his tunic, sobbing against his shoulder.

"At any rate," he added, "we both knoo our Meggie . . . She'll turn up on the doorstep, I'm certain. If no' on her own," he said with a faint smile, "then whoever has taken her will dump her there directly—wicked tongue and all!"

Alison gave a reluctant chuckle. Och, but it was true; Meghan certainly spoke her mind well enough.

"That's it, noo," Leith crooned. "Wipe the tears from yer eyes, lass. We must work together in this."

Alison did as he bade her and stopped weeping. She peered up at him, sniffling. He was right, she knew. And she had to be strong. For Meghan's sake.

"Noo," he proposed, "why dinna ye tell me everything, lass . . . and start from the beginning . . ."

Chapter 10

"**G**et off the horse, wench."

"Nay!" Meghan told him. "I'll no'. Ye canna tell me what tae do!"

He stood before her with his hands upon his hips, looking at her much as though she were a wayward child he'd like to toss over his knee and spank. To his credit, he did no such brutish thing. He merely raised a brow at her.

"We had a bargain, do you not recall?"

Meghan shook her head. "Ye perhaps had a bargain," she reminded him. "I merely suggested that it would be a pity for everyone tae see ye carry me in against my will—kicking and screaming."

Meghan was well aware that they were drawing an audience, but she didn't care. Let them all watch. They should see that their new lord was naught more than a ruthless Sassenach barbarian.

"Have it your way," he said, and reached out to pluck her off the horse. Meghan squealed in surprise. She expected him to toss her over his shoulder, but he surprised her by cradling her within his arms like a wee bairn. It flustered her so that she forgot to scream.

"What are ye doing?" she asked, scowling up at him.

"What does it seem I am doing?" he countered. "I'm carrying you over the threshold." He had the audacity to wink at her. "A loving husband and his blushing bride."

Meghan glared up at him. So much for her plan to show him for the barbarian he was. "You're no' my loving husband," she assured him. "Nor I yer blushing bride!"

He lifted her up to whisper into her ear, his breath warm and sweet against her face. It sent gooseflesh down her arms and legs. "Perhaps not, wench, but that's what my people see." He drew away and grinned down at her and Meghan suddenly ceased to breathe.

She couldn't find her thoughts suddenly, so discomposed was she by the intimacy of his embrace . . . his whisper . . . his tone . . .

Good lord, what was happening to her? Her body was reacting curiously, quickening, and her heart pounded against her ribs.

He seemed to realize what having his arms around her did to her, because his eyes were twinkling. "Go ahead and scream if you like," he dared her.

The rat—he'd understood her intent, and had thwarted her so easily. Meghan wished

she *could* scream. But truth to tell, she couldn't.
She could only stare at his lips, vaguely aware
that he bore her through the courtyard past the
prying eyes of his people and over the threshold of his door. He carried her up the stairs
then, and into his chamber. There he dumped
her unceremoniously upon the bed and walked
away.

The cad! He intended, she surmised, to show
her her place. Well, she hadn't wed him as yet,
and neither was she going to! Let him think so,
if it pleased him. Her brothers would come for
her soon enough, and then she'd have the last
word. Rotten misbegotten knave! Until then,
she was perfectly content to play his little
game.

"Ye canna simply lock me awa', ye knoo,"
Meghan announced, before he could close the
door behind him.

He stopped and turned to peer within. "Of
course I can," he replied and smiled coolly at
her.

If the truth be known, his arrogance both in-
furiated and intrigued her. How could that be
so?

"Watch me," he said.

And Meghan wasn't certain whether to be
angry or amused by his response. No one had
ever been so impervious to her. It seemed no
matter what she said, or what she did, he
would do as he pleased. She was certainly accustomed to despotic men, but somehow Lyon

Montgomerie was different. It was more than evident in the way he looked at her and in his actions—that he certainly was not indifferent to her appearance. Unlike other men, though, he was not reduced to babbling when he spoke to her. Nor did he seem particularly inclined to oblige her every whim. To the contrary, she'd never met a man who seemed so little concerned with her opinion of him. In fact, he didn't seem to care whether she approved of him or not. And more, he seemed amused by her apparent disregard of him.

The two of them seemed, in truth, to be engaged in some strange battle of wills and wits, and Meghan, for one, didn't intend to lose.

He turned once more to go, and Meghan said quite deliberately, "If ye're no' going tae stay and abuse me . . . would ye mind terribly sending in my grandminnie tae keep me company?"

If Meghan had hoped for a reaction from him, she'd hoped in vain, because he simply smiled tolerantly and said without hesitation, "Of course. I shall send her up directly."

Meghan smiled sweetly at him. "Thank ye." She batted her lashes coyly.

"You never cease, do you?"

Meghan's brows lifted. "Whatever do ye mean? I've no notion what ye're speakin' of," she assured him.

"Of course you do," he challenged her. "I can see it in your eyes, wench. You know precisely what it is you are doing, and it's not going to work."

"What's no' going tae work?" Meghan asked in her most innocent tone. "I've no idea what ye're referring tae. 'Tis merely the least ye can do. If ye're going tae keep us both prisoners here, ye might as well be kind enough tae let us serve our gaol together."

"Prisoners?" He lifted a brow. "Do not think of yourself so," he bade her. "You've my word you shall be given all due respect as my wife."

Meghan cocked her head at him, giving him her most willful glance. "I dinna remember agreeing tae such a thing, Sassenach. Though if it pleases ye tae think so . . . ha' yerself a merry time wi' the notion. Ye can gae noo," she said dismissively. And with a sigh, she laid back upon the bed, stretching out upon it as though it were her own and his presence of little consequence.

Lyon watched her make herself at home upon his bed, and experienced an immediate reaction to the sight of her lying there. She lounged upon it as though she had nary a care in the world . . . as though she were a sated mistress waiting for the return of her lover . . .

His mouth went dry, and though he'd planned to go, to prepare messages to send to David and Dougal MacLean, he suddenly didn't wish to leave.

Most particularly because she seemed to wish him to go.

Or did she?

He closed the door and smiled when her head popped up at once to peer at him. Her surprised expression at finding him still present shifted at once to that already familiar expression of bored disdain she had perfected so well. Their gazes locked and held as he approached the bed. The room went completely silent but for the sound of his own footfalls across the creaky wooden floor.

"I shall tell you what pleases me, wench," he said, leaning over her and pinning her to the bed between his arms. Her small gasp of surprise pleased him immensely.

"What?" she asked, blinking, but holding his gaze.

Lyon could see the question in her eyes. She wasn't so dauntless as she would like to have him believe. And yet she faced him squarely, her delicate chin lifting in challenge—tilted at a perfect angle so as to meet his lips . . . did he but lower his mouth to hers.

And Christ, what lips she was blessed with . . . full and pouty, perfectly shaped . . . He imagined them to be soft and luscious . . . imagined them wrapped about him in the most wicked way.

Her breast lifted with another soft gasp, and his gaze fell to her full bosom, lingering for an instant before returning to her face. It was all he could do not to bend for a taste of those sweet luscious lips. The scent of her rose to taunt him . . . that sweet elusive scent of her that awakened his body's hunger in a way no woman had in much too long a time.

"Seeing you here upon my bed," he whispered. "That pleases me."

She moaned softly in answer, and he could see that her own reaction shocked her, for it registered there upon her face with a startled blink.

God, he wanted her.

And yet he wanted her willing.

He wanted more than her body.

He wanted her to lie beneath him and call out his name in pleasure in the dark of night . . . and to think of him the first instant her long lashes lifted from sleep in the morn. He wanted to see the longing in her deep-green eyes, and the yearning in her body in the taut peaks of her breast—he wanted to feel them harden beneath the palm of his hand. He wanted her to moan with pleasure when his hands covered her breasts and wanted her to cry out when his mouth replaced his hands.

He wanted to initiate her into every wicked pleasure he had ever indulged in . . .

And more.

She did that to him somehow . . . this woman whose name he did not even know. This woman who looked at him askance, and pretended an indifference she couldn't possibly feel with that look she now wore in those beautiful eyes: a look of pure virgin innocence mingled with uninhibited curiosity. He sensed she hid a passion as deep as his own.

God help him, if it was the last thing he did . . . he was going to seduce her into his bed. And he was going to employ every device he knew to keep her there.

He was going to woo his way into her heart.

And he was going to bind her to him for always.

That he vowed as he stared down at her lovely face, flushed now with color.

He moved closer, savoring the heat between their bodies, hovering above her mouth, until the warmth of her breath teased his lips.

Meghan held her breath as he stared down at her.

Never in her life had she been kissed by a man—never had she desired it.

And yet . . . somehow she could suddenly think of little else but the way his lips would feel upon her own. She swallowed convulsively.

Poised above her as he was, with his beautiful lips so near to her own, and his vivid blue eyes locked with hers, Meghan felt utterly dizzy.

That look he wore . . . she wasn't so naive that she didn't comprehend what it meant. She'd seen Colin gaze that way at his women much too oft to mistake it.

"Ye're just like all the rest," she murmured huskily.

He shook his head and was so near that Meghan imagined she felt the brush of his lips.

Or had it been real?

"Nay," he assured her. "I am not, wench, and do not make the mistake of thinking so." His eyes gleamed wickedly, and Meghan immediately sensed that perhaps he spoke true. Perhaps, as with the others, her face had caught his eye, but his response to her was anything but familiar.

"Ye canna force me tae wed wi' ye," Meghan said a little breathlessly. "And I willna. Ye canna make me."

Was she trying so hard to convince him?

Or herself?

"Quite true," he agreed, smiling softly. "I cannot force you. But you will."

Meghan narrowed her eyes at him. "Dinna be sae certain o' yerself," she said. "I'm no' some foolish lass who sighs after every handsome lad. Ye willna win me wi' flattery."

His smile deepened. "You think me handsome, do you?"

Meghan's face burned. "I didna say such a thing," she denied. "Dinna put words in my mouth, Sassenach!" But she *was* surely thinking it. Never in her life had a face appealed to her more. It was the face of a man, not that of a boy. And yet Meghan could very much spy the deviltry of his youth in his every expression. He was a man who relished his pleasures

. . . and it was obvious to Meghan that his pleasure at the moment was her.

"I would not dare put words in your mouth," he assured her.

Never in her life had a man looked at her so. It was not solely the hunger so apparent in his eyes, or the intent written in the expression upon his face . . . Nay, there was something more . . .

"Not when there is something else I'd so much rather do with that lovely mouth of yours," he went on.

Meghan shivered at the silky tone of his voice.

He was a man who knew what he wanted and was used to getting it.

"Do you not realize what those lips do to a man?" he asked her pointedly.

Meghan shook her head, blinking. Was he going to kiss her now? It seemed to her that he meant to, for his eyes slitted and he tilted his face, as though to lock his mouth with hers.

She held her breath in anticipation.

Would she let him?

Should she?

"One day," he vowed, "you will ask me to show you."

"Nay—"

"Shhh . . ." His breath blew warm and sweet upon her lips. Meghan closed her eyes for an instant, letting the sensation brush over her. Good lord, but she felt defenseless against this

form of seduction. She knew how to deal with
men who leered, men who vowed their love
after first setting eyes upon her, and overeager
beaus, but she didn't know how to deal with
this man at all—nor with the strange way he
seemed to speak to her body. It answered to
him like a slave to its master . . . no matter that
her head and heart both said nay.

He withdrew a little, giving her space to
breathe, to think.

"I think you will," he asserted with an incorrigible grin.

"Nay, I'll no'!" Meghan assured him, with
more certainty than she suddenly felt.

"Then prove me wrong," he challenged her,
rising from the bed abruptly. Meghan blinked
in confusion at his unanticipated answer, at her
own keen sense of disappointment. He abandoned her there, leaving her to stare after him,
dumbfounded, as he walked away.

"You will wed with me," he said, "because
you know I speak the truth. It is the most obvious solution to our little dilemma." Then he
closed the door behind him.

What in God's name had just happened?

Had she wanted him to kiss her?

Surely not!

So why was she so disappointed that he had
not?

And why should she feel rejected, when he'd
made his intentions and desires clear from the
first?

Because for once, she hadn't been the one in control, Meghan realized.

And truth to tell, it galled her that he *had* been.

The knave! How dare he simply walk away and leave her so!

Chapter 11

 ~~~⌒⌒⌒~~~

It had taken every ounce of Lyon's will to leave her there lying upon his bed.

He'd wanted so badly to kiss those lips, to worship them with his own, but he wanted something else so much more. Aye, she might have kissed him back in the heat of the moment, but he understood that it was too soon. She would have regretted it after, because he wouldn't have stopped with merely a taste of her mouth.

Then, too, it had provoked the bloody hell out of him that she would compare him to all the rest of her swains.

Had she carnal knowledge of them? Is that what he saw in her expression when she looked at him? The thought both disturbed and intrigued him. He didn't like to think of her with another man, but the possibility that she would know a man's body and how to please him appealed as well.

He was a man with dark passions, he knew.

And he wanted a woman who was bold enough to share them.

And he wanted it to be the woman lying now upon his bed.

No other would do.

And that brought him to another matter entirely . . .

He had no notion how he was going to deal with Dougal MacLean over the matter of his daughter.

Lyon had met her only once, but she hadn't appealed to him in the least, and he scarcely even recalled what she looked like. And yet part of the understanding in his accepting this land from Dougal MacLean was that he would agree to give it back by virtue of an alliance. He'd put off the betrothal so long because after meeting MacLean's daughter, he hadn't been in any rush to fill his bed.

And now that he was, it wasn't Alison MacLean he wished to fill it with.

It was . . . whatever her bloody name was. He frowned at that. Christ, but she was as stubborn as they came. He wasn't going to glean her name easily from her, only because he desired it, and she knew.

Well, he was simply going to have to write the missive to David without it.

He barreled down the stairs, into the hall, and headed directly toward his table at the dais, ordering his pen and parchment from a lad who sat cross-legged upon the floor, petting a mangy cat. In his haste, he had forgotten to bring his writing implements with him.

The lad bounded up and ran to do his bidding, and Lyon stepped up on the dais and rounded the table. He drew out a weary breath along with his chair and sat to wait, trying to determine the best course of action to be taken. He raked his fingers through his hair.

Damned Scots.

He was going to have to word this precisely right, he knew, else he was going to end with yet another feud upon his hands.

Alison MacLean wasn't precisely ill-favored, it was merely that she lacked spirit. She'd sat there before him, her expression ranging from disinterest to horror at the prospect of wedding with him. At least that he didn't feel badly about. He had no doubt that she did not share her father's enthusiasm for the alliance. So he hadn't to worry about disappointing her. And yet he certainly didn't wish to wound her tender feelings.

He tried to conjure her face to his thoughts, but all that came to him were those crossed eyes . . . that nose . . . the miserable expression she'd worn. She sat there beside her father, looking entirely wretched, while her father had babbled on about the rewards of their proposed alliance, completely oblivious to his daughter's distress. Lyon had been aware of nothing but. How could he wed her anyway when it had been perfectly clear to him that

MacLean's daughter came into the bargain wholly unwilling?

Baldwin entered the hall. "Where's the wench?" he asked, looking bedraggled and seeming surprised to find Lyon alone. Lyon didn't think his old friend was ever going to forgive him for having to mount the bloody lamb upon his horse. As long as Lyon lived he didn't think he would ever forget the sight of Baldwin trying to mount with the rotten little beast in his arms. He'd finally managed only by straddling the animal over his saddle and then mounting behind it.

"I stink to high heaven!" he said, casting his arms out in disgust.

Lyon chuckled. "I'm sure you do."

"I hope you're happy," Baldwin said sourly. "Where's the mad wench?"

"In my chamber."

Baldwin nodded. "Of course."

"And where is *Fia*?" Lyon asked.

"Where do you think? I gave her to Cameron to place with the others."

"Well, you'll simply have to get her back," Lyon charged him, and couldn't help but laugh at his harassed expression. "She wants to see her grandminnie."

"You've got to be jesting!" Baldwin exclaimed. "You can't be serious!"

"Deadly in earnest," Lyon said. "She's something, is she not?"

Baldwin muttered something unintelligible

under his breath as he approached the table. "She's something else all right!" he agreed. "Are you bloody insane, Lyon? Whatever do you want with a lunatic wench?"

Lyon raised his brows. He could think of a few things—one in particular in direct relation to the throbbing condition he had concealed beneath the table. "What do you think I want with her, Baldwin?"

"Randy bastard!" Baldwin accused him.

Lyon merely laughed.

"I'm telling you, she's more trouble than it's worth," Baldwin said.

Lyon arched a brow. "I shall be the judge of that."

Baldwin sat upon the table. "She's insane," he said with conviction.

Lyon was tired of hearing it. "Nay," he disagreed, "I assure you she is not."

"What if she is?" Baldwin persisted.

"She's not. She's simply a cunning little wench, is all."

"And you seriously mean to do this?"

Lyon ran his hand over his jaw. "As serious as I can be," he replied.

"Christ, but you are!" Baldwin gave a low whistle, and shook his head.

The two remained silent an instant, considering the gravity of Lyon's decision.

"And what of MacLean?" Baldwin asked. "What will you say to him? He'll not be pleased, Lyon."

Lyon leaned back in his chair. "Aye," he agreed. "I know."

"He is counting upon this alliance, I do not have to tell you."

Lyon's lips twisted. "Well, we'll simply have to find the proper compensation for him, will we not? Every man has a price, as they say. As for David," he continued, "I am not so dim-witted that I do not understand why he gave me this land to begin with."

Baldwin nodded.

"He needs me here, else he'd never have risked the displeasure of these Highlanders to begin with—not when he is trying so desperately to win them over. Nay, he did not barter land from MacLean simply to reward an old friend. He's too shrewd for that. He placed me here because I'm damned good at what I do."

"This is true," Baldwin affirmed. "No one is better at commanding men."

Lyon leaned forward in his chair and over the table, peering up at Baldwin. "He also realizes that while I want this—and I do—I'd as soon leave it all as to sell myself any longer. I'm through with all that, Baldwin. I've gold enough to do as I will. Life is too short," he concluded.

"That it is. What can I do? How can I help?"

Lyon smirked up at him. "You can get your stinking arse off the table I eat on, to begin with."

Baldwin laughed.

"And then you can take *Fia* up to her *grand-daughter*," Lyon added with a note of wry humor.

Baldwin shook his head and hopped off the table, but, to his credit, said nothing.

"Thank you," Lyon added as his friend turned to go. "I realize this has the potential to make life difficult for the lot of us. Not only me."

Baldwin smiled. "You have done far more for me. Supporting you is the least I can do. Anything else you need just now?"

"Just one more thing," Lyon said. "Discover her name for me, if you will, that I might have it before the evening meal."

"Very well," Baldwin said, and started away just as the lad returned, bringing Lyon his quill, inkwell, and parchment.

Lyon took the items from his hands and then sent him on his way with a ruffle of his dark hair and a word of thanks. And then he set about writing the necessary letters: one to Dougal MacLean, one to David of Scotia, and one to her damned brothers as Lyon was certain they'd be wondering over her whereabouts just about now. It served little purpose to keep them in suspense. They were going to be brothers by marriage, after all.

In fact, while he was at it, he thought he might simply make it a wedding invitation and remind them to bring their own ale.

* * *

The little lamb was growing weary.

Meghan could tell by the way it seemed to wobble on its wee legs. And yet she knew the poor creature couldn't possibly make itself at ease enough in this strange place to fall asleep on its own.

"Poor wee thing," she cooed, and lifted the creature upon the bed, commiserating with it.

Weary as it was, it dropped down beside her, and she sat stroking its head while it grew still, listening to the sound of her voice. She'd always had a great love for animals—something she'd indubitably inherited from Fia. And having spent the entire day with this one, she was beginning to grow quite fond of the little beast. They seemed to have a natural affinity between them. In truth, strange as it seemed, she was even beginning to think of it as Fia!

She lay upon the bed, contemplating her prison as she stroked the animal's newly sheared coat. It wasn't a large room . . . nor was it precisely small. It was really quite unremarkable in every aspect, save for the gaping hole in the ceiling on the far side of the roof. It was growing dark; Meghan watched the gloaming sky fade to night before her eyes.

She knew her brothers had begun to search for her by now. She also knew they would worry, and felt a stab of guilt for putting herself at risk to begin with. She should never have taken the shortcut through the woods.

And Colin, she knew, would blame himself

most because he'd been the one to let her go.

Though Colin was the most indulgent of her brothers, he was quite protective of her still. He merely allowed her a little more freedom because he valued his own so much.

And yet, if it weren't for the fact that she knew they were home fretting . . . or out searching and thinking the worst . . . in truth she might not be wholly regretful of her circumstances.

No matter that she told herself she was content to be alone, she was fiercely lonesome, and this union could at least give her children some day.

"Ye knoo what?" she asked the wee lamb, which was resting peacefully beside her. Seeing it so at ease in her presence made her feel a sense of achievement. "The Sassenach is right," she continued, speaking low lest someone overhear her. "This truly might be the perfect solution, were I tae wed the brute," she reasoned. "What do ye think?"

She stared at the animal's serene face and thought of Fia when she'd slept. It brought a smile to her lips. How many morns had she gone tiptoeing into her grandminnie's room, only to find her stretched out upon her bed, lying so still, looking as though she had died in her sleep during the night. Meghan would approach Fia's bed with wide-eyed apprehension and a valor that she'd hardly felt. She'd stand there, watching her grandminnie's breast for some sign of life. But Fia always slept much too peacefully, and Meghan would wave a hand before her nostrils to feel the breath leave them in order to reassure herself. And then Fia would startle the life from her, coming awake so abruptly.

"Och!" she would complain. *"Canna an auld woman rest in peace?"*

Meghan would gasp in fright and then sigh in relief, and then feel wracked with guilt over waking her.

The memory filled her with sorrow. Fia had been her sole companion, and Meghan had lived in fear of losing the one person who had truly understood her. Her mother had been too brokenhearted to think of anyone ever.

Meghan didn't fault her mother for it, because it had been so apparent by the look in her eyes that her grief had been real. After her father's death, her mother's pain had been so great that it had seemed easier for her not to feel at all. She had spent hours alone simply staring from her window—and nights weeping in her bed. Meghan knew that, somewhere in her heart, her mother had loved her too, but her guilt and her pain had been too great for her to express it. Her father's jealousy had carried him to his grave, and her mother had never forgiven herself for her wayward smiles. Nor did she ever forget Meghan's da till the day she last closed her eyes. As for Megan's brothers, they were too involved with their own lives—Leith with his duties to the clan, Gavin with his God, and Colin with his women—to spend time enough with Meghan.

When Fia had died, Meghan had felt as though she'd lost her mooring, for while Alison was as true a friend as any could have, Meghan was more a mother figure to her in many ways; Alison had often shared her woes with Meghan, but Meghan had never felt comfortable to do so in return. It had always seemed Meghan's duty to be the strong one.

And she had felt so alone for so very long.

She peered hard at the little lamb's face and wished with all her heart that she could live such a simple life . . . a silly thing to wish . . . but she did.

Oh, to be more plain, like Alison . . .

Alison was lovely from within and it radiated without. Alison would someday find herself a man who would look past the flaws in her face and would love her for her soul.

Meghan's own face had always been a bloody curse. Women rarely received her warmly because of it, and men only wanted to possess her for it.

Now that Fia was gone . . . nobody seemed to care enough to know the heart within her silly body—not even her brothers! And Meghan had since resolved herself to spiritual solitude. She'd learned from Fia's example how to tend her own gardens behind the stone walls that sheltered her heart. And if she kept those walls erect, it was only because somewhere within she feared no one would like the imperfect soul behind the perfect face. She'd learned the importance of being content with herself and embracing even her flaws—especially her flaws—as it was foolish to place her happiness into someone else's hands.

Och, but she knew it was foolish to hope for unconditional love.

Aye . . . so this might very well be the perfect solution for all . . . save that Piers Montgomerie was no different from the rest.

Meghan was well aware of and none too pleased by the fact that that peace between their clans was not his true motivation. Like all other men, Piers Montgomerie was driven by lust. He lusted after beauty and perfection, and little did he realize that Meghan was a fraud. Her face might be pleasing, but her soul was fraught with flaws! She was not sweet and well-mannered like Alison—nor was she patient and warmhearted.

She was not perfect.

Never had been.

Never would be.

Chapter 12

It was the wee hours of the morn when the torches were once again returned to their sconces upon the walls.

It was the wee hours of the morn when the torches were once again returned to their sconces upon the walls.

They had searched the woodlands, the meadows, the loch's edge even, and still there was no sign of Meghan.

Leith Mac Brodie slumped behind the table where MacLean's daughter sat still, waiting, with her head cradled wearily within her arms. Her lovely copper tresses pooled about her upon the table. He resisted the urge to reach out and see for himself whether it was as soft as it appeared.

She peered up when he sat, looking as frightened as a wee rabbit startled by a pack of wolves. Her eyes were red-rimmed and her cheeks stained with tears. His heart wrenched a little at the sight of her, and his conscience pricked him.

They had yet to take her home, and he knew it would bear its own consequences come the morning light, but it could scarce be helped. He could spare not a man to see her safely to her father—could not spare them from the search for Meghan. And neither could he simply have let her go, not as a matter of principle, and certainly not in light of Meghan's disappearance.

He averted his gaze, rubbing at his temples, unable to face the lass as yet, as he knew she was like to have considered the consequences of her having spent the night unchaperoned in his home.

Damn, but troubles never ceased.

"Ye dinna find her?" Alison asked apprehensively, though hopefully, peering up at him, her eyes wide.

Leith met her gaze, shook his head, and sighed. "Nay, lass. We didna."

"And did ye search the meadow?"

Leith nodded.

"And the woodlands?"

"Aye, lass," he answered. "Colin and Gavin are still searching as we speak."

"Poor lads," she said, her expression full of concern.

Leith knew she was thinking of Colin; he recognized that forlorn look upon her face. He couldn't understand why Colin did not see the good in her. He couldn't perceive how his brother placed such weight upon the fickle face, and so little upon the heart. Alison MacLean was possessed of a beautiful heart and even lovelier soul. It was discernible in her eyes and in every expression that graced her sweet face.

And that hair, the color of Meghan's . . . it was her most remarkable feature. Even her eyes, crossed as they were, were like Meghan's . . . The two were not so dissimilar, he thought. As children they had looked naught alike, but it seemed to Leith that as they'd grown up together, the two had begun to resemble one another somewhat. It was peculiar.

He stared at her, thinking that a man could do much worse than to look into those eyes before he closed his own to sleep at night.

"Did ye find the wee lamb, perchance?"

He cocked his head at her. "Lamb?"

"Aye," she replied. "Do ye no' recall that I told ye I left a lamb for Meghan tae find?"

"Oh! Aye!" He straightened in his seat. "No sign o' the lamb either," he told her.

Her brows knit. "None at all?"

"None."

"It seems tae me," she said, thinking aloud, "that there should ha' been some sign o' the animal—hoof marks—something tae show the path it took awa' from the meadow. Dinna ye think sae?"

"The ground is dry," he pointed out.

She nodded, frowning. It was only then, with that small defeat, that he recognized the dread in her expression. Her face grew wan. Her eyes met his, and they were so full of fear that Leith once again had the most incredible urge to hold her . . . to fold her under his arms like a mother bird did with her hatchlings.

And it struck him then that she had yet to voice concern for her own situation. He knew she had to have considered the consequences of her remaining unchaperoned in his home. How could she not have? With every moment that passed, she was compromised all the more. As it was, dawn was quickly approaching, and they had not even sent a messenger to her da, letting him know of her whereabouts. As much as he loathed the thought of doing so—weary as he was, concerned as he was for Meghan—he knew he had to rouse himself once more . . . for Alison's sake.

"I came tae take ye home," he told her.

She seemed to take in a fretful breath, but nodded bravely. "Verra well, then . . . I am ready tae gae."

Guilt pricked at him once more. "I'm sorry we didna take ye sooner, lass."

"I understand why ye didna," she assured him, but it didn't help to soothe his conscience. "I couldna ha' expected ye tae do sae."

Leith nodded, as he didn't know what to say to her. She was right, of course; Meghan was his priority just now, but he knew her da well enough to know that she was not going to be well-received.

She seemed to understand what it was he could not say, for she told him then, "I came

knooing it would be sae, Leith Mac Brodie . . .
Dinna fash yerself over it, please."

Compelled to speak his mind, Leith reached
out and took her chin within his hand, lifting
it so that her gaze would meet his own. "Ye're
a guid lass, Alison. Dinna ye think otherwise.
My imbecile brother doesna deserve ye."

She smiled softly, and the sight of it lifted
him at once, but he wasn't simply saying so to
make her feel better. He believed it with all of
his heart. Aye, MacLean's daughter would
make some man a fine, fine wife.

"Come noo," he urged her, "let us gae and
deliver ye home."

She didn't come down for the evening meal,
and Lyon thought it prudent to leave her be,
as she needed time to think about his proposal.
No matter that he'd threatened to force her
hand, he would not, he knew. He might not
need her compliance, but he wanted it nevertheless, as he was well aware that forcing her
to wed with him would not bode well for peace
between their clans.

Nay, it was best to allow her time to think.

And it was just as well that she'd not appeared, for it had taken him long hours to prepare his letters. He returned to them directly
after supping, and only completed them when
the hall had fallen to silence for the eve.

His chamber was dark when he returned,
and he stood in the doorway, allowing his vi-

sion to adjust to the blackness before entering.

The only light that filtered within the room was that from the gaping hole within his roof. The shutters were nailed shut as they had been in peril of falling off when he'd moved into the manor a mere month before, and he'd thought it better, for now, to keep them closed rather than to have them not at all. At least they were secure.

There was much work to be done, and so little time. His chamber had been left to repair last, as he had only so many men to spare, and the entire manor had been in disrepair when he'd acquired it. It made no difference to him, at any rate. He had slept in worse places than this—hard cold stone floors and bare ground.

To him the bed was an indulgence.

And the woman within it a mystery.

Peering up at the yawning hole in his ceiling, he gauged the night sky. The stars were clear and the moon high, but it was hardly bright enough to illuminate his way across the room.

No matter, he knew his way well enough.

Having accustomed himself enough to the darkness, he made his way unerringly across the creaking wood floor, stopping when it seemed to sink beneath his feet midway across. He frowned, testing it, and then looked up again at the hole in the roof, shaking his head in disgust of the condition of the place. There was no telling how long the hole had been there, or for that matter how much snow and rain had dampened the floors.

Sighing, he made his way to the small desk that occupied his bedside. Upon it he kept his most prized possessions: his personal treatises. Placing the quill and inkwell down upon the desk, he slumped within the chair, wishing now that he'd carried up a candle to write by.

Tonight was one of those nights he knew sleep would elude him . . . like a lover veiled whose face he craved but could not see.

His gaze was drawn to the shadow stretched out upon his bed.

He tried to make her out, but could not. The room was entirely too dark, and his eyes too weary from staring so long at his scribblings. He'd had to word the letters just so. He knew how important it was to convey a precise message. And he was pleased with the outcome. He planned to dispatch the letters first thing in the morn.

David would feel thwarted, he knew, for he had his well-laid plans and liked to see them carried out exactly so, and yet Lyon also knew that his longtime friend was smart enough to adjust when the need arose.

David hadn't come so far as he had by being so inflexible.

As the ninth son of Malcom Ceann Mor, David had against great odds come to Scotia's throne. But neither had he come empty-handed, and that in itself had been a tour de force. He had in essence ruled most of southern Scotia already, Cumbria, and also Huntingdon and Northampton by virtue of marriage. He was, in truth, one of England's most powerful barons as well as Henry's brother by marriage. And he hadn't come so far so fast by making stupid decisions ... or by turning his back upon his allies.

The first thing David had done, in fact, upon his return to Scotia was to reward his friends— de Brus, FitzAlan, de Bailleul, de Comines, and Lyon among the many. Though Lyon was well aware that while David was sincere in his desire to reward those he favored, he'd also chosen his beneficiaries with a particular purpose in mind. It was his intent to bring the Highlanders under his yoke, and God's bloody truth, if anyone was capable, David surely was. David had placed his friends shrewdly, understanding well their strengths and their faults. And Lyon had been granted the most ungovernable bailiwick.

And he knew precisely why.

Nay, David would not oppose him.

MacLean, on the other hand, could prove to be a problem. Though Lyon didn't think so. The greedy old bugger had only agreed to yield this wasted slice of land in the hopes of gaining favor with David. Ultimately, that was MacLean's design, Lyon knew, though he'd claimed it was the return of his land and an alliance with Lyon. But an alliance with Lyon was an alliance with David, and Lyon was betting that MacLean would not risk David's disfavor to challenge Lyon. All these things he'd pointed out to David in the letter, as well.

As for the Brodies . . .

Lyon sighed at the mere thought of them.

He had understood long before he'd ever set foot upon this land that they, along with Iain MacKinnon, would be his greatest challenge—MacKinnon, by far, being his greatest concern. The Brodies, however, were certainly no small undertaking. They, like MacKinnon, comprised David's staunchest opposition.

Nay, men like these were not easily overcome, as they had no susceptibility to bribery. They chose their alliances with their guts, and fought their battles with their hearts. They were not blinded by gold, nor were they seduced by power. They clung to freedom and the right to their own will. They fought for their kinsmen, and did not fear death in the pursuit of their cause.

Damn, but Lyon respected the hell out of them.

Pain-in-the-arse Scots.

They were men after his own heart, but Lyon, in his mind, had not the bloody right even to lick their boots for he had compromised every value he had ever set for himself in the pursuit of personal gain. And if the truth be known, it had, like a sliver under one's flesh, begun to fester within his heart.

He did not like himself very well for the decisions he had made in his life. There was so much that he had aspired to, yet he had pursued all that he abhorred instead.

He sat back within the small chair and stared at the bed.

She could give him something to fight for.

She could give him a reason to change.

Though he had to win her first . . . and then convince her brothers.

Christ, but the mere thought of her filled him with something exhilarating . . . something compelling. She stirred his loins, aye . . . but more, so bloody much more . . . she stirred his heart, as well. She was cunning and brave, and she spoke her mind freely, revealing the convictions of her heart.

She made him yearn for more.

She made him hunger for far more than those luscious lips that must taste like warm summer rain.

Meghan.

Her name was Meghan.

He smiled, thinking about the tales Baldwin had returned with. He didn't believe a one of them . . . She simply didn't have *that* look in her eyes.

Nay, Meghan Brodie was no more a madwoman than he was a bloody saint.

He sat there, wondering whether he should spend the night in the chair, or whether he could trust himself to lie next to her upon his bed—God, but the mere thought of her lying there aroused him. The thought of her lying beside him *pleased* him in a deeper sense as well, and he decided that he damned well wasn't sleeping in a bloody chair. He wasn't a lad who could not restrain himself. He was certainly capable of lying upon a bed with a woman and not making love to her.

He was master of his desires, not the other way around, he told himself.

That settled, he stood and lifted up his tunic, tossing it determinedly aside. He pried off his boots with his feet while he untied his braies.

He slid them down and shrugged them off, leaving them where they lay, and then he crawled into the bed beside her.

Chapter 13

～○○○～

"What the hell!"

Meghan awoke with a start to the most ungodly sound, like that of a frightened, shrieking beast.

A shadow leapt from the bed and another leapt up and pranced wildly about her head, kicking her in the mouth.

"Ack!" she cried, and shielded her face with her arms.

If she remained here much longer, she was going to end up beaten to bloody death!

"What the hell is that animal doing in my bed?" Lyon Montgomerie shouted from somewhere in the darkness of the room.

It took Meghan a full moment to comprehend what must have happened, and then she couldn't help herself, she burst into laughter.

She heard him storm across the room and swing the door open. By the light of the open door, she saw the frightened lammie stumble from the bed to the floor. Montgomerie walked

out, leaving only for an instant before entering
the room once more, carrying a torch from a
sconce in the hall. He stood there in the doorway looking as wrathful as some pagan god,
and Meghan's laughter faded abruptly.

The sight of him took her breath away.

Standing naked in the open doorway, the
torchlight illuminating him fully, he was ex-
traordinary—a feast for the senses. Meghan
had certainly seen men nude before—she had
three brothers, after all—but this body was
magnificent beyond words.

His hair flowed down his back, like the lion
he was named for, gleaming gold by the flame
of the torch. His chest was broad and glistened
softly in the torchlight, and his legs were long
and lean, his hips and loins ... fully revealed
to her eyes.

Meghan couldn't tear her gaze away.

She blinked, mesmerized by the sight of him.

Her gaze lifted to his face ... to his eyes, to
find that they gleamed with unholy satisfaction.

God save her rotten soul, but she was just as
guilty as he for the thoughts that flew through
her head. She was no more immune to beauty
than were all of those silly men who babbled
like loons before her.

And he seemed to know it—seemed to read
her thoughts, for the look in his eyes was all
too revealing.

Would she have considered his proposal at

all if he weren't such a beautiful man? she
wondered suddenly. She liked to think she
would, but knew better.

Och, but she *was* a foolish lass who sighed
over any handsome face, and the very prospect
plagued her sorely.

How could she be guilty of the very thing
she most disdained?

Their gazes held, locked, sparred.

The expression upon her face was almost
more than Lyon could bear.

Women had gazed at him with that particular look of appreciation many times, but
never had it given him such a fierce satisfaction
as it did this instant. She was sitting upright
upon the bed—his bed—her hair mussed and
wild from sleep, her eyes fixed upon his face.

She was lovely—God, but she was—and
even the likelihood that she smelled like sheep
was not enough to keep his blood from singing
through his veins.

If he'd doubted her attraction to him before,
he certainly did not now. It was there in her
eyes for him to spy, raw and undisguised. He
savored it, like a well-earned victory. Her gaze
lowered, and he smiled fiercely. The mere implication of her thoughts tightened his loins.

"Care for a closer inspection?" he asked,
feeling utterly wicked under her scrutiny.

Her gaze flew up to meet his in surprise.

"Och!" she replied. "Dinna even think sae!"

"Think what?" he asked with false innocence. "What is it you would forbid me to think?"

Shuttering her expression, she laid down upon the bed and assured him quite pertly, "Ye've little enough I've no' seen before, Sassenach!"

Smart-arsed wench.

He had to commend her for her quick recovery. She was certainly no fainting miss, and he was inclined to believe her claim.

What had she seen before him? And who? How many?

"Is that so?" he asked, provoked by the mere thought.

She turned over upon the bed and dragged a pillow beneath her cheek. "O' course."

"Then you'll not mind if I remain unclad?"

"Why should I?" she replied, sounding unconcerned. " 'Tis yer home, yer chamber, and ye can certainly do whatever ye will."

Could he now?

He had to assure himself that no, he could not. Because what he wanted just now was to walk over to the bed, grasp her by the ankles, strip every last article of clothing from her body with his teeth, and make her his bride.

A slight smile curved his lips as he closed the door and started across the room.

"Do not mind if I do, then," he said as he rounded the bed, walking into her line of vision once more, forcing her to acknowledge him.

To her credit, she merely peered up at him and raised her brows slightly when he stood by the bed directly before her. He placed the torch within the sconce above the desk, wholly aware of what lay exposed and where her field of vision lay. And then he sat upon the chair by the bed, casting her a glance to find that her eyes were squeezed tightly shut.

His lips curved with the knowledge that she wasn't quite so unaffected after all. His smile deepened at the sight she presented—so like a little girl blocking her sight, as though to hide.

Such a delightful contradiction she was.

Her eyes remained closed while he arranged the items upon his desk. He pushed the inkwell aside, placed the quill beside it, and then opened one of his bound volumes, aware that she had yet to reopen her eyes. He could see her out of the corner of his eye, and her cheeks were adorably pink.

"Are you certain this is not disturbing you?" he asked her roguishly.

Her eyes flew open. "Who? Me?"

"You perchance spy someone else within this room?" His gaze was drawn to the movement in the corner, to the wee cowering lamb, and he waited to see how she would respond.

"O' course no'!"

Precisely what he suspected, and he was relieved to hear her say so.

Scheming little wench.

She flipped once more upon the bed. "As I

said, this is yer chamber; do what ye will!" she told him. "However," she amended almost at once, sounding startled as she spied the lamb and seemed to realize what she'd confessed to him, "ye should know ye are distressing my grandminnie!"

Lyon pursed his lips, trying hard not to laugh.

"You are only now recalling her presence?"

"O' course no'!"

He tried not to sound amused, though his shoulders shook with mirth. "So I am distressing her . . . though not you?"

"That's right!" she replied at once. "Ye've driven her into the corner awa' from the sight o' ye, can't ye see. Mayhap ye should dress, after all!"

"I see," Lyon said and chuckled softly.

He decided to put her out of her misery once and for all and reached down to find his braies from the floor by the bed where he'd left them.

"Tell your grandminnie I am dressing," he reassured her.

"Ye tell her!" she countered. "She's standing before ye, after all!"

"I thought you said she was deaf?"

"Uh . . . well . . . she is." He could hear the grimace in her voice.

"At any rate, I think she already knows," he told her, "as she's staring. And she doesn't appear particularly offended to me."

"Weel!" she snapped. "She is, and I can assure ye o' that!"

He grinned as she stepped into his trap. "I thought you said your grandminnie was blind?"

She lapsed into silence a long moment—thinking, he knew, trying to remember her lies.

"And yet she's offended by the sight of me?"

Silence was her response.

He damned well wished he could see her face.

She lay there stretched out upon his bed, and he had to remind himself that it was far too soon.

Meghan chewed her lip, trying to think of a way to save her lie.

She could hear the sounds of his dressing behind her and was grateful he was complying. She just couldn't look at him and keep her wits about her, nor could she sleep knowing he was in the room with her. His presence alone was enough to unsettle her. His nakedness wholly discomposed her and scattered her thoughts.

"W-weel," she stammered at long last, "ye did crawl into the bed beside her, did ye no'?"

"Good save, Meghan," he commended her, like the rogue he was.

She turned in shock at hearing her name upon his lips and demanded, "How did ye knoo my name?"

He was grinning down at her, one half of

his face illuminated by the torchlight, the other remaining in shadow.

He stood there, lacing his braies, looking down upon her, and Meghan shivered at the knavish look in his eyes. "Perhaps your grandminnie revealed it?" He winked at her.

Meghan frowned up at him. He was toying with her, she knew. He didn't believe her charade any more than she believed his claim.

And still she wasn't about to confess!

Not yet!

Perhaps she could convince him as yet . . .

"Did ye speak wi' my brothers, perchance?" she asked him. "Are they worried?"

"What?" he mocked her. "Do you not believe your grandminnie Fia told me your name?"

"Oh," Meghan said, smiling up at him, "weel, I would, o' course . . . save that Fia has been here wi' me all along. How could she possibly ha' revealed aught tae ye a'tall?"

"You have a point," he allowed. "And so Fia was not the one."

Once he was through lacing his braies, he sat down behind his little desk—one very much like the one Gavin used to study his manuscripts—and Meghan dared to stare at him in profile. She could scarcely help herself.

Och, but he was a beautiful man.

She stared at his lips, unable to keep herself from wondering how they might feel upon her own.

"I did not speak with your brothers," he said, relenting. "But 'tis not as though your name is unheard of, Meghan Brodie." He cast a glance at her, lifting a brow. "In fact, it seems your reputation precedes you."

"My what!" Meghan narrowed her eyes at him. "Just what is it ye're implying, Sassenach? What do ye mean, my reputation?"

"Naught at all," he replied, and winked at her once more, then returned to perusing his blasted papers, vexing her with his evasiveness. Och, but he couldn't leave it at that! He couldn't simply tell her she had a reputation and then not explain what he meant!

"What sort?" she persisted.

He turned the pages of his manuscript, seeming wholly engaged with the volume, and Meghan wondered if he was ignoring her on purpose.

Wretch.

At the very least he was prolonging her distress.

"Only that I was warned that Brodie women are all mad, and that their mates all end up dead."

"Me?" Meghan gasped in surprise, lifting her head up from the pillow. "*I* am mad?" It was one thing for *her* to say it, and another entirely for it to be said of her. "They think I am mad, as weel?"

He turned to her and winked yet again. The bloody misbegotten wretch!

"Who would say such a thing?" Meghan demanded.

She wasn't witless; she knew her mother and grandmother had oft been fodder for gossip, but she'd never imagined they would think such a thing of her as well! The prospect disheartened her at the very least.

Good lord, what had she ever done that anyone should think her mad?

Then again, what had her mother and grandminnie ever done? Her mother had grieved over a dead husband a little too devoutly, and, well, they'd simply never understood her grandminnie!

"How dare they say such a thing!" Meghan exclaimed, and despite the fact that she wouldn't have to try so hard to convince Lyon she was mad if he believed the rumors, her feelings were hurt. "Weel! It doesna seem tae keep them awa'!" she said, and knew she sounded petulant.

"Keep who away?"

She glared at him. "Men! Silly creatures—singing odes tae bloody faces and slobbering all over themselves at the mere mention o' breasts!"

He lifted a brow. "And when do you mention breasts?" he asked her.

"Och!" Meghan exclaimed. "Not I!"

He lifted his fingers to his lips and Meghan knew he was trying not to laugh. Well, she didn't particularly find this amusing!

"Well, maybe they've a wish to die?" he suggested. "The rumormongers swear that all men married to Brodie women end up with cocked toes."

"What silliness!" Meghan replied. She studied him, searching his face for his thoughts. She couldn't read them.

What *did* he want from her? "And what o' ye?" she asked baldly.

"What of me, Meghan?"

Meghan wished he would stop saying her name so; the mere sound of it upon his lips sent quivers down her spine.

"Ha' ye a death wish, too, Sassenach?"

"Not particularly," he answered, "though I vow I would die a happy man after a single night in your arms, Meghan."

Meghan's heart jolted.

Their gazes held.

Something stirred deep within her at his words . . . over the way that he looked at her.

Dare she reach out . . . remove a single brick from the wall encircling her heart?

"Why?" she demanded.

"You're a beautiful woman," he said simply.

"Mere flattery!" Meghan replied and glowered at him. Why did that answer seem to make her heart sink to her toes? "Ye men are all alike!" she vowed, and laid her head down upon the pillow, disappointed.

He stared at her a long instant. Meghan lapsed into silence, and he returned his attention to his papers. It wasn't long before curiosity got the better of her and she asked, "What are those?"

"Papers," he replied.

Meghan rolled her eyes. "I can see that verra well."

He didn't reply.

"What sort o' papers?" she persisted.

He set them down upon the desk, his expression harassed, and assured her, adding insult to injury, "Naught of interest to you, Meghan."

"Oh, really!" Meghan clenched her teeth. "And how could ye possibly knoo what interests me?"

He cast her a look that reminded her of Leith's barely tolerant glances. "Because they are merely dull treatises, that's why, and naught of significance."

"I see," Meghan retorted, gripping the pillow within her fist. "Naught a silly woman could possibly comprehend? Isna that right?"

"I did not say that."

Meghan glared at him. How could she possibly care what he thought of her? She scarcely knew him. And yet she *did* care. She wasn't certain who she was angrier at—herself for caring, or him for patronizing her! "Aye, Sassenach, but ye did! I heard it verra clearly!"

"Meghan, I did not mean to offend you," he said gently.

"O' course not!" Meghan exclaimed. "Whyever should I be offended simply because ye're an overweening mon!"

He lifted his brows. "If the light bothers you," he said, "I shall put it out."

"Oh, nay!" Meghan replied, incensed. "I am merely a prisoner here!" She turned over, facing away from him. "And a silly, brainless female at that! Dinna concern yerself wi' me!" she told him.

She had a few other choice words for him as well, but held her tongue and drew the pillow angrily over her head.

Bloody arrogant man!

Chapter 14

❦

"She's ruined!" Dougal MacLean raved. His fury boomed through the hall, unsettling even the dogs who rose prudently and slunk away with their tails tucked between their legs.

Alison wished she could join them.

"How dare ye deliver her tae me compromised, Mac Brodie!" her father raged.

Alison winced at the anger apparent in his voice. He'd been ranting more than an hour's time now and still his tone had not softened in the least. She wholly dreaded the moment when Leith took his leave because she thought her da might very well wield his strap against her bottom. The very thought of it pained her already, and she cowered at the thunder in his voice.

Poor Leith had taken the brunt of his furor with nary an angry word in return. Alison watched him, admiring his self-possession. His expression was neither belligerent nor diffi-

167

dent, but rather stoic, and the set of his wide shoulders resolute.

"I ha' already explained the circumstances," Leith said once more. "And I ha' offered tae make amends in whatever manner I may. I dinna knoo what more I can say."

Her father's face was florid. He slammed his fist down upon the table, and Alison flinched at the sound of it. "She is ruined!" he shouted once more. "There is naught ye can bluidy well do!"

"There is little need tae belabor the point, Dougal. I am well aware o' the circumstances!" Leith leaned forward in his chair, trying to make her father comprehend. He cast a solicitous glance at Alison. "But it couldna be helped, I tell ye. My sister is missing," he pointed out once more. "She is *still* missing, Dougal! And Meghan is my first responsibility, as she is my sister . . . Can ye no' understand? I couldna leave the search tae bring Alison home."

"My gaddamned daughter had no bluidy business there tae begin wi', Mac Brodie!" her father countered, shaking his jowls furiously.

"I-it was my choice tae gae!" Alison interjected, speaking up at last, startling them with her avid declaration. In the heat of their discussion, they seemed to have forgotten her presence entirely. Both turned to look at her now.

She peered at her father, beseeching him. She

simply couldn't allow Leith to take all of the blame. "Meghan is my friend," she said. "She would ha' done the same for me, Da."

"I dinna give a damn!" her father roared, slamming his fist yet again.

Alison winced, but didn't cower this time.

"Ye had no bluidy business staying until the wee hours o' the morn, daughter o' mine! Ye shouldna ha' come home a'tall after that!"

Alison straightened her shoulders, a little wounded by his implication. She narrowed her eyes at him. "Would ye rather I had made my way home alone, Da? Even after what happened tae Meghan?" Never in her life had she spoken so disrespectfully to her father, but she couldn't seem to help herself just now. "Is that what ye would ha' preferred, Da?"

Her question seemed to startle him as much as her angry outburst. He didn't seem to know how to respond; he looked at Leith and then down at the table. "Didna ye think I would worry?" he asked Alison after a moment's silence. And his eyes were suspiciously moist when he met her gaze once more.

Alison blinked at his unexpected response. "Ye were worried aboot me, Da?"

His brows collided. "Aye," he said bearishly and peered down at the table again, suddenly unable to face her.

Alison felt like weeping at his admission. She wished so much for the nerve to embrace him, but didn't dare move from where she sat.

It was not her father's way, she knew.

"I didna mean tae make ye worry," she told him. "I was only thinkin' o' Meghan, Da! I didna think o' the consequences!"

He shook his head. "Ye should ha' come tae me first, lass. Ye should ha' come tae me." He continued to stare down at the table, scratching the wood with his ragged nails.

"I was afeared tae, Da."

His gaze flew up to meet hers. "Afeared? Ye were afeared . . . o' me, Alison?"

Alison swallowed, and nodded.

His brows collided and his eyes grew moist once more. "How could ye be afeared . . . o' me, daughter?"

"I—because—"

Leith slammed his hand down upon the table suddenly, startling her. "Alison, ye dinna ha' tae say it," he told her. "Ye dinna ha' tae!"

Her father glared at Leith, suddenly furious once more. "Aye, Mac Brodie! She bluidy well does!"

And for once, Alison had to agree with him. "My da is right, Leith."

Leith's gaze sought hers, held hers, reassured her. "Are ye certain, lass? I swear tae God ye dinna ha' tae!"

Alison nodded. "Aye, but I do, Leith Mac Brodie," she said, "but I thank ye for offering, anyhoo."

He nodded, seeming to understand, and she turned to her father and said, "Da . . . I *had* tae

gae tae them, ye see . . . because I had a confession tae make." Her eyes filled with tears
she refused to shed. All of this was her fault
and it was time to make amends.

His eyes narrowed, scrutinizing her. "Confession? What bluidy confession would ye ha'
tae be makin' tae them, Alison? And why
didna ye come tae me instead?"

Alison lowered her head, unable to face him,
unable to speak for the shame.

"Ye're a guid lass," she heard Leith whisper
at her side, and it gave her the strength she
needed to lift her gaze once more to meet her
father's glare. "I stole the goat!" she blurted.

Her father's face contorted. "What bluidy
damned goat, Alison? What the devil are ye
speakin' of, lass?"

Alison took a deep breath and then proceeded to confess all. Everything, from her un-
requited love for Colin Mac Brodie, to her
stealing the goat that started the feud, to her
reasons why, to her failed attempt at making
amends and her desire not to wed Piers Montgomerie. All of it, every last degrading detail.

Her father listened to the story quietly, his
normally florid face turning the color of new
parchment. He shook his head gravely when
she finished, and said after a time, "Och, Alison . . . What ha' ye done . . . What ha' ye
done?"

"I followed my heart," Alison said despair-
ingly, wanting desperately for him to under-

stand—not to condone, but simply to understand. "I followed my heart, Da! I didna wish tae end like Mairi, ye see!"

He licked his lips and raked a hand over his thick jaw, then raised a hand to his breast, looking as though his heart were aching him. His eyes grew red-rimmed and welled with tears. Of all things she might have said to him, Alison knew this one made his heart bleed, for Mairi had been his favorite daughter, and he missed her so. She could never seem to measure up even to beautiful Mairi's memory. And yet, knowing she would fail, she had never even tried.

"Weel," he began when he could speak once more, "ye need no' fear wedding Montgomerie, daughter o' mine. I doubt he would ha' ye now. All is lost," he murmured. "I dinna know what tae do, Alison. All is lost."

"I'll wed her," Leith announced.

Alison lifted her gaze to his in shock. He couldn't possibly wish to . . .

"Ye?" her father asked, sounding as aghast as Alison felt. "Why should ye wish tae do such a thing, Leith Mac Brodie? I dinna mean tae disparage my own daughter, but ye only just heard her tell us that she loves yer own brother. Why would ye wed wi' her knooing that?"

Leith held Alison's gaze, assuring her without words that he meant every word he uttered. "Because I ha' great affection for Alison," he said quietly.

Alison's heart began to pound as it became clear to her that he was perfectly serious. "Ye do?" she asked him, bewildered.

"I always ha'."

He'd never once led her to believe he'd even noticed her. She had always thought he'd considered her naught more than Meggie's little friend.

"I . . . I did no' realize," Alison whispered in wonder.

"Och, lass . . . because ye only had eyes for Colin. But if ye will ha' me as yer husband, I would be pleased tae ha' ye as my wife."

Her father straightened within his seat. "Perhaps all is no' lost as yet!" he proclaimed. And then he sobered at once, peering at Alison and shaking his head, seeming to temper his excitement for her sake. "Though if Alison willna ha' ye, I canna force her tae wed where she willna," he said, staggering her with his proclamation.

Tears pricked at Alison's eyes. She understood what he was doing, and it warmed her heart, filled her with joy.

His gaze softened as he looked at her. "What say ye, daughter o' mine?"

Alison turned to face Leith. Leith smiled at her, and she knew the right thing to do.

"Aye," she exclaimed. "I will wed wi' ye,

Leith Mac Brodie. If ye truly want me, if ye truly do . . ." She shook her head, scarcely able to believe that he would. ". . . it would be my honor tae be yer bride!"

"I do, lass," he assured her, and her father leapt up from his chair with a whoop of delight.

"Tae bluidy hell wi' Montgomerie!" he proclaimed. "Tae bluidy hell wi' David o' Scotia, too! We're going tae ha' ourselves a bluidy wedding the likes o' which these Highlands ha' never seen! But first things first!" he said, nodding at Leith respectfully. "Let us gather ourselves together and search for Meghan. And we'll no' stop until we've turned every last stone!"

Lyon awoke at his desk in the wee hours of the morn, and his eyes were at once drawn to the bed.

Pale morning light filtered in through the hole in his ceiling, suffusing the room with a sweet glow. He didn't lift his head, didn't stir, didn't dare wake her as yet.

He wanted to watch her sleep.

She looked more like an angel than any mortal had a right to . . .

She slept like an infant, he thought, upon her belly, with her hands extended as though embracing the bed, like a wee bairn clutching its mother's bosom, her palms open and caressing the sheets, her face turned to one side and her long lashes pressed like ebony silk against her cheeks.

He stared, unable to keep himself from it, watching her sleep so peacefully. In slumber, her features were perfection ... her lips full and perfectly formed, her lashes long and soft against high exotic cheekbones, her nose perfectly aquiline, and her hair a luscious copper mass of shining ringlets spread over the pale sheets.

He hadn't dared to crawl in next to her ... not again last night, determined as he was to do this right. He could have seduced her, no doubt. The look in her eyes had assured him as much. Beneath that deliberate facade she wore, she hid a passion as fierce as his own.

He recognized it, and craved it.

And Christ, the way she'd gazed at him when he'd sat here bare before her.

The mere thought of it hardened his loins all over again, made his blood simmer and burn. God's truth, he wanted Meghan Brodie like he'd never wanted any woman in his life ... not even in his youth had he been so driven by lust.

And it was something more than her face that drew him ... something he could not put his finger upon. A pretty face alone had little to recommend it, and he'd walked away from many a bed for lack of interest. Particularly so in the last years.

This time was different.

Through the years, his desires had grown darker, and it had taken more and more to whet his appetite of late. He'd begun to think himself a little bit depraved that innocence no longer drew him as once it had. He remembered a time when a simple smile had been enough to make him hard as stone and ready to rut with any woman who had two legs to spread for him. And many had done so. He was the whore's son, after all, and it drew the sort of attention every lad craved from the moment he was able to spill his first seed.

His first lover had been an earl's wife. She'd been two and twenty to his ten and four. He hadn't been able to walk away from her bed, though he'd understood the peril to his soul.

His second had been a chambermaid who'd boasted to him that she'd lain with his father as well.

And the third . . . Well, she'd been a sweet infatuation of his . . . a lass three years his senior whom he'd dreamed of rutting with for weeks until he'd made her his conquest. And then she'd gone away and married her baron, and her memory was only a smear now upon his memory.

They were all a blur after that.

And now . . . he remembered not the faces, so much, but the appetite that had enslaved his very soul. He'd been so long a prisoner to his desires, and nobody but him had known.

He could never condemn his mother, for he understood her only too well.

And then one day he simply hadn't been interested any longer. The hunger that had consumed him body and soul had simply abated, and he'd found himself walking away from creamy round breasts that would have once set his heart to pounding and his blood to thrumming within his veins.

Nay, it had been a long time since a pretty face alone had been enough to stir him.

And though Meghan Brodie's face was sheer perfection, it was the look in her eyes that tempted him and set his heart to pounding once more. She'd roused his hunger, and it had awakened hard as stone. God's teeth, he'd scarcely been able to think of anything else since the moment he'd first laid eyes upon her.

She made him feel alive as he hadn't felt in far too long.

He wanted her, aye, but more than that ... he wanted to know what thoughts stole through that engaging mind of hers. He wanted to know what stirred her heart and made her burn. There was something bewitching in those deep-green eyes ... something compelling ... something that drew him ... something he wanted to know as intimately as one would a lover.

He wanted to be her lover.

He lifted his head from his arms, watching with hungry eyes the way she stirred.

And then he spied the lamb shivering in the corner, and frowned. Damn, how could they have forgotten the wee beast?

The poor animal probably needed to relieve itself—and was like to be half-starved, as well. He rose quietly from the desk, paused to take another long look at the woman lying so serenely within his bed, drinking in the sight of her . . . and then he set about taking her *grandminnie* out to piss.

Chapter 15

Meghan awakened to find herself alone. Not even Fia remained to bid her good morn.

She hoped Lyon had taken the poor little beast out to the meadow for a bit. She was certain it wasn't in the animal's best interest to keep it confined within a room all hours of the day. And yet it hadn't seemed so distressed while she'd been alone with it. But she felt a stab of guilt for having gone to sleep without concerning herself with its needs. She had been so weary. The day had taken its toll upon her, mind and body.

She'd lain awake for some time after their discourse, too aware of the man sitting there at the little desk. She'd lain with her eyes closed, wondering about the papers that held his attention—distracted him from her—until exhaustion had overcome her and she'd slept at last. But though she'd slept deeply, she didn't feel particularly refreshed this morn.

Nor did she feel especially benevolent toward Lyon Montgomerie.

Her brow furrowed. She wasn't certain why she felt so provoked by him, but she certainly was.

She had dared to hope . .

What?

That she might be wrong about him? That he might be different? That he might see her as something more than a pretty face?

Meghan yearned so much to spill her heart . . . to someone . . . to reveal every dark part of herself and every flaw, to be unveiled in the light of day . . . and to still be loved!

Piers Montgomerie, like all the rest, merely wanted a vessel.

The problem was that her heart was riddled with fissures. And her soul was exploding behind it, bursting to be set free. If she let them . . . the bricks in the wall surrounding her heart would come tumbling down so easily.

And if she revealed herself . . . and he were to be repelled by what he saw?

She couldn't take that chance.

And still . . . if she managed to bring peace with this union, all was well that ended well.

Right?

Then, too, she would be saving Alison from a marriage she surely did not want. Alison was her best friend, and Alison wanted Colin, Meghan knew—desperately! If Meghan wedded Lyon Montgomerie, it would buy Alison time at least to win her brother's fickle heart. Meghan was certain Colin could be content with Alison if he but gave her a chance. Alison might not be the fairest of women, but her heart was sweeter than honey and purer than gold.

Still and all, Meghan couldn't simply surrender herself so easily.

Pride would scarcely allow it.

She dared to want more!

She might concede to this union for the sake of peace, but Piers Montgomerie was going to get more than he bargained for, that she vowed. He was going to learn not to judge a soul by the mask it wore!

He wanted a face to wed, did he . . . Well . . . he could have the face, but not the heart!

And Meghan was looking forward to teaching the rogue a bloody good lesson!

Her gaze was drawn toward the desk . . . and curiosity seized her.

She didn't care if it might be wrong to pry. 'Twas certainly the least he deserved for so rudely locking her within his room . . . and for leaving his mysterious papers out upon the desk.

A little peek couldn't possibly hurt.

She went resolutely to the desk and found two thick, leather-bound manuscripts upon it. Turning over the first, she saw that it was untitled. Opening it revealed scribbled notations . . . pages and pages of them, all written in

Latin to the best she could determine. Her brows knit as she tried to make out the words. She recognized a few, but she had never really learned Latin. Her mother had been familiar with the language of the church, but Fia had not. Only her brother Gavin knew the tongue well enough to read script. The best Meghan could make out, by perusing the headings of each notation, was that they were entries taken from the writings of others: Aristotle and Augustine, Boethius and Anselm, and many more . . . too many to name—all dated, she assumed, to the year they were written.

Meghan's curiosity was piqued . . . and yet, she could hardly sit down to read the texts when she could not understand them. Frowning, she dropped the first manuscript down upon the desk, and turned over the other.

This one also was untitled. In the bottom right-hand corner was written . . . *Piers Montgomerie*.

Lifting a brow in surprise, Meghan drew out the chair and sat down before the little desk. She turned to the first page.

It was titled *Spiritualitas vs. Carnalis*.

But the script was written in the English tongue and that she understood very well, for Alison's mother had been an Englishwoman and had taught her daughter well. Alison, in turn, had taught Meghan.

Much too engaged to walk away now, she

laid the manuscript flat upon the desk and began to read . . .

Given that Lyon had only this morning dispatched his letters, David of Scotia was the last person he expected to find in his courtyard so soon.

David arrived with a retinue of five, looking harassed as he dismounted before Lyon.

"Christ bedamned! You must be foreknowing!" Lyon told him.

David's answering scowl was a testament to his mood. "What the devil are you speaking of?"

Lyon arched a brow. "Only this morn I dispatched you a letter, and here you are."

"So I am!" David replied, his tone curt.

Lyon slanted him a knowing glance. "What brings you to these parts?" he said. "Naught good, I suppose."

David shook his head ominously. "Naught good!" he agreed. "Damned misbegotten Highland rogues!"

Lyon slapped a hand upon his shoulder, his expression sober. "Come, then," he urged him, "let us converse within."

And the two made their way toward the hall.

"I'm afraid I bring distressing news," David disclosed.

"I gather as much."

"Lyon, old friend, I believe I've just made your charge here all the more complicated."

"I see," Lyon answered. "Well, that makes two of us, then, as so have I."

David cast him a curious glance.

"I shall explain within," Lyon assured. "We can argue over who shall go first over a tankard of ale. What say you?"

David's look darkened. "I'd say if you need to ply me with ale, Lyon, something tells me I'm not going to like this one whit."

"Then we are even," Lyon replied. "Because something tells me that if you felt compelled to stop and tell me about something you've done, neither will I."

"You always were a canny bastard," David told him. "And nay, you will not like this, I think. I hope you have something more than bog water to drink. I'm not in the bloody mood to grind my ale between my teeth."

"The ale is fine," Lyon said. "Just do not sit beneath the rotting ceiling or you'll discover splinters rained into your cup and plate instead—and then find yourself plucking slivers from your tongue the rest of the eve."

David's brows lifted. "That bad?"

"Aye," Lyon replied with a nod. "That bad." And then he grinned. "But better than having rats crawl up your arse while you sleep any day."

David chuckled. "I'm certain," he said, and shook his head. "Damned Highlanders! I'd rather be mauled by a pack of rats any bloody day than to deal with a single bloody one!"

"That bad?"

"That bad," David assured him as they entered the hall. He flung off his mantle and cast it over his arm. "Whatever possessed me to *want* to be king?"

"Because you bloody well love it," Lyon answered without pause. "And you were always better at chess than anyone."

David laughed. "Even you?"

"Aye, you canny bastard, even me."

It was getting late.

Squinting as the letters blurred before her eyes, Meghan set the manuscripts down. The texts, she'd discovered, were both a personal memoir and a corresponding treatise, with references to passages within the first volume.

It began with a rather poignant account of Lyon's youth, his days spent in study under the Archbishop of Canterbury. And it seemed to Meghan that though these had been his most uncertain years, years spent sequestered from his peers, they were also his most contented years. Though he'd questioned his soul, he'd seemed focused and certain of his life's ambition. While he'd studied beneath the scrutiny of the clergy, his ambitions had been of an academic sort; his enlightenment, while spiritual in nature, hardly adhered to the teachings of the church.

In fact, Meghan thought some of his beliefs quite heretical, even for her. Gavin would have apoplexy were he to read them, she was certain. He was nigh ready to tie Meghan to the pulpit for simply suggesting that her sanctuary was the woodlands, and that God's sermon came to her through the creatures of his creation. But these essays questioned the very existence and nature of God.

Within his first essays, he had explored in great detail his quest for spiritual truths and had been quick to dismiss the import of materialistic pursuits. It was very clear to Meghan, here, that his ambitions had been of a noble sort.

His next essay had been a little less conclusive and a little more discomposing.

Though he did not elucidate, something had happened to change his life's direction. He had by now abandoned his former aspirations to an erudite life and had resigned himself to a more . . . at first defensive . . . then offensive perspective. His objective seemed to be the pursuit of justice.

She was almost finished now with that particular essay though not completely, and though she wasn't certain she should continue—it felt a little as though she were peering through a looking glass at his soul—she couldn't seem to help herself.

The account drew her as much as did the man who'd written it.

She had no notion how long she'd sat reading, but knew that it had grown dark by the dimness of the room—not that there had been much light to begin with, as the only window that graced the chamber was nailed shut from within. The afternoon light was beginning to fade, and last night's torch had gutted itself sometime during the night. The remains of the supper they'd brought her were left almost untouched.

It was growing too dark to read.

Frustrated, for the treatise had grown ever more fascinating, Meghan rose from the desk and went to the window to examine the shutters, to see if there were some way she could brighten the room.

She found the shutters nailed firmly so that they could not be pried open, and no matter how hard Meghan tugged at them, they would not budge. She wondered who would do such a thing. Surely not Lyon Montgomerie? What manner of man could compose such a brilliant memoir and then board a bloody window shut rather than simply fix the shutters?

As she struggled with the shutters, she came aware of voices outside and below the window, and ceased her struggles with the shutters in order to try to make them out. She thought she would recognize Lyon's voice most anywhere, but the other she could not make out—not Baldwin's, she was near certain.

Searching for a knothole or a crack to peer from, she listened, but in vain, and then could suddenly hear the echo of voices carry up from the hall below.

Meghan rushed to the door and was surprised to find it unlocked. She frowned at the discovery, though it should have pleased her. He hadn't locked her in, after all. What was wrong with her that she should forget to try something so simple as the lock upon a door? She'd wasted entirely too much time sitting within his room, prying into his papers and his past, when she should have been making some attempt to get home.

Aye, it was entirely possible that a union between them would be advantageous to all, but Meghan didn't appreciate being coerced into anything. It would suit her much better were she to go home to her brothers and discuss with them the possibility of wedding Lyon Montgomerie. And if Lyon wished to wed with her, he could *ask* for her hand in matrimony, rather than bloody well *tell* her she was going to wed him!

She hadn't even drawn a comb through her hair, she remembered suddenly, but didn't care. And having slept in her dress, it was rumpled and even slovenly—och, she must appear every bit as insane as she would have him believe she was!

Making her way cautiously down the stairs, she examined her surroundings, and determined that it had been far too long a time since the manor had been in good repair. As the stairs creaked noisily beneath her careful steps, she didn't wonder any longer why the shutters had been boarded shut. She could perfectly understand why the very thought of repairing them might be overwhelming. And yet, *someone* had to begin the repairs *somewhere* with *something*, or the entire place was going to crumble down upon itself.

She spied them upon the dais as she descended the final steps—Lyon and his guest. At least Meghan assumed it was a guest, because he didn't look like one of Lyon's men-at-arms.

In fact, this man was dressed in finer garments than Meghan had ever set eyes upon in her life, and his bearing was anything but common. She knew at once that this was someone of import—someone who had the power to help her if he chose. And having determined that, she straightened her shoulders, and made her way resolutely to the dais.

Like a wolf scenting his mate, the instant she'd descended into the hall Lyon sensed her presence, and his gaze had lifted to find her watching discreetly from the foot of the stairs. And suddenly, he could hear not a word David was speaking to him, his attention wholly taken by the woman standing in the shadows.

"So it seems I misjudged MacKinnon," David disclosed, somehow oblivious of their audience.

Lyon was anything but.

Something like birds taking flight launched within his gut, and his breath strangled within his throat as her gaze settled upon his, her beautiful eyes slitting. Her chin tilted defiantly and she pushed away from the banister and marched toward them. His heart jumped.

"I can see now that it was a mistake to involve his son," David continued, "but what has been done cannot be undone."

Lyon nodded vaguely.

Meghan Brodie captured him as no woman ever had. She roused his body . . . made his soul yearn for something . . . something more.

He shook his head, trying to cast off the spell she wove over him. "Misjudged who?"

"Lyon?" David said, sounding vexed. "Have you not listened to a bloody word I've said to you?"

Lyon didn't see the point in lying.

"Nay," he admitted, but his eyes remained fixed upon Meghan's lovely face as she marched toward them, her expression foreboding. Even ungroomed as she was, looking every bit the part of a madwoman, he thought her beauty unparalleled. And God's teeth, whatever else she was, whether mad or simply shrewd as the devil, she was unshrinking as well, and Lyon braced himself, expecting the worst. There was little worse to bear than the lash of an angry woman's tongue.

David's gaze followed his.

"You have a guest!" he said with some surprise, and then as she approached, undaunted, with fire flashing in her glorious green eyes, he turned to Lyon and asked, "Lyon ... who is she?"

Lyon cast his friend a sheepish glance. "She," he replied with some hesitation, "is precisely the complication I was speaking of." And he shrugged.

Chapter 16

~~ ⌒◯◯⌒ ~~

Meghan decided she would appeal to the man's sense of loyalty. If he were countryman, she had some chance, at least, of gaining his support. If he were an English toad, then she was simply out of luck. It was impossible to tell by his manner of speech as he spoke like an Englishman, with the merest trace of a brogue.

"Are ye a Scotsman, sir?" she asked him, meeting his gaze as she approached the table. She straightened her spine and lifted her chin.

He cocked his head at her in puzzlement. "Aye," he answered, casting Lyon a wary glance. "And why do you ask, lass?"

"Verra guid!" Meghan exclaimed. "Because I wish tae gae home!"

The man turned to Lyon, looking all the more confused by her vehement demand. "What is this?" he asked. "What is she speaking of, Lyon?"

"Uh," was all Lyon Montgomerie could think to say.

Meghan turned to glare at him, and was pleased to see that he had the decency to flush at the prospect of an explanation.

She wasn't about to let him explain, however, because he would no doubt find some way to justify his actions. "He abducted me!" she charged, pointing an accusing finger at Lyon.

The man's brows lifted higher. "Lyon?" he said. "Is this true?"

Lyon had the good grace not to deny it. He nodded with lifted brows and an abashed grimace. "Afraid so," he admitted.

"Christ!" the man exploded.

"I was going to tell you as soon as you were finished," Lyon assured him.

"What a bloody pair we are!" the man declared. "Whyever would you do such a thing? Who the devil is she?"

"I am Meghan Brodie!" she announced, wholly annoyed with their apparent comradeship. "And I dinna knoo who ye are, sir. Ye dinna sound like any bluidy Scot tae me, but my brothers willna be pleased tae hear this, I assure ye!"

The man turned to Lyon once more. "Gaddamn, Lyon, but I anticipate you had a better reason than to simply warm your bed. Her very demeanor shrivels my willy!"

Meghan gasped in outrage at his crude remark, and her face heated.

Lyon chuckled softly. "I cannot claim I did
to begin with," he said, "but in my own defense, I must say she was somewhat more ap-
pealing yesternight."

The man chortled, and Meghan bristled. She
gritted her teeth and clenched her hands at her
sides. "I dinna see what is sae amusing!" she
assured them both and narrowed her eyes at
the arrogant stranger. "Who are ye, sir?" she
demanded of him.

He regarded her a moment, and then proclaimed matter-of-factly with an arrogant lift of
his chin, "I am David of Scotia."

Meghan blinked in surprise. *"King David?"*

"Aye, lass."

"Son o' Malcom Ceann Mor?"

"None other."

Meghan tilted her head at him in disdain.
"Ye dinna look like a king tae me, sir," she
accused him. "Ye look and sound like a bluidy
rotten Sassenach!"

He merely smiled at that.

"Och!" Meghan exclaimed, and was disheartened.

Or was she truly?

"I dinna suppose I can persuade ye tae send
me home?" she asked the man without hesitation, but also without expectation. There was
little chance of it, she knew, when he was the
reason Lyon Montgomerie was in Scotia to be-

gin with. The two were in league together. Bed-fellows!

"Give me a single reason I should question the judgment of one of my most valuable men," he answered.

"Because I dinna wish tae wed wi' him is why!" Meghan answered, lifting her chin.

His gaze flew to Lyon's in surprise. His brow arched imperiously. "*Wed*, Lyon?"

Lyon seemed to brace himself. He nodded. "Aye," he answered simply.

"You cannot wed with her!" David countered.

"That's precisely what I tried tae tell him!" Meghan interjected, pleased to see he was finally seeing her point.

"What of MacLean?" David asked, ignoring her.

Meghan bristled at his apparent dismissal.

"What of him?" Lyon replied mildly. "I have already dispatched him a letter of explanation, as I did with you. I assure you I'll not be wedding Alison MacLean."

"Lyon," David urged him, "consider what you are saying!"

"I'll not wed her," Lyon answered quietly, but tersely, and Meghan wasn't certain who she was more incensed for—herself, or Alison! Did no man know to look behind the facade of a silly face!

"The poor lass appeared as though she

might cry did I simply breathe upon her," Lyon said by way of explanation.

There was an immediate soberness between them as they stared at each other, seeming to be sparring without words.

David's expression was an unreadable mask but for his eyes, which flashed forbiddingly.

"Do you recall," Lyon said, "what you once claimed you would give to me upon a silver plate?"

David turned away, his jaw tautening. "I do," he replied.

Lyon's expression was every bit as firm. "This is not the way."

Meghan watched the two, considering their curious exchange. By the expression upon David's face it became quite apparent that Lyon would hold his ground, that David would give his.

What hold did Lyon have over this man?

It was also apparent by the look in David's eyes that he was unused to being opposed, and yet she knew instinctively he would yield.

"If you will not, you will not," David relented, "though I cannot and will not condone a marriage without consent. Christ, Lyon, but you have not even her brothers' blessings in this!"

Meghan held her breath.

"I will have *hers*," Lyon assured him.

Meghan inhaled a breath. "Nay, ye willna!" she swore, enraged by his arrogance.

David peered at her then, looking suddenly annoyed with her presence. Well! Meghan bloody well didn't care! This was her life! And she was certainly *not* going to stand idly by while two strangers decided her fate!

He returned his gaze to Lyon and yielded, "Are you so certain of this, Lyon?"

Lyon smiled. "What do you think, David?" He lifted a brow.

In answer, David arched a brow as well. "I think if anyone can, you certainly may, but if you do not gain it, I cannot, as I said, condone it."

Meghan could scarcely believe they were bartering the matter of her life before her so arrogantly!

"Very well," David said, "I can give you a fortnight to convince her, after which you must agree to release her if she remains opposed."

Lyon was silent, unresponsive, and Meghan, knowing this was the best she was going to get from David of Scotia, lifted her chin and challenged Lyon, "Unless ye are no' sae bluidy certain o' yer bluidy self, after all?"

Lyon met her gaze and his lips curved softly, his uncanny blue eyes flashing with seductive interest.

"I will agree if ye will agree," she boldly invited him.

He turned abruptly to David, looking suddenly quite satisfied with the arrangement. A quiver raced down Meghan's spine. Recalling the way he had left her upon his bed, ready to yield to him for want of a simple kiss, she wondered whether she had somehow made a mistake in challenging him so.

"You were ever the negotiator," he said to David.

David gave him a look that told Meghan he was hardly feeling a victor in this settlement.

"Fair enough," Lyon said. "I shall agree to a fortnight, after which if she does not agree to be my bride . . ." He peered at Meghan, and his smoldering blue eyes stole her breath. "I shall personally escort her home."

"Very well!" David announced, and Meghan had the immediate impression she *had* made a terrible mistake. Something in Lyon's expression told her she had lost already. And somehow, she got the feeling she'd played directly into his hands.

The image of him as he'd appeared standing in the doorway last night accosted her then, and her heart began to pound traitorously, thundering in her ears.

Wasn't it enough she had to vie with Lyon Montgomerie? Was she going to have to battle her own treacherous body, as well?

She had never thought herself so susceptible to the wiles of any man, but there was little use in denying the way this one made her feel— despite that she knew him to be as shallow-minded as the rest of his gender!

Well! She hadn't lost as yet! she reminded

herself. And she wasn't very good at losing, besides! Lyon Montgomerie might win after all, Meghan resolved, but she was going to make certain he looked thrice at his bloody rotten prize!

It probably wasn't the wisest thing Alison had ever done, but she had to speak with Leith. She had to tell him how much she appreciated what he was willing to sacrifice for her sake, but she had begun to feel the weight of her conscience ever since he'd taken his leave the other night. She knew he couldn't possibly love her, and she couldn't allow him to surrender his own chance for happiness with some other woman of his choice.

She found him in the courtyard with both Colin and Gavin, their heads together in solemn discussion. Gavin and Colin had evidently only just returned from yet another search, for Gavin still held the reins of his mount firmly within his hand. Colin had abandoned his own mount entirely, and it stood dutifully by, as Colin listened to whatever it was Leith was saying to him. Her heart twisted a little at the sight of him, but she told herself she was a fool. He had never shown her the least regard! Why should she care so much for a man who refused even to look her in the eyes?

Alison had to know, too, whether they had word of Meghan, as she was tormented with worry for her friend's sake. She couldn't bear the wait any longer; she had to know.

And yet, she waited still, unable to face Colin.

When both Gavin and Colin had taken their leave, and Leith turned to go as well, she ran after him, calling his name.

He turned to face her at once, his brows lifting in surprise. "Alison!" He reached out and seized her hand when it seemed she would stumble into his arms.

"Och! Forgive me for intruding!" she beseeched him a bit breathlessly. "But I had tae knoo! I had tae knoo o' Meghan! Please dinna be angry wi' me for coming yet again!"

"Dinna be sae silly!" Leith assured her. "I understand, Alison!" And he seemed genuinely pleased to see her.

Alison clutched his arm hopefully. "Is there news?"

He shook his head. "None at all, I am afraid."

Alison frowned. "I am sae worried!"

"And sae are we, lass, sae are we. But dinna ye fret. We will find her soon."

"I do hope," she said, and took a deep breath. "Leith," she began, peering up at him bravely. "I also came for another reason."

His brows lifted. "What is it, Alison?" he said with a look of concern.

Alison suddenly could not find the words to speak. "I . . . I . . . wished tae say . . . well, ye see," she stammered, "I feel a bit that ye were forced tae ask my father . . . well . . ."

He clasped her hands gently, seeming to understand what she was trying to say. "Alison sweeting, I was no' forced tae do anything a'tall, dinna ye see?"

Alison shook her head. "I canna think that ye would wish tae wed wi' me," she told him. "I knoo that ye feel sorry for me, and I wanted ye tae knoo that I willna be crushed if ye dinna wish tae take me as yer wife. I dinna need a man tae feel sorry for me, and I dinna wish tae make ye unhappy."

He smiled down at her. "Look at me, Alison MacLean . . . Does the prospect o' wedding ye seem tae distress me?"

"Well, nay, but—"

"Nay, but naught," he said, hushing her. "Come wi' me a moment." And then he drew her aside for privacy behind a horse and cart. "Will ye do me a favor?" he asked her.

Alison nodded, so grateful to him that she would have fallen at his feet and kissed them with her lips.

"Listen tae me wi' yer heart just noo, Alison," he said, and then drew her into his arms.

Alison gasped in surprise. Her heart began to hammer within her breast as he turned her face up to his and bent to touch his lips to her own.

She felt dizzy with shock as he kissed her sweetly, gently upon the mouth—just a tender kiss, but it was the first Alison had ever had in her entire life.

No man had ever, ever done such a thing to her.

No man had ever even expressed the desire to.

It confused her so, startled her so that she merely stared up at him in bewilderment as he lifted his face to peer down at her. She blinked in surprise.

"Did ye hear that?" he asked her, his voice tender.

Alison could not find her voice to speak, nor did she find the will even to nod.

"Listen tae me, and listen tae me well, Alison MacLean," Leith told her with certainty. "I want ye tae gae home noo," he directed her, "and think on what I ha' just said tae ye wi' my heart. Think aboot what is yer desire. Consider carefully whether ye would ha' me as yer mon. My offer stands as it was made, but I dinna wish tae force ye, either, lass. Gae home, then, and think o' this, and decide, and if ye will ha' me as yer husband, I would be honored tae take ye as my bride."

Alison shook her head and opened her mouth to speak.

"Shhh," he bade her. "Dinna say a word until ye ha' passed the night in thought. Do me the favor o' that. Will ye?"

Taking in a breath, before she should swoon at his feet with the shock of it all, she nodded.

"Guid, then," he said, and drew her out from behind the cart into open view once more.

He had to drag her out behind him because she would have remained there, so shocked was she by what he had said and done. She placed her fingers in bewilderment to her lips.

The messenger came as she stood there staring up at Leith Mac Brodie in bewilderment. Alison was scarcely aware of him, even, for he handed the missive to Leith and practically turned and fled whilst she stood there contemplating what had only just happened between them.

Leith broke the seal, and stared at the parchment. He turned it sideways, and then his face colored a bit. "Alison," he said. "Gavin is no' here, and I canna read this. Will ye do me the honor?"

Alison nodded, taking the parchment from his hands at once. She gazed at the paper without seeing the words for an instant, and then blinked and read.

"Lyon Montgomerie has her," she said, stunned. "He has Meghan."

"The hell ye say!" he thundered, and tore the parchment from her hands.

She peered up at him, blinking. "It says only that he holds her in custody for the charge o' thievery!"

Behind the protective barrier of rails, Meghan stood looking down upon Lyon's hall. Her vantage point along the tiny open corridor offered her a clear view of all who came and went, and she needed only step back into the shadows if Lyon entered the hall below. Neither did she fear anyone would come upon her here, as only Lyon's room could be accessed by the corridor, and no one seemed to dare climb his stairs, so Megan was able to observe her gaolers and make a plan.

The hall was empty now but for a few laggards who seemed disinclined to work whilst their master's eyes were not upon them.

King David had remained rather than continue along his journey to Edinburgh, and he and Lyon had closeted themselves to discuss matters of consequence. She wondered what those topics might be, as David's visits to the Highlands were rare. She was certain, however, their discussion did *not* concern her, as it was clear that her situation had been addressed and decided upon.

And she was hardly pleased with the outcome.

Yet neither could she argue it, as she had agreed to his bloody bargain, and to admit she had been outwitted only made her feel foolish.

Nay, she wanted to make him regret his shallow-minded covetousness!

More than that, she *needed* to go home.

The only way she knew that Lyon had come to his bed at all last night was because she'd awakened to his warmth upon the bed beside her. His body was gone, but his scent had remained, and Meghan, her heart pounding fiercely, had dared to turn over upon the warm sheets, embracing it. It was a brazen thing to do, but Meghan, having slept within his bed for the second night in a row, was having the most peculiar thoughts.

She couldn't seem to eradicate him from her thoughts—not that it was at all possible in her situation, she realized. How could she possibly when she was occupying his chamber, contemplating wedding with him for the sake of her kinsmen, and reading his most personal thoughts?

She was really growing quite desperate.

Studying the hall, she noticed for the first time that it bore a similar ceiling to the one Gavin had had constructed within their chapel. Only this one was older and not domed. It was flat, as there were rooms above the enormous hall, but it was braced along the walls with the same sort of beams that supported the ceiling of the chapel.

The same sort from which that silly raven had peered down at her.

She had felt so helpless to reach it.

Meghan stared at the beam closest to her, the craziest notion entering her head, and then she peered down at the hall below.

One would have to be truly mad to perch oneself upon such a place on high, she thought, and noted the placement of the nearest beam . . .

If she could but reach it—and she thought

she could—she could pull herself up onto it . . .

The thought of him looking up at her from below brought a cunning smile to her face. Well, perhaps she could convince him that she was mad after all. Determining that it was worthy of the effort, and certain she could see her grandminnie doing the very same, Meghan went to the far end of the rail and reached out, trying to touch the beam. Stretching, stretching, she lifted herself up on tiptoes and giggled with mischievous delight when she was able to wrap her fingers about the board.

She tested it, tugging it to make certain it was secure, and then smiled and stepped up onto the rail, humming a merry tune . . .

"Lyon!" came a bark from beyond his closed doors, and was followed at once by a sharp rap. "Lyon!"

Lyon removed his booted feet from the table and peered at David, knowing instinctively that the news would not be good. The two of them had been discussing Iain MacKinnon, and the best course of action to take with him. Lyon had suggested that David consider returning to discuss the matter with Iain directly. Iain, as Lyon understood it, was a fair man, and Lyon believed in direct personal confrontation. At any rate, sequestered as he was with Scotia's king, none would be so bold as to interrupt him here, lest the message be of grave import. Or . . .

"Enter!" he said, and braced himself as the door swung open to reveal a wan-looking Baldwin.

"Lyon?" Baldwin said apprehensively. "If I may beg pardon, I think you should come."

Lyon cast a glance at David to find his old friend eyeing him curiously with brows raised. Rising from his chair, Lyon knew instinctively by the look upon Baldwin's face that his interruption was about none other than Meghan.

What the devil was she up to now?

"I shall return," he said to David, and then asked as cordially as possible, "Have you perchance had the opportunity to sample the wine I sent you from Auvergne? I have some hoarded away for myself, I must confess. Perhaps you should like to try it now?"

David's brows lifted higher. "In other words, you would like me to occupy myself here alone whilst you go and deal with your guest?"

Lyon's lips curved upward. "You were ever a shrewd bastard," he said.

"As were you, of course," David returned, flashing a cunning smile. He sighed. "Very well, Lyon, go and deal with your wench. I will wait."

Lyon laughed. "I shall be quick," he promised, and abandoned David to his own devices. Preceding Baldwin out the door, he demanded of him, "What now?"

"Uh . . . I think you need to see this for yourself," Baldwin answered, and said not a word more.

Lyon grimaced. He suddenly wasn't certain he wished to know what she was up to, as he was certain Meghan was determined to make him pay in blood.

As he entered the hall, he heard her singing in the most god-awful voice, but didn't see her straightaway for the audience that had gathered at the sound. Christ, but the noise was as hideous as that of some ghoul from the black woods!

And her lyrics were none the better!

> "I must gae walk the wood sae wild," she
>   wailed,
> "And wander here and there in dread and
>   deadly fear!
> Alas, where I trusted, I am beguiled,
> And all for one!
> All for one!"

He didn't have to search long for her. He merely followed the gazes of his men to find her perched, of all places, upon a ceiling beam like some bird within a bloody tree. He halted abruptly at the sight of her there. She was crouched upon a high beam with her hand braced upon the ceiling for support—singing at the top of her lungs, totally unaware of her audience, it seemed!

"My bed shall be under the grenwood tree,"
she carried on.
"A tuft o' brakes under my head!"

God's truth, he didn't for one instant believe
her mad, but he had to admit that she had to
be just a little daft to perch herself up so high.

Damned lunatic wench!

"Meghan Brodie!" he shouted up at her, his
voice thundering through the hall. He didn't
wish to startle her, lest she fall, but her very
position was frightening him. "Come down at
once!" he hollered, but he worried for naught,
as she didn't seem the least bit disconcerted by
his presence.

She stopped singing and cocked her head as
she peered down at him. "Ye canna make me,
Sassenach!" she shouted. "And ye canna order
me aboot! Ye are no' my husband yet, nor are
ye my da, and I dinna ha' tae listen tae a bluidy
word ye say!"

"If I were your da," he assured her, "I vow
I would lay you over my knee and give you
the strapping you well deserve!"

"Och," she answered, unconcerned. "My da
didna ever do such a thing, and neither will
ye! Besides, Sassenach, I like it up here," she
announced, and with that she giggled, a sweet
childlike titter that made him uncertain
whether to laugh or scold her.

Damn!

With the deftness of one who might have

been climbing trees for all of her life, she surged forward to straddle the beam with her hand still balanced upon the ceiling.

Lyon's heart jumped, and like an aftershock, startled murmurs filtered through the room.

"Meghan!" he shouted, blood rushing to his head. "Get yourself down here now!"

"No!" she replied. "I willna!" And she surged forward to hug the brace, and continued to sing.

> *The running streams shall be my drink,*
> *Acorns be my food!*
> *Nothing may do me guid,*
> *But when o' yer beauty I do think!*

"Isn't that silly!" she declared. "Tae think a body would pine sae for beauty!" She cast him a pointed glance.

No one spoke a word, merely stared up at their demented guest. Lyon understood her barb was meant for him.

"My grandminnie used tae sing it tae me," she revealed to one and all.

"Meghan—" He asked her nicely this time. "—please come down."

"Why should I?"

"Because . . ." He glanced at his men, annoyed by their presence now. "Because I do not wish you to fall!"

"Why?" she persisted, staring down at him, and he had the distinct impression she was trying to embarrass him. Bloody rotten wench.

Lyon had to crane his head to see her. "Because . . ."

"Never mind! I knoo why!" she announced suddenly.

He knew better than to ask what conclusion she had come to.

Damn. She was showing much too much of those gorgeous legs of hers.

"Want tae knoo why?" she asked him when he would not respond.

"No," he answered resolutely. "I want you to come down from there, Meghan. Now!"

She adjusted her skirts, revealing far more of her luscious limbs than pleased Lyon. "Because ye dinna wish everyone tae see my bum!" she answered regardless of his refusal.

Snickers echoed through the hall, but were quashed at once by the glare Lyon cast them.

"Meghan!" he thundered.

She merely giggled.

His patience ended, he started up the stairs after her. "You will come down if I have to drag you down!"

"Oh!" she replied flippantly. "That will be fun!"

The hall erupted again with giggles.

Impudent wench.

"No, it will not be," he told her, "and neither will you think so when we have both cracked our skulls upon the ground!"

Meghan watched him climb the stairs and

then come to the rail's edge, scowling at her all the while. She lifted herself up, and the room below seemed to sway below her. She frowned back at him.

Och, but she did wish to come down now.

Despite her outward calm, she was quite uneasy at this great height. Perhaps this hadn't been so good an idea after all. She was sorely disappointed that King David had not been present to witness her stunt. It seemed she had bestirred herself for naught.

"Where is David?" she asked Lyon when he thrust out his arms for her, demanding once more without words that she get down.

He narrowed his eyes at her. "Busy," he assured her. "I'm afraid he will not be attending."

Meghan scowled at him, vexed that he should guess at her reason for asking. She knew by the expression upon his face that he had. She peered down at the hall below, at the faces that stared up at her. Och, but sitting up here so high above them all was the epitome of how she felt—alone and under everyone's scrutiny.

"Come down, Meghan!" Lyon demanded of her.

Meghan leaned to hug the beam suddenly, pouting, and said honestly, "No! I miss my grandminnie!"

He seemed uncertain how to respond to that, and Meghan's eyes watered. She missed Fia terribly, and feared that never again would she feel the closeness she had shared with her grandmother—that unconditional acceptance that came with pure love.

"Damn," he said, and frowned. "Don't you go and weep, Meghan."

His arms were reaching out for her, beckoning, promising warmth, and Meghan's resolve wilted.

"I promise to get her for you, if you'll only come down," he coaxed her, his expression full of concern.

He didn't understand, Meghan knew, and yet she recognized the small victory in his concession.

Maybe she would, in fact, convince him that she was mad after all.

Blinking tears away, she forced a smile, and allowed him to help her down from the beam, uncertain what, if anything, she had accomplished with her silly stunt—except to make herself feel lonely.

Except to make her yearn.

Bloody hell.

She would be stronger next time, she vowed.

She'd had them all thinking her raving mad—she could tell by the looks upon their faces as they'd stared up at her—and then she'd had to go and spoil it by listening to reason!

This time, however, she was determined to carry her scheme through.

Deciding that Fia didn't look enough the part of an old woman, Meghan tore herself a piece of Lyon's sheets and formed it into a scarf to tie about the lamb's head. That done, she surveyed her handiwork. She hoped her grandminnie would forgive her for it, but it couldn't be helped. *Now* she looked more like Fia.

And this was war between them!

"Ye look *verra* lovely," she told the lamb, quite pleased with her handiwork. She gave the beast a quick pat to its head and smiled down upon it.

Strange, but she was growing quite fond of the wee animal. In a peculiar way it was almost as though she had acquired a new friend. She was only sorry she was forced to handle it so rudely. Her grandminnie would have given her a tongue-lashing for it, she knew, as Fia had fancied herself a guardian to all creatures great and small.

She apologized to the wee lammie, for her grandminnie's sake, and when she was satisfied that both she and Fia were prepared to face their prospective audience, she urged the lamb out of the chamber door. Once out, she lifted it up to bear it down the narrow stairwell and hoped with all her might that they were all at the noonday meal because she wanted to make the greatest impact with her entrance.

She wanted to shame Lyon Montgomerie

into doing the honorable thing—or at the very least embarrass him until even his bloody toes turned red!

If truly he yearned for peace he could ask her brothers for her hand in matrimony, and let her decide yea or nay for herself—instead of abducting her like some barbarian and then resorting to wiliness to lure her into this devil's bargain!

She frowned behind the little lamb as she made her way down the stairs. God's truth, she might have bargained with the devil, in truth, but she was determined to save her soul!

Trying not to trip as she bore the lamb down the final steps, she entered the hall and was well satisfied to find that conversation came to an abrupt halt as she entered. Peering over the fidgeting lamb, she spied the confederates together at table and made her way purposefully toward them.

Lyon had spotted her already, she was pleased to see, though David was in the middle of his discourse and didn't appear to notice. Until she placed the lamb before them upon the table.

"Guid evening," she bade them. "We've come tae join ye at table."

She smiled at David as he turned to peer at her with a bemused expression that nearly made her laugh aloud.

"We?" he asked her.

Meghan smiled sweetly and nodded. "O' course."

David eyed the lamb warily. "I usually prefer my mutton well done," he told her with lifted brows.

"Och! Mutton!" Meghan exclaimed, sounding perfectly affronted at his declaration. "This is no' mutton!" she informed him brashly. "*This* is *Fia!*"

She saw that Lyon rolled his eyes, and tried not to appear pleased by his reaction.

David turned a questioning glance to Lyon.

"Humor her," Lyon urged his liege.

David turned once more to face her. "Fia?" he dared to ask. "What is a *fia*, might I ask?"

Meghan sighed in exasperation. "Why, Fia is my grandminnie, o' course! Ha' ye no eyes tae see wi', sir?"

The lamb began to bleat as it trampled a dish near David's trencher. David slid his chair backward across the dais in alarm. He stared at the creature, aghast. "This lamb is your grandminnie?" he said, repeating her outrageous claim as though he could not believe his ears.

"Och! No' ye too!" she complained and rolled her eyes. Her hands flew to her hips. "What did he tell ye?" she demanded, casting Lyon a vexed glance. "I dunno why he should think her a bluidy lamb!"

"Perhaps," Lyon interjected, his tone mordant, "because she *is* a bloody lamb." He was frowning at her now.

So let him frown! Meghan resolved. She hoped he was humiliated.

She glared at him in turn. "I told ye, Sassenach! This is no lamb! This is my dear sweet grandminnie! And ye ha' insulted her quite enough!"

She turned to David once more, narrowing her eyes at him. "That brute ye would ha' me wed," she informed him pettishly, "is a verra poor host, I should tell ye. Why he tossed my grandminnie oot in the meadow yesterday morn!"

She stared at him expectantly, as though anticipating he should *do* something about her complaint. "Ha' ye naught tae say aboot that?" she demanded when he did not respond, and tried not to laugh at the harassed expression he wore.

"Lyon?" he said warily, turning to face Lyon once more, clearly taken aback by her behavior.

Meghan lifted her chin as she too turned to face Lyon Montgomerie, tilting a victorious look at him.

She was either a very shrewd actress, Lyon decided, or she was deadly in earnest.

He could no longer bloody well tell, and he frowned.

Christ, but the damned beast was dressed in a bloody wimple! And he didn't care to look so closely at what she'd formed it of, because the cloth looked entirely too familiar, and he hadn't as yet had the opportunity to procure more.

David turned to glare at the bleating lamb. "Let me get this aright," he said, addressing Meghan. "This lamb, you claim, is your grand-minnie?"

Meghan nodded, lifting her chin—the bloody wicked wench! "O' course!" she persisted. Lyon tried not to laugh at the blatant challenge flashing in her green eyes as she met David's gaze once more.

"I see," David remarked calmly, turning again to Lyon. He lifted his brows. "Lyon, you would wed this woman?"

Lyon was uncertain how to respond: while he did not wish to impute her before David, neither did he enjoy being made the bloody fool.

"Where might we sit tae eat?" she persisted, seeming entirely too pleased over the havoc she'd wreaked. "Or did ye plan on starvin' us as well?"

"Meghan," Lyon said softly in warning, through now playing games.

"Ye said ye would make us *both* welcome!" she reminded him pertly. "And sae far ye've no'! Are ye a liar as well as a thief?"

Lyon eyed the bleating lamb in growing frustration. He cast a glance at David, who was staring now, quite displeased, and for the first time in his life, his face burned with chagrin.

"Meghan," he warned, clenching his jaw.

If she was serious, he determined, then she was truly mad . . . and if she was not, then she was undermining him before his friend and his liege. Feeling obliged to take the situation in hand, to save his food if not his face, he stood and lifted the noisy beast from his table, placing it at his feet.

"My pardon if it offends you, Meghan, but your *grandminnie* is not welcome at my table."

"How dare ye!" she exclaimed, and sank to her knees at once, unfazed by his growing ire. Lyon peered down in trepidation to find that she was crawling beneath the table to reach the wee lamb, shoving at David's knee. "Get oot o' my way!" she demanded.

Bloody hell, but she *was* mad!

She was a goddamned beautiful lunatic!

"What the devil is she doing, Lyon?"

"There, there! Poor Fia!" she cried out, and then peered up accusingly at Lyon from under the table. "How dare ye!" she declared once more, crawling out from under the table at last. "Ye willna win me like that!" she swore, and having said that, she stood, brushed herself off, and quite rudely reached between him and David, seizing a loaf of bread from the table. "If Fia isna welcome, then *I* am no' welcome!" she proclaimed, and reached down to snatch up the lamb into her arms, as well. "Hmmph!" she said, and gave them her back. And without a *by your leave* she left them, hurrying toward the stairs, with her grandminnie and his food in tow.

David stared after her, bemused. "What the hell was that?"

Lyon sat staring after her as well. Crazy-as-the-devil wench. "Naught more than stubborn Scot pride, I think," he answered, and his brows drew together as he watched her stomp her way up the stairs to his chamber. His face contorted. "I hope." And then, "Pardon the interruption . . . what were you saying?"

"Never mind!" David declared. "I've changed my mind! I should think twice were I you, Lyon! That woman might be beautiful, but she's daft besides! You'd be better suited to wed Alison MacLean!"

Lyon wasn't willing to concede. "I respectfully disagree," he said. "And I've already made clear my reasons why. Aside from that, Alison MacLean is entirely too—"

"Sane!" David interjected. "What the devil has come over you, Lyon?"

Meghan Brodie.

Meghan Brodie had come over him.

A stubborn-as-the-devil miss with flashing green eyes and a temper as fierce as the Highlands that had bred her.

"How the hell should I know?" he answered, frowning.

The slam of his chamber door reverberated throughout the hall. Lyon could hear her

stomping across his room, bearing the weight
of the lamb within her arms.

"As a friend, not your liege . . ." David began.

The floorboards creaked ominously. Lyon
peered up, making a mental note to fix them
soon. He could hear her muffled ravings and
her subsequent tantrum, designed specifically
for his ears, he was well aware.

She continued to stomp, punctuating her
every rant with another stomp, bringing an unwilling smile to his lips . . . until he heard the
first crack . . .

David continued ominously. ". . . I beg you,
think with your head and not—"

It happened so fast, Lyon hadn't time to re-
act. "Meghan!" he shouted.

The floorboards gave even as he surged from
his chair.

She came crashing down through the ceiling.

David leapt up and out of the way barely in
time.

The little lamb gave an unholy shriek as it
followed her down.

Meghan landed with a crash, smashing
trenchers and cracking her forehead upon David's tankard.

The lamb landed upon the floor with a sick-
ening thud.

Meghan murmured, "I—I decided tae j-join
ye a-after a-all." And she closed her eyes and
her head landed in a plate full of mutton.

For an instant, Lyon was too stunned to move.

The hall fell into a stupor.

David stood beside him, staggered.

She lay before him much too still.

He turned to David. "Find me a physician!" he snapped, dispensing with formalities for Meghan's sake, and reached out to scoop her at once into his arms, his heart pounding with fear.

Chapter 17

Lyon bore her up the stairs, barking orders to his men: one to bring water, another to bring rags.

She was bleeding somewhere upon her beautiful face, but it was too soiled with food and blood for him to tell precisely where she was injured.

He kicked open his door with an urgency born of fear.

She began to murmur unintelligibly within his arms. "Fia," she whimpered.

His heart twisted a little. He carried her to his bed and laid her gently down upon it. What was he going to say to her? How could he tell her? "Shhh," he urged her.

She opened her eyes, and stared up at him with a dazed expression upon her face. "W-where is Fia?" she persisted.

"Sleeping," he lied, and winced as a vision of the animal's twisted form flashed through his head.

She closed her eyes. "No' dead . . ."

"Shhh . . ."

"Sleeping," she murmured. "Dinna mean tae wake her," she whispered, drifting off once again.

She lost consciousness again.

David came into the room then, his concern evident in his eyes. "They say there is only a midwife to be found," he said. " 'Tis the best we could do. I sent one of your men to fetch her. How does she fare, Lyon?"

"She spoke," Lyon said gravely, peering up at his longtime friend. "She asked after the lamb."

David shook his head. "Poor creature," he said low. "I ordered the carcass lifted."

Lyon nodded, and then muttered an oath beneath his breath. "Where is the water to wash her, damn it! I can see naught for all the blood!"

David placed a hand upon his shoulder.

"I should have fixed those floorboards!" Lyon said in self-reproach. "I should have bloody well fixed them!"

"You could not have foreseen this."

"Nay! I saw their condition days ago," Lyon confessed. "I should have fixed them!" He shook his head in self-disgust. "I should have fixed them!"

"And I should never have interfered in MacKinnon's affairs," David countered, much too calmly for Lyon's state of mind. He could scarcely think, yet alone reason, and David would speak to him of politic matters?

David's voice was drowned in a torrent of his own thoughts. Where was she cut? Was she hurt elsewhere besides? And what was he going to tell her about her poor lamb?

Christ, she was bleeding too much!

"I should not have taken his son," David continued, his voice grating upon Lyon's nerves. He couldn't think. "Because of me Lagan MacKinnon lies dead. I should not have interfered in the MacKinnon's affairs, and because I did, your task is made all the more difficult."

At the moment, Lyon didn't bloody well care!

"And my goal lies all the more distant," David added as well.

"I cannot think of this just now!" Lyon said, and thrust his hands into his hair, maddened by the wait, feeling helpless but to stare.

"What good does it do me to regret?" David persisted.

"None," Lyon answered impatiently, understanding David's meaning at once.

These were all things he knew, of course. And yet . . .

"Precisely," David said. "What is done is done."

Lyon tautened his jaw stubbornly. "Now is not the time for lectures, David. Help me with these sheets," he demanded, spying the shredded linen she had used for Fia's scarf. "They are taking too long!"

Seizing the cloth in his hand, he ripped it in half, handing the bigger piece to David. He tore a smaller piece for himself and began to clean the blood from her face—gently, lest he hurt her more. He found the wound near her temple, within her hair, and pressed the cloth to it in an attempt to staunch the flow.

David continued to tear the linen. " 'Tis not as though you purposely left the floor to rot," he pointed out.

Lyon gently pushed the blood-soaked hair from her face.

"She truly is lovely," David remarked.

"Aye," Lyon agreed, watching her face closely for some sign of lucidity. At the moment, beauty didn't concern him, only that she would be well.

His men arrived bearing water and rags.

"About bloody time!" Lyon snapped as he was handed a rag already soaked with water. He ordered them all from the room, and began to clean her face once more. "Send the midwife in the instant she arrives!" he commanded them before they went.

"It appears to be the single cut," David said, watching. "Allow me to hold the rag. You inspect the rest of her to be certain there is no other wound."

It was precisely what he intended to do.

Lyon released the blood-soaked rag into David's hands, and did as suggested.

David lowered his voice. "And what shall you tell her about . . . the lamb?"

"I've no idea," Lyon admitted, and proceeded to remove her soiled clothing.

She stirred, moaning softly as he undressed her, and he peered at her face expectantly. She didn't reopen her eyes, and he stared at her, contemplating what he would say to her when she awoke. At worst she believed the lamb to be her grandmother. At best it was a beloved pet. Either way she was going to be aggrieved.

At the moment, however, he was too concerned for her to feel anything more than sorry for the animal.

He removed her sleeve, drew it down, and his heart wrenched to find that her arm had been twisted in the fall. It was swollen about the elbow, already turning an ungodly shade of crimson-blue.

"Mother of Christ!" David exclaimed. "I think she may lose the use of that arm!"

Lyon cast him a black glance.

The hell she would, he vowed, and at once set about untangling her from her gown.

Leith had insisted he bring her home.

He'd kissed her once more, a gentle peck upon the lips before bidding her farewell, and

Alison had yet to walk inside. She stood in the shadows of her father's home, watching him go, her fingers pressed to her lips in something akin to awe.

Leith Mac Brodie wanted to wed with her.

Her?

She still could not believe it, though he had sworn it with his heart in his eyes. She had never thought a man would ever look at her so.

She didn't know how long she stood there, but he was long departed when a voice startled her from her reverie.

"Alison?"

Alison saw the man coming from the woodlands, and she turned and walked quickly toward her father's hall, ready to shriek for help, and horrified at her own stupidity for waiting so long like an idiot to watch Leith go. It had been a stupid thing to do.

"Alison MacLean!" the man called out.

Alison lifted up her skirts to flee, but he shouted out, "Wait, I mean ye no harm. I bring news o' Meghan!"

Alison spun to face him, responding instinctively to the note of alarm in his voice. "Meghan! What o' Meghan?" she demanded.

He came near enough so she could see his face, and then she recognized him. "Cameron!"

"Aye, lass, ye remember me," he said. " 'Tis Meghan," he hurried on. "There isna time tae speak long. Ye must come."

"Come?"

"Tae Montgomerie's!"

"Me?" Alison asked in surprise.

"She has had an accident, Alison, and I dinna knoo how tae say it, but they told me she didna look sae well when I left there. They sent me for a midwife, and I knoo ye spent much time wi' her and her grandminnie. I didna knoo where else tae gae for help. She needs ye noo, lass!"

"Oh, no!" Alison exclaimed, and her heart nigh leapt from her breast in fear. "But how shall I gae? He would knoo me!" she said doubtfully. "I think he would knoo me! Will he let me tend her?"

The old man suddenly seemed to share her concern. "I dunno," he said. "I dunno."

"Wait!" Alison said. "I knoo what tae do! He shall no' recognize me when I am through, and he'llna turn me away if he doesna knoo me. Wait here for me, and I will return in a trice!" She clutched the old man's arm. "Thank ye. Thank ye for coming tae fetch me. Wait here noo, if ye will, and I shall be back anon. Wait!" she begged him, and raced into the hall, taking care that her father did not see her, as he believed she was still within her room.

Meghan needed her now, and she would not fail her dear friend—she would not!

Meghan awoke to the sound of voices. She couldn't seem to gain her bearings.

She heard everything, was keenly aware of her surroundings in the oddest sort of way, but her lids were too heavy to lift. Nor could she move. It was as though she were sleeping still and could not awake.

"I ha' reset the bone," said a woman's voice from somewhere beyond the haze. Meghan faintly recognized it. She tried in vain to open her eyes, to look upon the bearer of it. " 'Twill need time tae heal," the woman continued gravely. "Dinna let her use the arm, and if ye must . . . bind her tae the bed until she awakes."

"I shall remain with her," she heard a familiar male voice say in a low tone. "How long will the *drogue* last?"

"Until the morrow," came the woman's reply.

Drogue.

They'd given her a *drogue* . . . like the ones her grandminnie sometimes used . . . Her heart lifted with hope.

"Fia?" she murmured.

Shadows descended like a shroud over her senses.

"Fia?" she persisted.

She sensed more than felt the hand at her brow . . . not a small one with calluses on the tips of fingers raw from pulling herbs . . . but a large one . . . as gentle as it was coarse.

"Hush now, Meghan," the man's voice commanded her, though not unkindly, and the familiar sound of it reverberated through her very soul.

Lyon?

Meghan heard herself whimper softly, and was surprised by the distance of the sound. Strange, it didn't sound like her at all, didn't feel like her, though she knew it was.

What was wrong with her?

And why did her arm hurt?

And why had they drugged her?

"Och, ye really should bind her tae the bed," the woman said, concern in her voice. "Ye dinna want her tae injure the arm any more."

Meghan shook her head. She didn't want to be bound to the bed. She whimpered, trying to tell them nay.

"Poor wee thing," the woman lamented, and once more the familiarity of it struck her.

Who was the woman?

"Fia . . ."

The woman let out an audible sigh. "Crazy auld Fia has been dead nigh two years noo," she said. "The two were unseverable; where ye spied the one, the other wasna far behind."

It wasn't Fia.

Fia had been dead *nigh two years now*. Meghan's heart fell as she remembered that. It wasn't Fia.

Who was it?

She heard weeping again and wondered if she were the one sobbing.

She felt so weighty, so dizzy . . . so insubstantial . . .

"Fia . . . Fia is her lamb, as well," Lyon confided to the woman.

Dear God, the lamb.

Meghan groaned as slices of memory began to return to her. She'd been holding the wee lammie within her arms, dancing with it across the room—with a few well-placed stomps for special effect—so happy that her plan had gone so well.

"Aye, but she seems to think the lamb is her grandminnie," another man's voice disclosed.

Silence.

"Och!" exclaimed the woman after a moment. "Poor wee thing, but it doesna surprise me," she said grimly. "She comes from verra bad bluid, ye see. 'Twas merely a matter o' time before Meghan Brodie succumbed tae the madness as well."

"She seemed well enough to me."

"Sae were her mother and grandmother in the beginning," the woman pointed out sadly. "And then *it* came over them, twisting their minds. Och, but 'tis a shame, too, as Fia understood the magic o' the woodlands well."

Naught had come over her mother and grandmother, Meghan wanted to scream. They had simply been misunderstood. Who was this woman who would befoul her mother's and grandmother's names?

"I'm afeared she'll end like them if something isna done—and soon!"

She wanted to speak up and tell the woman that she was wrong—all wrong! It wasn't true! But she couldn't open her mouth to speak. Nor could she lift her lids. What had they given her? The heaviness seemed to be dragging her down into oblivion.

Meghan fought to stay awake . . . fought until finally, the will to sleep was too great . . .

"What can be done?" Lyon asked the old woman.

"I ha' a potion," she answered, and those vaguely familiar eyes began to gleam with the color of gold, though in the dimness of the room, it was difficult to tell their true color. "I am something of an apothecary," she disclosed. "But the price o' this particular potion is high," she cautioned him. "And ye willna relieve me of it for less than a handful o' gold."

Lyon wasn't entirely certain it was necessary to do anything at all to cure Meghan's so-called madness, but if the old woman's *médecine* was harmless enough, he might consider the prescription, no matter the cost. "What sort of potion, woman, would cost me a handful of gold coins?"

She smiled, a brilliant smile that seemed to smooth the wrinkles from her brow, making her appear much too young. Her hair was covered with a scarf that concealed much of her face, as well, and was tied entirely too tight about her chin besides. He wondered that she could bear it.

"A powerful potion," she assured him, eyeing him first, then casting a glance at David. "Made from roots."

"I have never heard of such a thing," David interjected.

"Of course no'," she replied, drawing back and peering at him, obviously insulted by his challenge. "It is the root of a tree found in the Far East alone."

"You have been to the Far East?" Lyon persisted, at once doubting her claim.

"And you have seen this tree with your very own eyes?" David added as well.

"Och, nay," she confessed, "but I do ha' the root wi' me even noo."

"And you have seen it work its magic?" David inquired, saving Lyon the trouble of asking.

"Nay. But ye will need tae take my word."

" 'Tis rather convenient a tale, I should say." Lyon eyed her speculatively. "And you just happen to carry with you this root of an unknown tree—"

"Do ye not also carry upon yer person yer most valuable possessions?" she countered.

"I have none," Lyon claimed, and was aware of David's surprised glance.

"Ah, but ye do," the woman demurred.

"This tree root," he continued, overlooking her remark, "it comes from a land where you have never been, and you claim it a cure for madness, though you have never seen it work?"

"Ye are no' a believer o' médecine, I take it?" she asked him, cocking her head inquisitively.

He wasn't a believer in anything at all, if the truth be known, except in life and in death. All else, according to his mind, was merely illusory. He lifted his brow. "I believe your nose scents gold, old woman!"

Her eyes narrowed. "No' precisely," she yielded. "What I *do* scent is something far more valuable than gold!"

"And what makes you think I've anything of value betwixt these walls? Look about you," he charged her. "Do you see the hole in my roof and the one in my floor? Tell me, does this strike you as the home of a wealthy man?"

"These auld eyes," she said, "see more than ye think. For instance, they spy the look in yer eyes when ye gaze at her." She glanced down at the bed where Meghan lay, resting peacefully. "It is the look of a man who loves a woman."

"And then shall I pluck out my eyes," he asked acerbically, "and place them within your palms to pay for the potion? All for the love of a woman? Do you think me a fool who can be taken advantage of over some sentiment you *perceive* I bear?"

The light in her eyes faded.

She seemed disappointed.

"Perhaps I was wrong," she said and turned away to make a few last-minute inspections of Meghan's sleeping form. "She'll sleep until the morn, I think. Dinna let her rest upon that arm, as it must heal exactly as I ha' set it. As for the wound upon her head," she continued, "it bleeds, but it is no' deep. Simply leave it be and it will heal upon its own."

Lyon watched her gather up her belongings— her potions, her needle, and her thread—and was grateful she had not had to use the needle upon Meghan's lovely face.

"If she should need me," she began, "I shall—"

"Wait!" Lyon urged her.

She spun to face him, the gleam in her eyes once more apparent.

"Are you so certain it will work? This potion . . ."

She gave him a discerning glance. "Nay, there is never a surety. But the root is said tae purify the mind and return its lucidity. It is said tae make the weak mind strong, and to create genius in that which is already keen."

"Very well," he relented, "I shall pay your price, old woman. Work your sorcery!"

"But there is one last thing," she apprised him, her eyes narrowing. "There is yet another price tae be paid beyond that ye will render tae me."

"Another price?" He gave her a deprecating glance. "More gold? Perhaps you'd rather jewels or cloth?"

She smiled, flashing teeth that were far too white to be so old. "Nothing such as that," she assured him. "Though this price is tae be paid by her, as well." She nodded at the bed where Meghan lay.

"And what price might that be?" Lyon persisted, his tone fraught with sarcasm.

"The potion is sometimes disfiguring."

His brows collided. "Disfiguring?"

"Aye," she said, giving him a knowing look. "Tae the face. There are those who form a reaction tae it," she explained. "Sometimes merely a pox ... sometimes more ... but ye canna knoo until it happens just who will, and who willna. If ye think it more important tae ha' a pretty face than a keen mind ... dinna give her the potion. But ... if she truly matters tae ye ..."

Her implication hung in the air for him to ponder.

He narrowed his eyes at her. "And is that all? The potion is safe aside from that?"

She seemed pleased with his response, for her smile manifested now within her peculiar eyes. "Aye," she answered, and then declared, "I ha' the root wi' me noo, but 'tis useless to ye withoot the elixir. I shall ha' it prepared by this eve. Ha' the gold in hand when I arrive," she commanded him, and with that, turned and left, leaving him and David to stare at each other in wary contemplation.

Lyon turned to the woman lying so quietly upon his bed. The old woman had claimed he loved her.

Did he?

Could he?

He knew he wanted her, knew he craved her even.

But love?

Love was something he had never believed in.

So what was this strangeness he felt? This bond he shared with the woman lying within his bed?

Obsession?

David departed before eventide, with the intent of paying the Brodies a visit.

It was their right, Lyon knew, to be informed of Meghan's accident. Were the situation reversed, he would appreciate the same courtesy. Right or wrong, however, he had refused them visitation, and David had agreed to uphold his decision, and to soften the blow of his refusal with a personal appearance. It was more than Lyon had a right to ask of David, since the Brodies surely would not accept Lyon's decision so blithely.

Lyon was perfectly aware that he was being

unreasonable, but he also understood that if her brothers came to see her . . . and Meghan asked to leave with them . . . he would look at her in the condition she was in . . . and he'd not be able to refuse her.

He wanted the chance to win her.

It had suddenly become crucial to his state of contentment. He didn't understand what it was about her that drew him, but she did. Her very presence had somehow banished shadows from his life, like the morning sun, which dispelled darkness with its glorious appearance.

The old witch—it was how Lyon began to think of her—returned as David rode from the courtyard. She seemed to appear from the night mist: he was alone one instant, and not the next. She handed him a vial, dispensing instructions for the administration of its contents. She'd laced the potion with mandrake, she'd claimed, something for the pain, and he was to measure it out to her judiciously lest he poison her. And then she had demanded her coin forthwith. After wishing him well, she vanished as swiftly as she'd appeared.

Clutching the precious vial within his fist, Lyon climbed the stairs to his chamber. When she awoke, he wanted to be with her. When she first opened her eyes, he wanted to be the one she saw.

And if she did not awake this eve, he would be content to simply watch over her . . . as long as he knew she would open those beautiful green eyes eventually.

He entered the chamber, closing the door behind him, and went to stand before the bed. She looked so fragile lying there amidst his rent sheets and her own dried blood. The very sight of her made his heart wrench.

The torchlight cast dancing shadows over the bed, animating her face despite that she slept undisturbed. She was beautiful even now, though her poor face was bruised and wan. She looked more like an angel lying there so serenely, though he had to own he preferred the imp in her to the cherub any day.

The very thought of her temper and wit made him smile.

Guilt stabbed at him as he watched her.

He had no doubt she would recover, for she was strong and her wounds were minor, but he couldn't help but feel responsible.

Had he not taken her against her will, none of this would have happened. She would likely, at this instant, be safe at home with her brothers.

And yet, God save his rotten soul, he still could not find regret for his actions.

She stirred, whimpering softly, calling for Fia once again, and he frowned. Lifting up the vial in his hand, he contemplated its contents. It was entirely possible the elixir was a sheer waste of time . . . that there was naught wrong with her at all . . . as he suspected.

But . . . what if he were wrong?

What if there were, in truth, some family madness she was cursed with, and he had in his hands the means to cure her?

He liked to think he was a better man than to sacrifice her sanity for the privilege of gazing upon a perfect face.

He watched her an instant longer, his heart sinking when she began to weep softly in her sleep. God damn him to hell if he could be so shallow as to allow her to suffer for his pleasure.

His mind made up, he sat upon the bed beside her and proceeded to open the vial. There was enough within it for a sennight's supply, the old woman had said. The results would be immediate, she'd claimed.

Well, the morning would bring answers enough. If he observed no significant difference when she awoke, he simply wouldn't continue the treatment.

But if the differences were apparent . . . Well, then . . . he had the means within his hand to help her, and he would be a selfish bastard not to use it.

And with that resolved, he set about administering the potion.

Chapter 18

Meghan was uncertain at what point her dreams became substance, but Lyon's face was the first thing she saw when she awoke. He sat upon the bed, staring down at her, his expression concerned.

She'd been dreaming of him—strange dreams, pleasant dreams, but his was a constant presence—and she couldn't say she was surprised upon opening her eyes to find him watching her.

"Welcome back," he said quietly, his lips curving into a soft smile. His deep-blue eyes gazed at her with such warmth that it stilled her heart.

Surely she imagined the tenderness . . . He couldn't possibly feel aught for her but lust.

Meghan tried to return a witty reply, but when she parted her lips to speak, only a moan of pain came from between her parched lips. She lifted her head and peered groggily down at her arm. "W-what . . . happened?"

"Do you not recall?"

Meghan did, though she wished she didn't!

Her arm? It hurt. It served her right. She averted her gaze to the bed, tears welling in her eyes. The entire ordeal made her feel both guilty and childish at once. It didn't matter that she'd been pretending; he must think her a spoiled brat to have thrown such a wicked tantrum.

And her fit of fury had gained her what?

And what of the poor wee lammie? She was afraid to ask, but had to know. "W-where is . . ." she began, and choked on a sob.

"Fia?"

Her face burned with guilt, but she nodded, daring to peer up into his glittering eyes. His expression was softer yet, no condemnation there to be seen.

He shook his head. "I . . . am . . . so sorry, Meghan, but the la—*Fia*," he amended, "she . . . is . . . gone."

Meghan gulped back another heartfelt sob, feeling incredible shame.

"There was naught to be done," he continued gently. "But know that it—that *she* did not suffer," he offered in condolence.

Tears rolled down Meghan's cheeks. She didn't have to pretend grief.

"Poor, poor wee lammie!" she sobbed, bringing a hand to her mouth in remorse. " 'Tis all my fault!"

He shook his head. "Nay," he argued.

" 'Twas not—" He narrowed his eyes. "Poor wee *lammie?*"

Meghan couldn't bear that she'd been the cause of the poor animal's death. If it hadn't been for her tantrum... "Aye, it *is* all my fault!" she cried. "If only I hadna—"

"Nay," he said quietly, though with a lingering frown upon his face. "It was not your fault, Meghan. You couldn't possibly have known the floor would give way beneath you. If the fault lies with any, then it lies with me, as I knew the ceiling was weak and in disrepair. I should have fixed it long before now," he said, and shook his head with a look of self-disgust.

His gaze met hers once more, and Meghan recognized the regret in his deep-blue eyes. He didn't have to ease her own burden of guilt, she knew, and yet he was attempting to do that. Meghan appreciated his efforts, though she knew full well that she had to accept much of the blame. She should never have used the lamb so selfishly. It had been cruel enough that she had forced it to remain locked within the room with her. She simply hadn't considered the animal's feelings and needs.

She swallowed the knot in her throat and averted her gaze; the look upon his face was making her entirely uncomfortable.

Och, he couldn't possibly be so bad as his essays would have her believe. The man who gazed at her now with such compassion over the loss of an animal was certainly not the same man who had proclaimed himself able to shed blood so easily for the mere price of gold.

"Weel," she said weakly, and it was the best concession she could make to the man who had stolen her against her will, and was now trying to steal her heart, "ye couldna possibly ha' known ye would abduct me and lock me awa' in yer chamber, noo could ye?"

He smiled a little at that. "Of course I could," he countered. "Did you not realize that all men are base and weak of will?" He winked at her. "I saw your face and simply could not resist."

Meghan had to quell the urge to roll her eyes at his proclamation. She tried to lift herself from the bed, and grimaced as pain shot through her arm.

"Do not move," he commanded her. "Rest, Meghan."

She seemed to have no choice in the matter.

Meghan felt, after that small effort, so weak. Even had she wished to refuse him, she couldn't have. She was too weary to fight.

He produced a small vial from within his hand.

"What is that?" she asked him.

"Something for the pain."

A faint sheen of perspiration moistened her brow, and her body trembled still from the meager effort of trying to lift herself from the bed.

"How long did I sleep?" she asked him. "It

seems an eternity, and yet I would sleep again."

" 'Tis the *drogue*," he said, lifting the vial as though to inspect its contents. He was quiet a moment, and then turned to study her.

Under his scrutiny, Meghan felt a bit like a fly in a spider's web.

"Though your arm was not broken, Meghan," he said, "it was displaced and had to be reset. It'll plague you for some time, I think. But this—" He lifted the vial to show her. "—should ease it."

Meghan winced, and lifted her hand to her forehead, to the ache there. God's teeth, but her entire face felt bruised. Her cheeks hurt, and she had a headache, besides. Her entire body hurt, in truth. It was the least she deserved, she told herself.

Dear grandminnie would be sorely disappointed had she lived to see that Meghan had had so little regard for a wee creature's life.

"Your face remains unharmed," he assured her, "all but for that wound upon your head." He reached out then, parting her hair gently, inspecting the wound for himself, and Meghan flinched at his touch. "You'll not be able to see it when it is healed, hidden as it is."

Meghan glowered at him. Why did his reassurances make her feel bitter, rather than relieved?

"Pity," she replied, before she could stop herself. "Were my face scarred, ye would ha' little reason tae keep me, noo would ye?"

He withdrew his hand then. "Is that what you believe?"

"Aye," Meghan answered without doubt. "Ye said yerself it was my face that drew ye." And wanted to add that he'd kept her despite the possibility that she might be mad—so it wasn't her mind that interested him, in any case. She had no doubt he would discard her if her face no longer appealed to him, but she didn't say as much, because saying such a thing would imply that the notion disturbed her, and she certainly didn't care whether she appealed to him or nay!

At least he had the decency not to deny it.

He merely stared at her without answer.

Her gaze was drawn once more to the little desk, to his manuscripts lying there. His essays confused her. The man sitting before her now, tending her so gently, speaking to her so kindly, could not possibly be the same who wiped blood from his sword without remorse.

She didn't know what to think of him . . . what to feel.

Lyon, equally bewildered, contemplated her accusation.

He couldn't deny it, though he wanted to. But neither was he so certain of it as truth. There was something about the woman lying within his bed . . . something other than the perfect face and body . . . something in her eyes that beckoned to him . . . challenged him.

In truth, he was no longer certain that her face alone had motivated him to begin with . . . and yet . . . neither could he put his finger upon the attraction. He could scarcely claim he knew her mind and loved her for it. Nor could he profess to adore her heart, though he saw evidence of her goodness in the tears that stained her face over a mere beast of the fields—it didn't matter whether yesternight she had thought the animal her grandminnie or not; this morn he saw lucidity in her eyes—potion-induced or not—and he knew without doubt that she understood her true relation to the animal. And still she wept.

He also knew he would administer the rest of the vial to her.

The old witch had claimed she'd laced it with something for the pain, as well, and he could see the strain of Meghan's injuries in her every expression, her every move.

She was watching him, he realized, and seemed to be waiting for a response.

He lifted his brows. "I don't suppose it would do any good to deny it?" he asked her, and popped open the vial. "When I only admitted as much."

"Nay," she returned, "we both knoo what it is ye want o' me."

"Do we?" She couldn't possibly know what it was he wanted of her, as neither did he.

But he wanted her, that much was certain.

"I'm no' stupid," she told him.

He cast her a glance. "Perhaps not," he conceded. "Now, however, I want only your tongue."

"Ye're just the same as every other mon!" she accused him then, narrowing her eyes. "Why do ye want my tongue?"

To draw it into his mouth, suckle her sweet nectar; that's what he wanted with her tongue.

"Why else?" he asked, and smiled slightly. "I wish you to take your *médecine*, is all."

"Ye want tae knoo what I think?"

"Depends," he answered, "but I'm certain you're going to tell me."

"I think ye're no' sae bluidy wicked as ye like tae think ye are," she informed him baldly, and thrust out her tongue to receive her dram of *médecine*.

Lyon blinked, merely staring for an instant at the tender flesh she offered, imagining ... the feel of it ... the taste of it ...

His loins tightened.

"Nay?" he asked, his voice hoarse.

He had to shake himself free from his thoughts in order to tip a few drops upon her sweet waiting tongue.

She swallowed, and he licked at his suddenly dry lips.

"Nay," she answered, and her gaze moved once more to his desk.

Lyon couldn't help but note the direction of her eyes.

His manuscripts remained just as he'd left

them, and yet . . . why did he feel she knew their contents?

It was highly unlikely, as he didn't know many men or women who could read or write their own names, much less read a manuscript of its nature. He was well aware that it was onerous reading at best, interspersed as it was with both Latin and French. One thing he could scarcely claim to be was an engaging scribe. Much of the text, in fact, was incomprehensible as there were pages and pages of fragmentary ruminations—left so on purpose, for much of its content would gain him little more than persecution—interspersed with unclear references to the second manuscript.

His scribblings were naught more than the discourses of a man attempting to comprehend his own life's purpose.

What was it going to take to bring him peace?

He hadn't ever truly experienced contentment—satiation perhaps, but not contentment. And yet, though he'd never experienced the one, he understood the difference innately. It was a far, far different thing to satisfy the body than to satisfy the soul.

His body had many times known gratification, but his soul had always been left wanting.

He watched her as she stared at his manuscripts, watched the expression upon her face . . . and knew.

She'd read them.

And yet . . . had she read them all . . . she couldn't possibly make such a claim as the one she'd only just made to him.

He was not as wicked as he believed.

But he *was* wicked

The evidence was manifested now within his braies. Even wounded as she was, the sight of her lying within his bed filled his loins with raw heat.

How far had she read into his manuscripts?

Did she know his darkest desires . . . his pleasures?

The notion that she might . . . that she knew . . . and yet would still claim such a thing made his heart pound fiercely.

How far had she read?

"I'm afraid I *am* as wicked as I think," he told her, feeling compelled to warn her. He smiled softly then, feeling quite predatorial, despite that she lay helpless within his bed—or perhaps *because* she lay so helpless within his bed.

That was the nature of the beast . . . the darkest side every good man fought to deny. But Lyon understood his beast all too well; it was not defeated by turning his back upon it.

Nay, but you had to stare it in the eye, know it well in order to master it.

"You see," he reasoned, "you cannot possibly *know* how wicked I think I am, therefore you cannot begin to suppose whether I am, or not, so wicked as I think. I could think myself only slightly wicked," he told her. "In which case you are safe enough lying there within my bed. Or . . . I could think myself absolute evil . . . and *you* cannot possibly conceive which of the two is true. Can you now?"

She sucked in a breath, instinctively understanding his challenge, and the effort lifted her breasts, drawing his gaze there. She swallowed.

His gaze lingered.

"I—I think I can," she answered a little breathlessly.

"Though you cannot be certain, Meghan." He cast a glance at his papers, wanting her to know that he knew . . . needing to know how far she'd gone. "Do you read?" he asked her casually, though his look was anything but that.

She followed his gaze to the desk. "A-aye," she answered hesitantly. "I—I do."

"Do you?" His gaze returned to her face.

Meghan's breath snagged at the intensity within his deep-blue eyes.

"Aye," she replied.

His eyes slitted, and her heart quickened its beat, tripping painfully.

He knew.

He knew she'd been reading his essays. Was he angry?

She thought not . . . and yet . . . the look in his eyes was anything but harmless.

"I think I need not ask how far you've read,"

he said low, his voice softening to a mesmerizing note. "Because if you'd read far enough, Meghan Brodie, you would scarce claim such a thing to me . . . that I am not so wicked as I think. *I am*," he advised her once more. "And you'd do well to remember it."

Meghan suddenly found it difficult to breathe.

Her heart pounded like thunder in her ears. Though she knew instinctively he'd not harm her—he hadn't as yet, though she'd given him ample cause—she sensed the truth in his threat. She *would* do well to remember. Somehow, she had forgotten the tales told of this man. She'd forgotten how he'd won this little piece of Scotia. She'd somehow, from the very first, forgotten to fear him, when she'd had every reason to.

And yet . . .

"Ye dinna frighten me," she told him, though the hammering of her heart within her ears belied her bold claim.

"I know," he said, and smiled. He winked at her. "But let us see if you can say that still . . . *after* you have finished the manuscripts."

Meghan lifted her chin. "Do ye gi' me permission tae read them?"

"Nay," he answered, his eyes glittering with challenge.

Meghan's brows knit. "Nay?"

"Nay, Meghan," he countered, rising from the bed and making his way toward the desk.

He lifted up the manuscripts and suspended them before her. "Rather I am *daring* you to read it." And he tossed them upon the bed. "See if you can still look me in the eye *afterward* and say then I am not so bloody wicked."

A knock sounded upon the door.

Lyon abandoned the manuscripts to her to answer the door.

Cameron stood there. "Baldwin says for ye tae come quick," he relayed.

"What is it?"

Cameron peered within the room, casting a pointed glance at Meghan, then nodded and said, "He says for ye tae come, is all."

"Damn," Lyon said, understanding the unspoken message. He turned to Meghan. "Are you comfortable, Meghan?"

She lifted a brow. "As comfortable as a wounded prisoner can be!"

He grinned at her, seeming satisfied enough with her reply. "I shall be back directly then," he told her with a wink. "In the meantime, enjoy the read . . . *if you dare.*"

And with that challenge, he left her to her curiosity and his manuscripts.

Chapter 19

"Tell him Leith Mac Brodie says we're no' leavin' till we see our sister!"

"Tell him yourself!" Lyon charged as he approached the armed gathering within his courtyard.

His men parted, giving him room to enter the circle they'd formed about his mounted guests. He had to admire these bloody Scots, riding in as they had, just the three of them against his greater numbers. Christ, but these Highlanders were nothing if not fearless.

"Damn ye all tae hell, Lyon Montgomerie!" the stockiest of them proclaimed. He charged his horse at Lyon, but his men moved forward at once, blocking him, and he jerked the reins back, bringing the horse to a protesting halt. "Ye ha' no right tae take what doesna belong tae ye!"

"So says the man who now owns five of my goats and a bloody cow, as well!"

"Ye started it, mon! Ye canna thieve from us

255

and no' expect us tae retaliate! And ye canna take our only sister in turn for a handful o' bluidy goats and a milk cow!"

"*Who* started this?" Lyon countered, unable to believe the gall of that single remark. It was *his* goat that had been discovered in *their* hands, not the other way around, as he recalled.

"Ye did, Sassenach!" said the third Brodie.

Lyon didn't even feel the need to reply, ludicrous as it was. Damned Scots. "You've bloody short memories," he said to no one in particular. "And who makes these rules?" he asked of Leith Mac Brodie. "Who dictates what eye is to be plucked for another?"

"Honor makes them!" Leith Mac Brodie returned.

"Whose honor?" Lyon contended.

The two of them faced each other, neither relenting.

"The fact is I caught your sister in the act of stealing from me," Lyon told him. "I did no more than to arrest her."

"Liar!" shouted the bigger Brodie.

Lyon turned to face him directly, his jaw taut with restrained anger. "No man has ever called me that and walked away with his bloody balls still attached to his body."

The impudent Brodie returned his glare, undaunted, his hand going to his sword. Lyon watched his every move but didn't respond save to raise his hand when his own men drew their own weapons.

"Aye?" the other man replied. "Weel, Colin Mac Brodie has noo! My sister steals from no one—no one, d' ye hear me!—no' tae save her own bluidy life! Speak that lie once more, Sassenach, and ye'll rue every syllable tae come from yer mouth!"

Lyon's hand went reflexively to the sword at his belt. He flexed his hand upon the hilt, reminding himself that he was speaking to Meghan's brother—reminding himself, too, that Colin Mac Brodie stood now for his sister's honor. He'd like to think he'd do the same were the situation reversed.

"You can call me a bastard," Lyon told him as calmly as he was able, "because 'tis the bloody truth. And you can call me a thief if it please you, as I'll not mince words, but do not _ever_ again call me a liar, Colin, or I'll slice your goddamned tongue from your mouth and feed it to you with my fist. Do you understand?"

Colin's eyes burned with fury. "If that was said tae strike terror into my bones, Montgomerie, then ye failed! Give us Meghan, or we'll bluidy well show ye the meaning o' terror!"

"I'd have you remember where you are, Colin Mac Brodie," Lyon apprised him. "Do not try my hospitality."

Colin spat viciously upon the ground. "Standin' before a lyin', thievin', bastard Sassenach!" he answered. "That's where I am!"

"Colin!" Leith Mac Brodie barked at his brother. "Cease!"

Lyon nodded at Leith. "Wise man." He turned to Colin. "You should heed your brother, whelp."

Colin launched into an explosion of expletives.

"Aye, he should," Leith Mac Brodie interjected. "But dinna mistake me. I *will* be leaving here wi' my sister, Montgomerie. Ye ha' no bluidy right tae keep her."

Lyon said naught; he merely removed his hand from his sword and crossed his arms.

"I will no' gae withoot her," Leith asserted.

"Aye," Lyon countered, "you will, as your sister is in my custody by David of Scotia's command."

"Tae hell wi' David!" Colin hissed. "That Sassenach-lovin' bastard holds no sway in these parts!"

"Aye," Lyon said, "he does, as he does with me."

"Return Meghan tae us," Leith Mac Brodie persisted. "And we shall gae and the bad blood be ended between us."

"Nay," Lyon said, and uncrossed his arms. "I've decided that Meghan is the solution to our little dispute."

Leith Mac Brodie urged his mount forward suddenly and approached him. Their gazes locked, held. "Solution?" he asked, coming to a halt before Lyon, looking down upon him

with narrowed eyes. "What is it ye are pro-
posin', Sassenach?"

"I've decided to make Meghan my bride."

"The bluidy hell ye ha'!" Colin Mac Brodie
erupted.

Lyon ignored him. "That should put an end
to our disputes once and for all," he pointed
out, "as what is mine shall in essence be yours
and what is yours shall in essence be mine. No
more quarreling."

Leith Mac Brodie remained silent, scrutinizing him.

"Meghan wants no husband!" Colin proclaimed, spurring his mount forward as well.
"Sae ye can bluidy well forget that, Montgomerie!"

"I'll no' agree tae such a thing," Leith announced, after a moment's contemplation.
"No' unless I see my sister and she agrees tae
the same wi' her own lips. No other way,
Montgomerie."

"Well," Lyon said, "then you have wasted
your time in coming here today, because
Meghan is not seeing guests. She is indisposed,
as you well know."

"Montgomerie," Leith warned him, his lips
thin with anger now, "I canna force my way
past yer guards today, but hear me weel . . . I'll
no' rest until I see my sister where she belongs.
And if ye willna let me see her noo as a show
o' faith, I willna promise tae fight fairly. I will
leave here, as ye leave me little choice, but

Meghan is my flesh and my blood and I'llna abandon her tae ye sae easily.''

Lyon ignored the prick of his own conscience.

He wanted this too badly, he knew.

"I am asking for a fortnight," he said stubbornly. "Give me that time with Meghan, and thereafter I will allow her to decide freely. If she chooses to leave, she may go of her own accord. That is the best I can do."

Leith seemed once more to contemplate his request.

"Ye expect us tae simply abandon her here, Montgomerie?'' Colin countered. "Knooing she is wounded and in need of us? I dinna think sae, ye rotten bastard!''

"Return her tae us, woo her properly," Leith said.

It was a reasonable enough request, but Lyon could not agree to it.

"Nay," he answered. If he returned her now, he knew, he'd never see her again.

He needed time.

And right or wrong, he was willing to wield his sword to keep her.

"Sassenach bastard!" Colin spat. "Lay a hand upon my sister and I'll do some slicin' o' my own!''

Lyon met Colin's gaze, assuring him, "I give you my word I'll do naught to your sister she does not wish me to.''

The quietest brother rode forward then and

whispered into Leith's ear. The two spoke an instant, and then Leith nodded, and turned to face Lyon once more. "Yer word?" he said. "And what assurances ha' I that yer word is honorable, Montgomerie?"

Lyon considered his answer carefully, and then spoke truthfully, as there was no other way with him. "None at all," he replied, "save that I value honesty above all else."

Leith contemplated his words, and then announced, "No' good enough!" He motioned for his men to follow. "We're goin', but ye've no' seen the last of us, Montgomerie! My sister is no' some beast tae be bartered!" He whirled his mount about and spurred it away, forcing his way through the circle of Lyon's men. "I'll see her a bluidy auld maid before I see her unhappy!" he swore as he thundered away, his brothers at his heels.

"Sassenach bastard!" Colin said and spat upon the ground as he followed his elder brother.

Lyon watched them leave, and for the first time in a long time, experienced a twinge of guilt for his actions.

It confused him.

He'd done things in his life for which he should have prostrated himself upon the ground, and yet he hadn't felt guilt then. He'd always done whatever needed to be done, with the least amount of brooding, because to dwell upon them brought madness. But this moment, as he watched Meghan's brothers ride out from his courtyard, he felt a prick of conscience.

It was as though Meghan Brodie, somehow, in the space of a single day, had revived him in whole, body and soul.

It was as though he'd been slumbering and now reawakened—by a smart-arsed, canny-eyed wench who might or might not be mad, as well.

He shook his head and turned toward the manor with the intention of returning to her, and then stopped and forced himself to turn about and walk away.

He would go to her soon enough, but just now he needed time to think. Nor could he so easily face her after refusing her brothers so coldly.

He didn't particularly like himself at the moment, and he needed to determine why, when he'd felt far less remorse for worse.

Meghan completed the second essay, and forced herself to set the manuscript aside and contemplate it, before going on to the next.

Sometime during the years in which the second essay had been written, *Piers* Montgomerie had ceased to exist and *Lyon* had been born. What had begun with noble cause—his pursuit of justice—had ended with a far, far different tone. Meghan had no notion what had happened to him, precisely, as he didn't elaborate within his texts—perhaps naught at all and it was simply a consequence of the life he'd led—

but he'd ceased to claim any noble incentives
at all. In fact, he seemed quite resigned to his
own avidity, and even irreverent when his pursuits conflicted with those of others. And the
detached manner in which he spoke of himself
within the text was both unapologetic and yet
self-reproachful. In truth, had Meghan not read
the previous essay, she might have taken him
at his word: she might have believed him no
more than an evil greedy knave, concerned
only with his own personal gain. It seemed to
Meghan, however, that he was not content to
be what he was. It seemed to her that he had
embarked upon a search and somehow had
ended empty-hearted.

He was testing his limits in an effort to . . .
what?

Had he lost something of himself along the
way and tried to recapture it? Had he found
himself numb and yearned to feel again?

She knit her brows and pondered those questions . . . She couldn't quite discern what drove
him . . . couldn't quite put together the two
sides of this man.

Still, she didn't view him as wicked precisely, no matter that he thought so of himself . . .

But there was still more to read, she knew.

Perhaps, in truth, she would think so after.

With her good hand, she lifted up the manuscript once more, set it upon her lap, opened
it, and turned another page.

The next essay was titled simply *Plaisir*.

She wasn't familiar with the word . . . *Plaisir* . . . *plesir* . . . *plesur* . . .

Pleasure?

Something like fluttering wings erupted within her belly and soared into her breast.

Her heartbeat quickened as she turned the page and read . . .

I am my mother's son. I understand her too well to condemn her for her carnal vices.

Her heart beat faster as she continued . . .

I can deny it if I so choose, but the evidence lies sleeping now within my bed, her body bare and replete by my own body and my hands and mouth.

Meghan's heart tripped. How could she continue to read this essay, when it was so obviously a private matter? And yet how could she not?

He wanted her to read it.

Had dared her to, even.

Beauty is my vulnerability, he wrote, and her heart leapt at the words. Curiosity bade her go on . . .

. . . has always been my weakness. Beauty turned my eyes from the université, *my hands from justice, and my heart from piety. And in my covetousness I walked away and never looked back. And where is it I walk to? Where is it that I stand?*

Where is that boy who once yearned for knowledge and virtue?

I doubt now his existence, as no trace of him seems to remain.

Meghan paused, inhaling a quivering breath, her heart aching for the man whose words spilled like lifeblood upon these brittle pages. She caressed the bound parchment . . . feeling it beneath her palm . . . wishing it were the sweet face of that little boy of whom he spoke so distantly. She heard the confusion in his chosen words, the condemnation, too, and wanted to tell him that no man who agonized so, no matter how wrong his choices, could be so wicked.

She took another deep breath, her heart pounding, and continued . . .

If one must conclude that happiness is associated with the fulfillment of one's nature, as Socrates suggests . . . then I should be well sated . . . and yet I am driven here once again to pour my words upon these pages in hopes that I should find that part of me which remains absent from my soul.

While I cannot deny the physical pleasure my body receives in the carnal act, the satisfaction is fleeting. And I sit behind my papers now . . . knowing only too well that next time it will take so much more to bring back the trice of contentment which Eros brings.

It makes me weary to think of it only.

Plato, I think, claims Eros to be passionate rather than calm, and thus demanding, irrational, and even obsessive, and Protagoras observes it as one of the impulses that may overcome one's knowledge of good. On this I can agree wholeheartedly, as I have experienced the above in full. But Eros defined it as the desire for the beautiful? I'm afraid this I must dispute, though my eyes and actions might call me a liar.

In truth . . . I have wallowed in beauty like a swine wallows in cool mud, surfeited my body in ways to be delineated in this very text, shocking though the experiments might be, and it is my contention that Eros is far more than a desire for merely the beautiful.

It is a desire for something more, as well . . . something which my soul understands, but my heart has yet to see.

It is that which drives me from bed to bed, I think . . . and compels me again to leave.

The truth is that I have yet to find true contentment in pleasure.

Does that state of true contentment known as happiness exist beyond the realm of human imagination?

If so, it is certain that pleasure and happiness are not equal as argued, for the separation is easily measured within the confines of the soul. And knowing as much . . . I cannot, in good conscience, return to the bed just now . . . even knowing what pleasures await me there.

This descent into intemperance has left me deplete of desire.

Her heart pounding fiercely, Meghan paused once more for breath. In reading, she'd entirely forgotten to breathe, so entranced was she by his heartfelt words.

This was by far the most personal of his essays. None of the others had been nearly so revealing, nor had he spoken of himself in such a forthright manner.

Why did he wish her to read this essay?

Meghan would have buried such a manuscript ten feet under after writing it, in fear that anyone would know her most personal thoughts.

Why had he simply handed it over to her so easily? Even dared her to read it?

Was he trying to frighten her away?

Surely not—not when he'd made so little pretense about wanting her for his own.

What was it he wanted her to discover in these pages?

She nibbled her lower lip, contemplating.

Perhaps if she continued reading, she would learn the answers.

Below the passage she'd read was a reference to works she had no knowledge of—by men called Plato and Socrates. Some of their arguments, it appeared, he'd copied into the second notebook, and were therefore impossible for her to read, as she did not understand the Latin text. She turned the page, and gasped at the crude sketches which accompanied the detailed text. She stared wide-eyed at the raw drawings of man and woman in positions and acts that she would never have conceived of. Her breath quickened and her heart tripped.

God have mercy upon her wicked soul, she could not stop now, no matter that she knew what next she would read . . .

Chapter 20

⌒◯◯⌒

Lyon hadn't meant to stay away so long.
But neither had he been able to face her, lest he feel obliged to confess what he'd done. Sending her brothers away when they must have been worried sick after not seeing her for three days and then discovering she was hurt was certainly not the proudest moment of his life.

Why had he done such a thing?

Had he fallen so far into iniquity?

God help him, it was just that . . . for the first time in his life he wanted something so sorely.

Meghan Brodie.

Her name alone made him burn.

She was becoming an obsession.

It seemed he could think of naught else but her. In the time he'd known her, he'd abandoned his promises to old man MacLean, disappointed his sovereign, and now turned away worried kinfolk for fear they would seize her from him.

What the devil was happening to him?

He'd spent the morning alone digging a grave for a bloody lamb named Fia! And then had remained by the grave after burying the damned animal, swilling his ale under the high afternoon sun. His skin was blistered now, but the burn upon his flesh was nowhere near that which smoldered through his loins. The mere thought of her there . . . within his bed . . . reading his manuscripts . . . made his heart thunder and his blood blaze through his veins.

He thought about his words and wondered if she would be shocked by them, repelled— thought about his drawings and wished he could see her face when first she'd set eyes upon them.

Would she be appalled?

Amused?

Aroused?

His heart hammering as it had not in years, he climbed the stairwell to his bedchamber, wavering a bit in his drunkenness. He'd returned from the gravesite and had remained within the hall below, swilling more ale whilst he'd stared at the hole he'd had boarded within the floor of his chamber . . . trying to imagine what it was she was thinking behind the door . . .

What it was she was doing . . .

His breath quickened at the thought of seeing her once more.

He swallowed the last of his ale as he

reached the top of the stairs and hurled the empty tankard down the stairwell, listening to it clatter its way down, uncertain whether it was a warning to Meghan or a self-recriminating gesture.

It didn't matter. He was too besotted to care.

He opened the door, and stood wavering upon his feet, acclimating himself to the dimness of the room. His eyes were drawn at once to the lone taper lit upon his desk. The tiny flame illuminated her face and little else, and his breath caught at the sheer beauty of her profile.

God, but she was lovely.

Meghan heard the warning clatter beyond the door, but had no time to leave the desk before the door swung open to reveal Lyon standing there.

Her heart leapt against her breast, and she dropped the quill upon the desk, afraid he would catch her penning her own words upon the pages of his manuscript.

Despite the fact that the room had grown dim and she'd had to squint to see the pages, she'd scarcely been aware of the passage of time.

And now he was here, filling the doorway with his presence.

He came into the room, swinging the door shut behind him, and her heart quickened its beat.

"Is that fear I spy within your eyes, Meghan?"

Meghan couldn't find her tongue to speak, so expressive was his look. After having read his essays, the brightness of his gaze took on an entirely new significance. Och, but she could hardly look him in the eyes without wondering if he thought of her in those ways he had written about.

"Have you changed your mind now after reading those pages?" he persisted.

Meghan's breath caught as he approached her.

She didn't know what to answer. Certainly, she *should* be shocked by their content, but she wasn't. And perhaps she should think him wicked, too, but she couldn't—because if he were so wicked then so was she, because his private thoughts made her feel . . . warm . . .

Much too warm.

And his presence now made her heady with anticipation.

She closed his manuscript before he could spy her scribblings, and pushed it guiltily aside.

He came to stand beside her.

Meghan's heart thundered as he lifted up the manuscript and held it, inspecting the binding. He didn't open it, merely stood there holding it between them, and she prayed he'd not. She wasn't certain whether he'd be incensed by her boldness . . . or merely amused that she should think herself learned enough to add her own observations to his. He would read them soon enough, she was certain, but she was afraid it would be now, when her musing was as yet incomplete and her thoughts too scattered to form into comprehensive words.

"Answer me, Meghan." He tossed down the manuscript and Meghan let out a sigh of relief.

"Nay," she answered, and averted her gaze, staring at the bright-yellow flame as it danced atop the burning taper.

"Nay?"

She held her breath as he knelt beside the desk, and cast him a glance but didn't dare look him full in the face.

How could she ever again when she knew what he was thinking?

When she shared his thoughts?

She couldn't forget his words . . . or his drawings . . . Couldn't keep her heart from hammering as he stared so expectantly at her.

"Nay, you will not answer me?" he asked her, his voice no more than a husky murmur. "Or nay, you do not think me wicked, Meghan?"

Meghan's face heated. "Nay . . ." She turned to look at him then, and the intensity in his eyes seized her breath. "I—I d-do no' . . . th-think ye wicked," she told him, and sucked in a breath.

He cast a glance at the arm she had cradled

before her within her lap. "Does it pain you still?"

Meghan nodded. "A bit," she confessed. Though in truth, she'd not thought of it overmuch whilst she'd read through his manuscripts—nor whilst she'd sat writing at his desk. Her thoughts had been so immersed within the manuscripts that she'd forgotten even to feel.

He produced the same small vial he had once before from his belt, and opened it. The sweet scent of herbs tickled her senses. "Give me your tongue, Meghan," he urged her, and the silken sound of his voice sent a quiver down her spine.

Meghan stared at his mouth, recalling all the wicked things he had confessed to doing with his own tongue. Och, she wasn't ignorant in the ways of men and women, but she had never dreamed a man would wish to do such things to a woman's body!

That he could crave the taste of her . . .

Did he?

The very notion sent gooseflesh rippling over her.

The way he was staring at her made her feel as though he did.

"Give me your tongue," he demanded once more.

Meghan swallowed convulsively and did as he bade her. She hugged herself, cradling her injured arm, trying to still the trembling of her body as he moved the vial over her tongue, dripping *médecine* into her mouth. The liquid tickled her buds. Meghan blinked as he withdrew the vial. She swallowed, her eyes drawn once more, against her will, to the manuscript that sat upon the desk between them, its leather cover illuminated by the candle's twisting, flickering light.

"Tell me what you're thinking," came his softly spoken command.

Meghan's gaze returned to his face.

Their gazes locked, held.

She swallowed once more, no more capable of revealing her own thoughts than she could cease thinking of his.

"Have you been reading all afternoon?"

"Most," she confessed, and her voice was soft and low, strange to her own ears.

Her confession thrilled him.

The blood hummed through his veins. He wasn't certain what he'd hoped to accomplish by having her read his manuscripts, but he was pleasantly surprised.

Relieved.

Intrigued.

By the look upon her face.

Was she not what he had supposed?

Was she more like his mother than some virginal Highland lass whose brothers had kept her sheltered from greedy eyes and hands?

Was that why she was as yet unwed?

Was she deflowered and unpure for the marriage bed?

All these thoughts and more poured through his mind. He wasn't certain how the answers should make him feel, but one thing was certain, he didn't care this instant—couldn't care less if her body had been explored by unknown hands and eyes before this day, because they were untouched as yet by his own. And if he had his way, there would be naught of her left to his imagination. And when he was finished with her, there would be no memory remaining of another man's hands upon her delicious body.

The taper's flame began to fade as it burned down the wick, the only evidence of the passing of time, for the air grew still between them, the tension as delicious as anticipation should be. The room was left deep in shadows but for the almost nonexistent glow from the candle, and what muted light came from the hole in his ceiling. The flame was a soft illumination upon her lovely face, casting a buttery-yellow light upon her pallid cheeks. And the flicker of the flame was a glimmer in her eyes—eyes that were hardly wicked as his own must seem, but hardly innocent either.

He had to know . . .

How innocent?

His own body tautened at the mere scent of her flesh.

"You're trembling," he said softly, his voice thick with hunger.

"M-my arm," she whimpered.

He wanted to hear that she did not think him depraved.

He wanted to take her beautiful face into his hands . . . taste her sweet mouth . . . wanted to slide his tongue between those luscious lips and drink of her.

"I have something that will ease it . . ."

The candle flickered between them, making it appear her dark-green eyes widened a bit in fear, but it was a trick of the candlelight, he hoped, for in the next instant they were filled only with a curiosity he wanted more than life to satisfy.

"If you will trust me," he added.

She seemed to understand that his meaning was deeper, because she hesitated before nodding. And yet she nodded and it sent his pulses leaping.

He reached down, holding her gaze, and separated her kirtle from her undergown. Watching her face, he gathered it within his fist and jerked it, renting a strip from it. She gasped, but her gaze never wavered. Lyon's heart thundered within his chest at the implication. Not knowing his intent, she trusted him still, allowed him his will. He tore his gaze away long enough to examine the strip he'd rent, and then folded it and rose to his feet.

"Extend your arm a bit," he bade her. "Just a bit . . . I know it hurts, Meghan."

Once more she did as he asked her, and he slid the strip about her arm so that it cradled it comfortably and then he lifted it about her neck to secure it. He couldn't help but wonder if she would be so compliant within his bed . . . within his arms . . . lying beneath him . . . or whether she would bend his will to her own, wield her power over him, reduce him to naught more than a lover grateful for every soft touch his darling bestowed.

"Lift your beautiful hair for me," he urged her.

She did, gathering the strands with her good hand, and he slid his hands about her neck, reveling in the feel of her warm silken skin beneath his touch. He tied the sling at her nape.

His hands lingered . . . his fingertips caressing lightly . . .

Meghan's heart beat faster.

Swallowing, her breath quickening painfully, she released her hair so that it fell and covered his hands.

And still he did not remove them.

He wrapped his fingers about her nape, then, and slid his thumb beneath her jaw, gently turning her head up to look him full in the face.

"I said you were lovely, Meghan Brodie," he whispered fiercely, "and so you are."

Meghan gulped back the retort that came naturally to her lips.

Jesu, but she *did* like the way he looked at her.

No matter that she told herself she did not . . . she did! Och, but her heart seemed to blossom when he gazed at her so. It made her feel . . . wanted . . . cherished . . .

And yet she needed so much more.

She wanted him to gaze at her and think her beautiful within as well. Because someday, someday . . . Meghan knew she'd no longer have beauty to fall back upon. Someday, as with Fia . . . she would lose her youthfulness and then they would all call her mad and view her as though she were some curiosity to be hidden away. Even her brothers had been guilty of it with Fia; they had felt nothing but shame for the woman who had raised them.

Aye, beauty was but a curse.

Her father had been driven to his own demise in obsession over it, and her grandfather had all but discarded her grandmother in pursuit of it once Fia's own beauty had fled her.

Aye, Meghan was afraid to embrace his words, afraid to take pleasure in them, lest she end like her mother and grandmother before her.

Alone.

She wanted him to accept all of her. She wanted him to see that she was more than the sum of her parts. She wanted him to look into her eyes and know that there was a brain behind her silly face . . . and thoughts . . . and feelings.

She wanted him to hear her words and respect them.

She wanted him . . .

She wanted him to kiss her . . .

His fingers tangled within her hair. Gooseflesh erupted over her flesh. Meghan held her breath as he looked down upon her, his eyes glittering with the reflected light of the dancing candle flame . . .

And with something else . . . something that truly *was* a little wicked . . .

Meghan averted her eyes to the desk, to the manuscript lying there.

"Look at me, Meghan," he demanded of her.

Meghan did, and her heart skipped a beat. It was wholly impossible to look into his eyes and not imagine the things he'd done . . . the desire he made no effort to hide. A delicious shiver raced down her spine.

"Look me in the eye," he commanded her, his voice naught more than a husky whisper, "and tell me, Meghan Brodie . . ."

The sound of her name upon his lips sent another quiver down her spine.

"Do you think me wicked now?"

Meghan blinked.

How to respond? She inhaled a shuddering breath.

Did she tell him aye, accuse him, when she

knew in her heart that she was as wicked as he?

Or did she deny it and let him think her wicked too?

She could not find her voice to speak. Her lips parted but no words came.

"Tell me, Meghan."

"I—I dinna think . . . I dunno," she whispered.

"I think you do," he murmured and bent, brushing his lips softly against her brow. She moaned softly at the sweetness of the gesture, tilting her head back, melting beneath his lips, and he moved lower, kissing the bridge of her nose. Meghan held her breath, closing her eyes, and he then kissed each of her lids. She ceased to breathe at all as the warmth of his mouth descended toward her lips.

But he didn't kiss her. The scent of ale accosted her . . . ale and man . . . and something more . . .

"I d-dunno," she swore, and expelled a breathy sigh.

And she truly did not. She had no notion what to think, what to feel, what to do . . . He was stirring her senses as though he were a master weaver and she the silken thread upon his golden loom.

She was suddenly so warm . . . and so . . . hot . . . heady . . . dizzy . . .

Och! It seemed as though a veil fell over the room.

Meghan wasn't certain but it seemed she wavered a bit in the chair . . .

And the candle flame . . . it seemed to dance away before her eyes, teasing her vision.

The pain in her arm faded along with the clarity of the room. The only thing she was acutely aware of . . . was the hands that cupped her face so tenderly . . . the lips that drew away from her own, leaving her mouth yearning . . . the eyes that watched her so intently . . .

She blinked, peering into his face, feeling intoxicated by his very presence.

The *drogue* was taking effect. She willed it away, not wanting it to dull her senses.

"Do you think me wicked?" he asked once more, and Meghan could scarcely breathe for his nearness. His blue eyes gleamed as they scrutinized her, scattering her thoughts.

She shrugged. "I canna . . ." She swallowed. ". . . canna make such a judgment."

His eyes slitted, piercing her. "Cannot or will not, Meghan?"

"Canna," she whispered. "I dinna knoo ye well enough, Lyon Montgomerie."

"I beg to differ . . . You know me better than anyone else upon the face of this earth, Meghan Brodie," he told her. "I poured my soul into those pages."

Her face burned. She tried to look away. "I . . . I didna read them all," she lied, unable to look him in the eyes after having such intimate knowledge of him. Her heart beat so loudly she was sure that he must hear it as well, was sure that in the silence of the room it was amplified.

He forced her gaze back. "How much?" he pressed. "How much did you read?"

"I . . . I dinna remember."

He lifted a brow. "You do not remember, Meghan?"

Meghan shook her head.

He released her suddenly, and stood once more, looking down upon her. Her heart hammered as he slid aside the candle upon the desk. Without warning, he reached down, plucking her up from the chair. Meghan gasped in surprise as he sat her upon the desk, and then seated himself before her.

"Shall we rouse your memory, then?" he suggested, and reached down, sliding his hand beneath the arch of her foot. Meghan's heart leapt into her throat at the intimacy of his caress.

His written words came back to her with the first touch: *I lave her feet with my tongue. It is as though I am a slave to my passion . . . and this the ultimate gift as I humble myself at her feet in worship . . . craving the taste of her flesh like a man with strong drink, and inebriated with the desire only to please . . .*

"W-what are ye going tae do?"

"Shhh," he commanded her.

His gaze never left her face as he began to massage her bare foot, stroking the arch and caressing her skin gently.

"Do you remember what I wrote of this, Meghan?"

Meghan's breath quickened at the question. She nodded as his fingers massaged her foot, gently lacing through her toes. And then he raked the seat backward from the desk and Meghan thought she would swoon as he lifted her foot to his beautiful mouth, watching her face all the while as his tongue darted out to lap at her toe.

Wicked.

A shudder flew through her.

She knew she should protest—God only knew that she should—but she couldn't. She couldn't find the words to deny him . . . to deny herself . . . even knowing where this could lead.

Feeling paralyzed with uncertainty, and dizzy with anticipation, she watched as he drew his tongue along the arch of her foot, tasting her flesh where his fingers had caressed. And then her heart leapt against her ribs as he drew her toe into his mouth, gently, suckling it, his eyes gleaming with a hunger she could but yield to.

Gooseflesh raced over her limbs as he massaged her calves, pushing up her gown as he moved toward her thighs, all the while continuing to suckle at her toe . . .

God have mercy upon her wicked soul, but she could not bring herself to still his hands as they climbed upward . . . like warm velvet across the flesh of her thighs . . .

He withdrew her toe from his mouth. "I want you for my own, Meghan Brodie," he told her without ceremony.

"Ye want my body," she answered breathlessly, scarcely able to think for the way his hands were making her feel.

He didn't want her . . . He wanted her body . . . There was a difference, Meghan understood. She fought to remember that.

"Aye," he whispered, his voice low and husky with a desire he didn't attempt to conceal. "I'll not deny it. I *do*," he confessed, and fell to his knees before her.

"I want your body, Meghan," he whispered. "I wish to know you. . . ." He spread her legs, settling himself before her, and Meghan's heart thundered within her breast as he shoved up her skirts and cast her a last hungry glance before leaning forward to blow out the taper.

Under cover of darkness, he moved in to kiss her where no man had ever laid his eyes upon her before.

". . . to know the taste of you upon my tongue," he said, "upon my lips," and he moaned as the warmth of his mouth opened over her most private place. Meghan gasped, and her head lolled backward, enveloped by a sweet heady pleasure unlike anything she had ever experienced before. Wrapped within a cocoon of sensation, she fell backward against the wall, crying out . . . not in protest, or in pain, but in utter and helpless surrender.

His heart hammering, Lyon closed his eyes and concentrated not on the burn of his loins, but the taste of her upon his tongue.

This time it was not for him, he told himself.

As much as he craved the taste of her . . . as much satisfaction as he received in the pleasuring . . . for once, it was not a means to an end, his end, but an act of giving. He wanted to give her this with all his heart.

He could see in her eyes that she was not completely lucid, and he didn't simply desire her surrender . . . he wanted the gift of her heart along with that of her body.

Nay, this time it would be different.

Because she was different.

Deep in his soul, he sensed that in her arms he would find all his answers. All the revelations he sought seemed buried behind the mirror of her gaze.

He craved them madly.

Answers.

Closing his eyes, he adored her with his mouth . . . his lips . . . his tongue . . . wanting to please her . . . needing to please her. She fell backward, whimpering with pleasure, and the sweet sound of it sent desire clawing through his loins. His body hardened, pulsed with need, but he ignored it, seizing her good hand into his own, and anchoring it about his neck. Sheer and utter exultation filled him as she responded by thrusting her fingers through his hair, clutching him in ecstasy.

Aye, he was well aware she was drugged ... that she might not have allowed him so much liberty otherwise, but he'd never confessed to moral restraint. He'd never intended mercy in his pursuit, nor did he play fairly.

He played as he fought as he loved ...

To win.

Only this time, the prize was hers to receive. Not his.

He wanted to hear her cry of release ... wanted to feel her tremble sweetly against his lips ... taste her honey ... wanted her to cry out his name.

And then when at last she slept ...

When at last she dreamt ...

When she awoke in the morn ...

He wanted her to remember every instant of pleasure he'd given her.

He wanted her to think of naught else but him every waking hour of the day—as he did with her.

She was in his blood.

He was obsessed.

He wanted to look upon her beautiful face and see her flush of desire.

And he wanted her to look him in the eyes and beg for more.

He worked feverishly, denying his own need, his heart pounding and his blood thrumming through his veins, worshipping her body with every lap and every suckle. She wrapped her thighs about his neck in utter abandon, and he felt a fierce satisfaction in her pleasure.

And when she cried out at last, embracing his head as though she were clinging to him for her very life, he felt joy as he'd never experienced in his own completion.

Closing his eyes, inhaling the sweet feminine scent of her, Lyon kissed her and then each of her thighs in turn. He kissed her belly then and lifted his head to her breast, listening to the thundering beat of her heart.

Who would have thought after all this time without a bloody woman . . . he would find such perverse pleasure in his own denial. Christ, but he did!

He held her, taking thorough gratification in every throbbing pulse of his own manifested desire.

Aye, this time was different, he assured himself, and he didn't give a damn if she was mad or not—if she was bloody mad, let him be mad with her—he wanted Meghan Brodie for the rest of his life.

Chapter 21

"**B**less ye, Cameron!" Alison MacLean said, and bent to kiss the old man upon the cheek. "Thank ye again for coming tae fetch me when Meghan fell. And bless yer true Scots heart for doing this for me noo!"

The old man blushed fiercely, his face mottling with color. "'Twas naught," he replied. "Dinna thank me, lass, as I didna want the bastard mon upon my birth-land, anyhoo, and I dinna appreciate the way he takes what he wills—arrogant Sassenach!"

"I knoo!" Alison agreed. "But I couldna do this withoot ye, Cameron, and I can thank ye if I please!"

The old man nodded. "Ye were a brave lass," he said, "going in there like that tae help yer friend."

"How could I no'!" Alison declared. "Meghan Brodie is my verra best friend! She would ha' done the same for me," she swore. And Meghan would, she knew. It had twisted

Alison's heart to see her friend lying there in so much pain. If she could have lifted her up and carried her from that wretched place, she would have! As it was, she'd had to tend Meghan and then hurry away lest he should recognize her face.

Cameron nodded again in agreement, and Alison went on, "I was sae worried! I had tae see wi' my verra own eyes that she was weel." She'd not thought of her plan until King David had sounded so uncertain of Meghan's sanity. It had startled her, as Meghan Brodie was the sweetest, smartest person Alison knew! But Alison had taken advantage of David's uncertainty and had formed this hasty plan. She hadn't known how well it would go, but it was worth a try. "Anyway, Montgomerie didna recognize me sae all is weel. But I canna risk myself again sae soon, if I am tae gae back and trade places wi' Meghan later. Sae, then, be sure tae give her this," she instructed, and pressed a small sack into the old man's hands. "'Tis verra important! And ye tell her just what I told ye, all right?"

"Aye, lass," Cameron said. "I remember it all, I do."

"Verra good, and this is for ye," she added, and held out a few gold coins.

"For me?" he asked, peering up at her in surprise.

"Aye," Alison answered, smiling brilliantly. "For ye. And thank ye again, Cameron o' the

MacLeans, and gae on wi' ye. I'll need ye soon enough again if my plan is tae work. Run noo tae Meghan and tell her tae follow my instructions precisely."

The old man smiled as he took the coins from her. "Aye, lass," he agreed. "I'll give her the sack the verra instant she is alone, I will."

"Thank ye." Alison said with feeling, and threw her arms about his neck in appreciation. "Ye're a sweet auld mon," she said and drew away. "Gae quickly noo," she urged him.

"No sooner said than done," he promised, and turned on his heel.

Alison watched him wend his way through the forest until he was gone from her sight, and then she turned and hurried home. There was much to do before her final performance, she knew.

She had colored her face with a thin layer of mud, not enough to make her appear grimy, but enough to dry her skin and give her the appearance of wrinkles, and she had been thankful for the dim light of his chamber that he could not make out her eyes, for though she'd met him only the once, she knew they were revealing, crossing as they did so oft.

She didn't worry he would suspect her later, because by the time Cameron snuck her in to trade places with Meghan, he would be ready to believe anything. And her hair and eye color were close enough to Meghan's, that as long as she kept her face concealed, it would give them more than enough time to sneak Meghan out and carry her home. And then she would simply slip away herself, remove her wimple and makeup, and leave with none the wiser. And Meghan would be home and safe and just in time to see her wedded to Leith.

She smiled at that, certain that Meghan was going to be surprised with the turn of events. Alison could scarcely believe it herself, but Leith Mac Brodie had been so kind to her. And if she'd initially believed his proposal one of mere pity, she no longer thought so. He sent her gifts, one each day, and Alison was beginning to wonder what it was she ever saw in Colin Mac Brodie. A handsome face alone was not nearly enough to recommend a person, she knew, and Colin Mac Brodie had never treated her kindly. How could she have been so blind to Leith? How could she have done to him what Colin had done to her? She'd nearly discarded Leith without a second glance merely because his face was not as comely as Colin's.

"Ye should be ashamed, Alison!" she berated herself. And she certainly was!

And that brought her to another thought entirely . . .

Could she have misjudged Piers Montgomerie as well? She knew what she'd spied in his eyes—the way he'd looked upon Meghan as she'd lain so still within his bed. It seemed to Alison that he had gazed upon her with genuine distress. And perhaps it was no more than he should feel, as it was his fault Meghan was hurt to begin with.

And yet . . . Alison could have sworn there was something more in his eyes when he gazed upon her . . .

And he *had* purchased the potion at an exorbitant price—one she had set only to make him think her greedy—but whether he did so for his own sake or that of Meghan's wasn't clear. Perhaps he did so to alleviate his guilt or perhaps her beauty was his utmost concern. Neither did it matter, as far as Alison was concerned, for Meghan had a right to choose her own husband. If Lyon Montgomerie wished to woo her once she was home, then that was another thing entirely.

Let him court her properly as would any self-respecting man.

And with that decided, she lifted her skirts and ran the rest of the way home, not wanting to be discovered, not even by her father, lest he forbid her to do what she knew she must.

For once in her life she was doing something that mattered, and Alison didn't care what the risks were.

Meghan needed her.

The fact that she could make such a difference so exhilarated her that she wanted naught more than to run home and share the news with her father. She wanted to run and tell Leith what she'd done and what she planned, but she didn't dare, lest the two of them, in their silly male pride, forbid her to help and insist upon saving Meghan themselves. Nay, she wasn't about to tell them! Male pride had gotten them thus far, and it was time to use their wits, not might!

Foolish men!

With the morning sun upon her face, Meghan lay wholly afraid to open her eyes.

The very thought of what she had done . . . of what she had allowed . . . heated her cheeks. And sweet Jesu, it warmed her body as well!

Last night, though she'd been sated and drugged besides, she had lain there, unable to sleep. And even now, this morning, the memory of their wicked embrace made her belly stir with desire she hardly could deny.

But she could scarcely sleep forever, no matter that the *drogue* kept her weary enough to do so.

Cautiously, she opened her eyes to the bright light of morning.

Lyon Montgomerie's face was the first thing she saw.

He was kneeling by the bed, watching her. Meghan started, blinking in surprise.

"I mean to steal your heart, Meghan Brodie," he swore, and Meghan's heart leapt.

She feared, somehow, he already had.

Her heart quickened its beat. "H-ha' ye been watching me all morn?" she asked hesitantly, feeling both flattered and distressed all at once.

She had dreamt of him, his lips upon her flesh, his hand upon her breast. And in her dream . . . she had awakened to find his head cradled between her thighs . . . as he had been last eve. In her dream, he'd peered up at her, grinning wickedly, his eyes flashing with an unmistakable amatory gleam as he'd slid his hand along her belly to her naked breast, whispering, "*It's only me.*"

Meghan shuddered at the memory.

"Time to get up!" he said. "I have something to show you."

Meghan gave him an exasperated glance. "Ye are a despotic mon!" she told him, taking comfort in her pique. "Do ye never tire of ordering people aboot?"

"Never," he admitted, grinning roguishly at her, his look much too boyish to be aught but engaging.

Meghan grimaced as she tried to rise. He moved to help her.

"I can do it myself!" she exclaimed. "Stop being sae bluidy nice. I dinna wish tae like ye!" she told him honestly. "Dinna ye realize?"

He chuckled at that. "Though you do?"

Meghan gave him a withering glance. "I didna say such a thing!"

"But you are thinking it?"

"Och, but ye are arrogant, too."

Lyon merely shrugged at that.

"Then I shall resolve to be less so," he vowed, and inhaled a breath at the sight of her.

He could scarcely keep himself from staring.

Damn, but he couldn't seem to get enough of her.

He'd fallen asleep with his body hard as stone, and nevertheless with a smile upon his face. And this morning he'd felt himself scarcely able to leave her, though he'd had matters to attend to. He'd left her only long enough to see them well in hand, and then had rushed back to her side.

What the devil was wrong with him?

He felt as reckless as the boy he'd once been, eagerly chasing every skirt that passed him by, starved for the sight of creamy flesh and greedy for the female scent.

Only he no longer wanted the rest.

He wanted this one.

He couldn't stop smiling.

"I ha' told ye, Lyon Montgomerie, I dinna want ye tae be sae accommodating! Move oot o' my way," she demanded, ripping the tattered bedsheets off and sliding her legs over the side of the bed.

Lyon sucked in a breath as her movement placed him kneeling before her once more.

She seemed to realize this belatedly and her brows lifted in surprise. Her gaze flew to his and her cheeks pinkened.

He merely smiled at her, wholly satisfied with her reaction. He wanted her to remember, wanted her never to forget. He wanted her to be his, body and soul; he knew very well that her heart would come if he mastered her body. He understood women only too well, and knew how to please them. He damned well wasn't going to waste his God-given talents when he wanted this more than he wanted to breathe.

He lifted a brow. "Are you asking for more, Meghan Brodie?"

"Och!" she exclaimed, gasping in outrage. "Ye *are* a wicked rotten knave! I've changed my mind! I *do* knoo ye well enough tae make such a judgment! Ye are!"

"Aye," he murmured, "you do," and he bent to plant a swift, but chaste kiss upon the bridge of her nose.

Her hand flew to her face at once, her fingers touching her nose where he had kissed her. "Why did ye do that?" she asked him, seeming confused by the innocence of the gesture.

"Because you are adorable," he answered simply. "Come, let us go." He rose, drawing her up with him by her good arm, though gently, lest he hurt her. "There is something I wish to show you this morn, and I hope it pleases you."

He insisted she close her eyes as he led her along behind him, taking her to some unknown place.

Meghan had no choice but to follow, as her curiosity was too great to deny.

When he bade her open her eyes at last, they

were in the meadow, with no one else in sight. The bright sunlight, after being secluded so long within his chamber, made her squint. She had difficulty focusing enough to see anything at all, and then, she only saw Lyon standing there before her, gazing at her expectantly, as though he were awaiting her response.

Her brow furrowed. "I thought ye wished tae show me something. I see naught."

He was grinning at her.

She tilted a glance at him. "Why do ye look at me so?"

He lifted his brows, and his eyes shone with a boyish gleam that snuck its way into her heart. "Because," he said playfully, " 'tis not oft one beholds both the sun and the moon together, Meghan Brodie!"

Meghan tried not to roll her eyes at his exalted praise, and was thankful for his shameless cajolery as it helped her to keep him at bay. Accustomed as she was to men's empty flattery, it no longer stirred her heart to hear it.

Except when Lyon Montgomerie spoke it, it seemed.

Her heart quickened.

"You are both the fiery brilliance of sunlight, Meghan, and the bewitching serenity of moonlight," he told her, and his ardent tone managed to seep into the cracks of the wall surrounding her heart—despite that Meghan sat behind it, casting mortar at every fracture.

"And *ye*, I fear, ha' missed yer calling, Lyon

Montgomerie. Ye should ha' been a troubadour begging entrance at every manor.'' She eyed him sharply. ''Ye are a shameless flatterer! And I ha' told ye I am unmoved by pretty words, and still ye persist—why?'' she demanded.

He stood there, looking entirely too beauteous for Meghan's peace of mind—his smile too radiant, and his words entirely too blithe—and she wanted to loathe him for making her yearn for more.

''Because you've turned me into a besotted lad,'' he answered unrelentingly, ''who would do aught for merely the favor of a smile from his darling.''

Meghan frowned at him. ''I am no' yer darling, lest ye forget!''

She eyed him circumspectly. He wore a deep-blue tunic that brought out the vivid color of his eyes, with a strip of green and blue plaid about his waist and black braies that hugged his long lean legs. He stood tall before her, with his long hair stirring like silk in the breeze. It shimmered like spun gold beneath the mid-morning sun.

She could scarcely forget the way it had felt clutched between her trembling fingers, the way it had gleamed last eve by candlelight as he'd played her body so masterfully.

Och, but if ever a man could be called beautiful, Lyon Montgomerie was fiercely so!

And yet there was naught about him that made one doubt his masculinity. He was as hard and as beauteous as the hills that surrounded them.

And it didn't help much to see that he seemed at ease here upon the land she loved so passionately. It was as though he'd been carved from the very stone, in fact, as those ancient cairns that bedecked this soil of her birth.

Despite her claims to the contrary, he *was* stealing her heart—curse his rotten soul!

His pretty words confused her—made her sigh for more.

But how?

When she knew better.

Was she so feckless that she would abandon her convictions so easily?

Were all her principles naught more than chatter?

Her condemnation for those who would not search beyond a face nothing more than hypocrisy?

Meghan only knew that his words of adulation made her heart beat faster and her knees melt like wax beneath a flame.

And och! She was as guilty as any man with covetous eyes, for she stood wholly entranced by the mere sight of him. When she looked into his gleaming sapphire eyes ... her breath caught at what she saw there within their beautiful depths. And when she lowered her gaze to his mouth, which smiled at her with such sensual promise, she wanted to open her arms and beg him come to her once more.

As he had last night.

It seemed she was naught but a bloody impostor, and she didn't know herself anymore!

Her cheeks heated at the turn of her thoughts, and she averted her gaze.

He reached out suddenly, drawing her chin up with a finger. "Meghan, lass," he whispered, much more soberly now, "why does it bother you so that I think you bonnie?"

Ashamed of herself, Meghan withdrew her face from his touch.

He stood there gazing at her, and she felt utterly exposed beneath his scrutiny.

"Can it be that you do not see what I see?" he asked her softly.

She lifted her gaze to his. "I *knoo* what ye see!" she assured him. "And I canna—I am no'—" She couldn't find the words to make him understand.

"Yours is the most lovely face I have ever set eyes upon!"

He didn't understand!

Couldn't possibly.

She wanted to be *more* than a face and body, didn't he see? She wanted to be a heart and a soul and a brain, as well.

Leith had always appreciated her mind, respecting and needing her counsel, but out of fear that she would leave them perhaps, he had made her ashamed of the face she saw in the looking glass. To please him, as a wee lass

she'd worn rags and never a ribbon in her hair.
Her brother Colin boasted of her beauty, but
never cared to know her deeper thoughts. And
though she was closest to him of all, she didn't
recall ever once, not once, having had a mean-
ingful conversation with him about such things
as life and death and God. It was a pitiful state
of affairs when she could say such a thing! And
while Gavin was concerned enough with her
spiritual pursuits, he discarded her philoso-
phies entirely, and Meghan was only too aware
of how he viewed those women who succumbed to their vanities.

Meghan yearned for someone to accept her
as she was—all of her, not simply in parts!

She was terrified that behind the shell of her
face and body was a woman who just could
not be what everyone believed her to be. She
was afraid that if they looked deep enough
they would not like what they saw. She had
listened to suitors enough to know that they
did not see her as she was, only how they
wanted her to be. They looked upon her face
and made her a graven image, sang odes to her
beauty and threw petals at her feet . . . as
though she were some pagan virgin being led
to her sacrificial altar! They set her upon a sa-
cred pedestal and refused to let her down, even
when she screamed and begged and yelled.

"Meghan," he whispered, and lifted her face
once more, "look at me."

Meghan did and swallowed at the intimacy with which he gazed at her.

"I do not care if I feel a fool for speaking my heart," he said.

Heart? Meghan thought. Hah! Like every other man, he spoke with the fickle fire of his loins. Heart, indeed!

"I have never," he swore, "wanted anything as much as I do you."

"Me?" she asked, tilting her head in challenge. "Or is it my body ye crave, Lyon Montgomerie?"

He lifted a brow. "I'll not lie to you," he answered, and slid his hand along her cheek, cupping it gently.

Meghan shuddered in response. And like a wanton she responded by tilting into his caress. Och, but she couldn't help herself! He slid his hands beneath her hair, then to her nape, curling his fingers about her neck.

For an instant, they merely stood staring at each other, while her heart beat a warning in her ears.

Deny him noo, this instant! she told herself, *before ye no longer can.* Deep in her heart, she knew he would not force her. Last night was evidence enough if she doubted her instinct. He had pleasured her, and then had lifted her up into his arms and laid her within his bed, never appeasing his own body.

Walk awa', Meghan Brodie.
Walk awa' noo!

"I want . . . more than anything . . . to make love to you, Meghan Brodie," he whispered, and Meghan was lost in that instant. Her heart leapt as he drew her closer. Faltering in her step, she went to him, and he wrapped his arms about her, gently, so as not to injure her arm, and Meghan was at once defenseless within his embrace.

His arms were too warm . . . his hands too reassuring . . . the beat of his heart much too close . . .

His hand slid upward along her back, gently, though she could feel his hunger in the trembling of his fingers as it joined the other hand at her nape. And then sliding them both at once to cup her face within his two hands, he lowered his face to hers.

Her breath left her. Her heart jolted. It occurred to her in the instant before his lips touched her mouth that he hadn't kissed her at all last eve.

Not upon her lips.

Nay, but his mouth had found more intimate places to caress.

The very thought of it . . . the very memory of where his lips and tongue had been, made her knees buckle beneath her. He caught her, and she cried out softly, not for the pain in the arm cradled between them, but because in that instant . . . his lips met her own, and it was the sweetest, most wicked sensation she had ever known.

Meghan moaned softly. So warm . . . and smooth . . . his lips moved over her mouth, molding with her own, like warm wet silk— hard yet gentle, too. Meghan thought she would die with the thrill of it. His lips were moist and sweet, but insistent, and his tongue slipped out to trace the seam of her lips, sending quiver after delicious quiver down her spine.

Meghan slid her arm about his neck, but she wasn't certain whether her reaction was meant to support herself, or to clutch him to her lest he leave her wanting. Parting her lips as he coaxed her to, she moaned again as his tongue slid within her mouth, drinking of her will as surely as though it were a goblet tilted to his lips.

Closing her eyes, she savored the moment . . . never wanting him to stop.

"I want you," he murmured. "I need you, Meghan."

Meghan sighed softly in reply.

"I want to be inside you," he said feverishly. "Do you understand?" And a quiver shuddered through her at his words.

Emboldened by her own desire, Meghan slid from his embrace to the dewy grass, dragging him by the hand down with her. He followed her, the look in his eyes both hungry and fierce, and like a wanton she lay back upon the grass in blatant invitation. She didn't care if she was brazen . . . she wanted more of what he'd given her last night.

She wanted more.

He moved over her, gently covering her, taking care with her arm. And then he kissed her once more, and it was slow and tender, his lips coaxing her own to part. And once again he slid within, tasting the very depths of her mouth.

Sweet Mary . . . never had she imagined . . .

Meghan could no longer think . . .

He severed the kiss suddenly, startling her with the abrupt departure, and lifted himself to look down into her face, leaving her to stare up at him in a haze of dreamy, bewildered pleasure.

"I want to see you," he murmured. "All of you, Meghan."

In that instant, she forgot to breathe. Her heart hammered against her breast, and she swallowed convulsively. No man had ever seen her unclothed. No man. Not even last evening had he laid eyes upon her, for he'd extinguished the light beforehand. Meghan was suddenly both frightened and exhilarated by the thought of baring herself to his scrutiny . . . beneath the bright-blue heavens, no less.

If she allowed him to undress her, she knew . . . there would be no turning back.

If she let him look upon her . . . and then she looked into his eyes . . . and spied that same adoration there . . . she could not deny him . . .

He hadn't meant to do this so soon.

Hadn't meant to ask.

And then before he could stop himself the words were out of his mouth—and God help him, he was not saint enough to rescind them when she so eagerly drew him down into her arms.

And yet . . . he suddenly needed to know that she wanted this as much as he did.

"Meghan?" he whispered, and watched her face intently.

Her beautiful green eyes were undeniably glazed with passion, but he wished to hear from her own two lips that she wanted him to make her his own.

Never in his life had this simple act of sharing bodies been such a momentous decision.

He brushed his knuckles along her jaw and his heart jolted when she leaned so sweetly into his touch once more, closing her eyes.

"Tell me what you wish," he demanded softly. "Tell me what you want."

"More," she whispered, and that was all Lyon needed to hear. He shuddered with pleasure over the single word, and bent to kiss her mouth once more before sliding down to kiss her belly. And then down further . . . wanting more than anything to taste her once more.

But first things first . . .

For the moment, he passed over the treasure that awaited him, and removed her slippers, set them aside. And then he drew up her skirts

slowly and kissed a thigh, then the other. He
wanted everything off her body this instant,
and were she not injured, he thought he might
have rent the clothes from her flesh, so desperate was he to see her in full.

He drew the dress up, raising her bare bottom to lift it past her hips, and the feel of her
soft flesh within his palm sent fire once more
through his loins. Drawing her up by her good
arm, he raised the gown, kirtle and undergown
both, untangling her sleeve first from her injured arm before lifting it up and over her
head. He tossed the dress aside, his heart hammering against his ribs.

At then at last she was revealed to him fully,
and he found himself dumb with awe. He
sucked in a breath for she was lovelier than he
could ever have imagined.

For the longest instant, Lyon could merely
stare at the creamy flesh he'd uncovered. Her
legs were as long and lean as he'd known they
would be. A vision of her walking with the
baby lamb in the forest, her luscious hair wild
and free, her skirts clinging to her long limbs
came to him, and he blinked, overwhelmed.

And her breasts . . . Christ . . . he craved the
feel of her hardened nipples against his tongue
. . . her soft round flesh against his palm . . . exquisite.

"Meghan," he whispered, "you cannot be
real!"

Meghan's heart quickened at his words.

She lay before him, wholly revealed to his eyes, and the expression upon his face warmed her as the sun never could.

Jesu, but she loved the way he looked at her.

She thrilled at the hunger so evident within his gleaming blue eyes.

And she didn't care just now what it revealed of herself; she wanted only for him to adore her body the way he had last night.

She wanted his lips upon her own ... his hands upon her, caressing ...

He lowered his head once more, all the while watching her with wicked eyes that glittered as with fever, and Meghan lay frozen in anticipation.

What wicked place would his mouth seek now?

What unspeakable things would he do to her?

And then she knew ...

His lips brushed softly against her breasts, the touch delicate and even reverent, and she gasped at the feeling of his tongue caressing her there. She whimpered, closing her eyes, arching for him, and he rewarded her by taking her full into his mouth, suckling like a babe at his mother's breast. The sensation made her quiver with delight, and she discovered some heretofore unknown connection between this place ... and that other ... some sweet thread of pleasure that seemed to uncoil as he suckled

. . . until the thread was a taut ache in her belly
. . . and her hunger undeniable.

She wanted to be his . . . wanted him to have
her . . . wanted him to do anything to her . . .
anything . . . wanted to please him, as well . . .

"Lyon," she whimpered, reaching out and
lacing her fingers into his hair.

Dear God, she couldn't speak . . . couldn't
think for the things his mouth was doing to her
. . . he moved down her belly, kissing her as he
went . . . and Meghan wanted to say that it
wasn't enough. Somewhere deep within her
there was another ache that his mouth couldn't
appease . . . that his lips and tongue were only
heightening. She wanted to tell him but she
didn't know how. Didn't know what she
wanted . . . what she needed.

"Tell me," he whispered. "Tell me what you
want, Meghan."

He stopped long enough for Meghan to
gather her senses. She peered up at him, pant-
ing softly.

"I want to please you," he said.

"I—I want tae see ye, too," she told him,
greedy for the sight of him as well. "Show
me," she commanded him.

His blue eyes glimmered with a fierce satisfaction, and a knowing smile curved his lips.
Meghan held her breath as he began to untie
the plaid at his waist. He slid it off and cast it
aside. And then as she watched, breathless
with anticipation, he drew off his tunic and

cast it aside as well. He stood, then, and removed his boots, and began to unlace his braies. Though modesty would have had her turn away, Meghan refused. She stared, eyes wide with expectation over what would be revealed to her. She lifted her gaze to spy the look of relish in his eyes, and her body quivered in response.

He wanted her to see him.

Wicked man.

Wicked as she.

He stood there a moment; their gazes locked, entwined like lovers, and Meghan gulped in a breath as he drew the braies down at long last and shrugged them off. He cast them, too, aside.

Jesu, but he was beautiful.

He stood before her in all his glory, unashamed.

And then he fell to his knees. And Meghan forgot to breathe as he reached out and took her legs into his hands, positioning her so that he was settled between her thighs once more.

"In the East," he began, his voice husky and low, "a maiden's defloration is done in the presence of both mothers of the wedding couple, with loving care and a gentle finger. Are you a virgin, Meghan?"

Meghan drew in a breath at his bold question. She was and yet why was she not offended at his asking? The look in his eyes held no condemnation, no expectation, but she was suddenly afraid to answer. He must have been with many women—was she doing something wrong?

"It matters not," he swore, seeming to read her thoughts. "I only wish to make this pleasurable for you. I do not wish to cause you pain, Meghan, and there is a way to lessen it."

She nodded almost imperceptibly.

"A virgin?" he asked once more.

Again Meghan nodded, words failing her, her throat too tight to let sound pass.

Her disclosure seemed to please him, because he smiled down at her. "Will you trust me?" he asked, and Meghan nodded once more.

His smile deepened.

"Close your eyes," he commanded her, "and feel, Meghan. Only feel. Can you do that for me?"

"Aye," Meghan answered breathlessly and did as he bade her. She closed her eyes and felt him lift her knees and part her legs to his scrutiny. Her body shivered, suddenly aware of every sensation . . . the gentle breeze upon her flesh . . . the heat of the sun bearing down upon her like a lover's body . . . the moist bed of grass she lay upon.

And then once again his lips were there . . . upon her . . . and she moaned in delight.

God have mercy upon her wicked soul, but she loved him . . . loved his mouth . . . loved the way he adored her . . .

He suckled her and lapped her gently, and then she felt the pressure of his finger, sliding in as he kissed and reassured her. He pushed within suddenly, and Meghan felt only the slightest pain as he severed her maidenhead. She heard him groan, the sound an echo of her own desire, and then he withdrew his finger, and she felt him cover her, felt his hands prepare her, and then once more the pressure.

Only this was not his finger.

He entered her with a single thrust and Meghan gasped at the feel of it—pleasure and pain together, though the pleasure far outweighed the pain. He waited an instant, seeming to know that she needed him to, and then he began to move within her, stroking her in the most delightful way, and Meghan was lost in a whirlwind of sensation.

"Oh, God!" she cried.

He slid a hand beneath her waist, lifting her, and continued to move within her, filling her and withdrawing, and Meghan thought she would die from so much exquisite pleasure. He was slow and purposeful, and seemed to know exactly what to do . . . how to move. Warmth flooded her, and something new kindled within her belly. She focused upon it, feeling it as it grew, following it with all of her heart and her soul. She lifted to each thrust, tilting her hips greedily to take him fully. And then, without warning, something exploded within her, and her body shuddered with sensation unlike any she'd ever known.

She cried out in exultation.

Lyon heard her, felt her convulse about him, and it was what he'd waited for, what he'd craved. He held her hips within his hands and released himself from his careful restraint. His own body convulsed as he thrust a final time, spilling himself for the first time in so damned long. He cast his head back and cried out.

God help him, it felt so right.

So good.

And in that instant of completion, Lyon suddenly found what he'd been looking for all his life.

And it was a feeling unlike any he'd ever imagined.

Soul-deep contentment.

Damned if he hadn't found it in the arms of a woman, after all.

And her name was Meghan Brodie.

Chapter 22

Rolling white clouds feathered the heavens above, swirling across the blue sky like furls of spun silk.

Meghan had never imagined she could feel so free. She could scarcely believe she was lying in the middle of a meadow, fully revealed beneath God's eyes, and relishing every moment.

For the first time in her life, she felt no shame in herself. She lay enfolded within his embrace, feeling his heart beat against her cheek, and felt only exhilaration at the sensation of lying so uninhibited within his arms.

He made her feel this way.

And she couldn't help but smile.

She stirred, lifting her face from his chest, thinking that she should dress, but he pressed a hand to her head, drawing her back to cradle her head against him.

"Stay with me," he urged her.

Meghan wished in that instant that she could

lay there forever, listening to the quickened beat of his heart. She wondered if her own still beat so fast.

"How is the arm?" he asked her, sounding concerned. "Did I hurt you, Meghan?"

"Nay," Meghan assured him. He had done anything but that. In truth, he had been cautious to a fault. It was difficult, having been privy to his written words, because she couldn't help but yearn for the unrestrained passion he had written of in his manuscript. He hadn't been that way with her at all . . . He had been gentle and solicitous instead.

"Good," he said, and lifted her head gently from his chest. "I almost forgot," he told her, "the reason I brought you out here, Meghan."

Meghan had forgotten as well.

"Sit up," he commanded her, and helped her to rise.

Meghan blushed as his gaze slid appreciatively over her body, lingering at her breasts. He curved his lips roguishly.

"What is it?" she asked, returning a demure smile of her own.

"Look about," he commanded her, turning his head from her abruptly. "Do you see naught at all?"

Meghan did as he bade her, and saw nothing more than she had before: a meadow wide and green, resplendent with posies and heather. Colorful and bursting with life . . . except for a small plot of soil that had been freshly turned . . .

She peered up at him, her brows drawing together in bewilderment.

"I hope you do not mind," he said. "Nor was it my wish to make you sad, Meghan."

"I dinna understand."

"I buried Fia here for you."

Meghan blinked in surprise. "Ye did?" She was staggered by the gesture. She hadn't asked about the lamb, only because she hadn't wished to know its fate, had assumed they would use the animal for its meat. Tears sprang to her eyes, though she knew it was foolish. It was naught but a lamb, she told herself. And his gesture . . . She didn't know what to make of it.

He stared at her, seeming to be searching her face for answers. "I . . . I know how much she meant to you," he said. "Aye, and I buried her. I hope you do not mind," he said again, more than a little hesitantly.

Meghan shook her head, discomposed by his confession. She wasn't certain what to think of a man who would bury a lamb, simply because she had claimed it was her grandminnie, despite that he didn't believe her.

Or had he?

Was he so willing to accept the body without the soul? As with Gavin, did her thoughts not matter to him? Her mind not at all?

Well, it didn't matter at this instant, as she

was overwhelmed by his kind gesture. It was the sweetest thing anyone had ever done for her.

Gulping down the knot that rose in her throat, she turned to gaze at the tiny plot of soil, not more than three yards from where they stood. "When?" she asked him, turning to look into his eyes. "When did ye do this?"

"Yesterday," he told her, "when I left you. I came here. I am sorry if it was not the right thing to do, Meghan. I simply thought—"

"Shhh," Meghan commanded him, and lifted her finger to his lips. "Hush, Lyon Montgomerie . . . and kiss me again."

She didn't have to ask twice. He trembled as he drew her into his arms, and lapped the tears from her eyes with the tip of his tongue.

"Be mine," he begged her, and gently covered her mouth with his own.

Meghan's lips parted in helpless surrender, though she refused him an answer.

How could she reply nay when it was already so?

And neither could she yield her heart so completely.

They spent the entire afternoon upon the meadow.

It wasn't until late that Lyon returned Meghan to the hall, bidding her go upstairs and rest before it was time to sup.

Meghan could scarcely protest as she was

weary in a way she'd never been in her life. And her arm hurt terribly, besides.

She didn't wish to, because she didn't like the drowsy way it made her feel, but Lyon had left the vial of *médecine* upon the desk for her, and she was in too much discomfort to care if she supped at all. She was going to go take some of the elixir and lie down upon the bed, for it seemed that every step she climbed toward his chamber left her all the more fatigued.

He had asked to carry her up, but Meghan refused to be coddled in such a way. Her will was as yet her own, and she was perfectly capable of climbing stairs upon her own.

In her weariness, however, she was blind to the figure standing in the shadows of the corridor leading to Lyon's bedchamber.

"Meghan!" came an anxious whisper as she reached for the door.

Startled, Meghan whirled to find the old man Cameron stepping from the shadows toward her.

"Is he comin' after ye?" he asked at once, peering anxiously about.

"Lyon?" she asked him, startled.

"Aye!" he exclaimed.

Meghan frowned at his strange behavior. "Nay, but he didna say where he was off tae," she informed him warily. "If ye're needin' tae speak—"

"Nay," he answered. " 'Tis *ye* I wished tae

speak tae!" He held out a small cloth sack and pressed it into her hands. "This comes tae ye from Alison, lass."

"Alison!" Meghan said, suddenly feeling more alert. "Is Alison here?"

"Nay, lass," he said, "but I met her in the woods. She bade me give ye this, and tae tell ye that it was she who came tae tend ye after the fall."

Confused, Meghan took the sack from his hands. "It was Alison? But they didna tell me!"

He gave her a look of reproach, lifting heavy red brows. "Neither did he tell ye that yer brothers came, did he, while he was oot there wooing ye? I'm sorry but I spied ye together lass."

Meghan's face warmed. "Leith and Colin and Gavin came?"

"Do ye ha' others?" he retorted. "Aye, lass, they came yesterday, but he wouldna let them see ye. In any case, they didna realize it was Alison who came tae tend ye, as she came disguised as an auld hag."

"But how—"

"When they asked me if I knew of a physician, I answered that I knew of a midwife. They sent me oot after her, and I sought oot Alison."

Meghan could scarcely believe that Lyon would fail to mention that her brothers had come to see her. He had to realize she would be concerned for them, and they for her. It didn't make sense to her that he could be so generous about the lamb, and then so ruthlessly deny her brothers and herself.

"Alison has a guid plan," Cameron revealed. "Dinna fash yerself, lass, we'll get ye home tae yer brothers soon enough."

Meghan was confused. How could he make love to her so sweetly, say such warmhearted things . . . and then keep something of this nature from her?

She shook herself free of her thoughts, of the memory of his touch, forcing herself to consider her brothers. "What sort o' plan?" she asked.

"The sort that should work, I think," he said, and bent to whisper it quickly into her ear.

Chapter 23

Staring at the manuscripts that were spread before her, the small vial of *médecine* clutched within her fist, Meghan sat transfixed at the little bedside desk.

It was, in fact, an ingenious plan.

If she had ever wondered about Alison's shrewdness, and which of them had the keener mind—and she had not, she had always known Alison was the more clever of the two—she certainly didn't wonder now.

Meghan could never have conceived such a cunning scheme on the spur of the moment. As Cameron relayed it to her, she was to use the potion primarily for the pain, and the pouch of face powders and colors to validate the outlandish tale Alison had woven for Lyon's benefit. She was to disfigure her face, make herself as unappealing as possible with the powders, until he no longer recognized her so well, so that when Alison came to replace her, he'd not suspect the two of them were different women.

With their hair and eye color so similar, and her own face covered with a veil, along with the doubts placed within his head by Alison's shrewd tale, Lyon was certain to believe it.

Aye, it was a perfect plan.

Even if it failed, Meghan had every faith Lyon would simply let Alison go, as he wasn't a cruel man. The worst that could happen would be that they would be discovered and they would have gained naught by it.

Meghan would remain with Lyon, and Alison would be sent home to her father with a scolding.

Not so terrible a thought to remain with him, if the truth be known.

And if it worked . . . Well, then . . . with Cameron's help, she would be home with her brothers soon enough. And when Meghan was safely away, Alison would simply remove her disguise and slip away with no one the wiser.

The question was . . . did Meghan truly wish to leave?

She considered that a long and anguished moment and decided that it didn't matter what she wanted. She owed it to her brothers to go to them. And if Lyon respected her enough to court her properly, then Meghan was certainly willing. No matter whether he held her heart or not, this was not the right way to go about it, she knew. Her brothers would never accept him this way, and she loved them all too much to choose between them. If Lyon wanted her

truly, if he cared for her, if he loved her—aye,
she dared to hope—then he would want her to
come to him of her own free will.

As for the deception . . .

She set the vial of *médecine* down upon the
desk.

If Lyon wanted her for more than her body,
well then, this was the way to discover that,
too, and Meghan refused to feel guilty for simply trying to find her way home.

And less so for attempting to learn the truth
about the man who would have her heart.

With that decided, she opened up the little
pouch, tugging the ribbon loose with her teeth,
cursing her bad hand that she could not do this
properly. That done, she set the pouch down
upon the desk and removed a few items from
it—a small piece of looking glass, a tiny box
secured with ribbon, and a little bottle filled
with a substance that appeared to be fine-
ground meal.

To begin with, these would be enough.

Casting a glance first at the door, she struggled with opening the small bottle, popping
the cork with her teeth at last. She poured a
small amount of the flour upon the desk. Keeping her attention upon the door, she powdered
her hand and then her face, making certain to
blend it well. That done, she lifted up the small
box and, with her teeth once more, she untied
the ribbon that held the lid secure. She set it
down then and lifted the tiny lid to find a sub-

stance like black ash within. She lay the mirror flat upon the desk, and dipped in a finger, bringing it to her eye, giving herself ghastly circles beneath. She was generous with the ash, but blended it well, and when she was through, she looked more like the living dead than a living, breathing being.

Scrunching her nose at the sight of herself in the distorted little glass, Meghan inspected her handiwork with a critical eye. Then she dipped her finger within the ash once more and added it to the powder upon her face, blending it well, and then dabbed on more powder to soften the effect.

When she was finished, the sight of herself within the tiny mirror was enough to make her grimace in disgust.

Deciding she had used more than enough for the first time, she re-covered the box, blew the remaining powder from the desktop, replaced the stopper within the bottle, and then placed the items once more within the small pouch. With her injured arm it was impossible to bind the box again, and so she did not even attempt it. She lifted the pouch carefully, so as not to spill anything, and then bent to place it carefully beneath the bed. When it was still visible from where she sat, she went to her knees upon the floor to better push it out of sight. No sooner had she done so when the door burst open.

Startled, Meghan sprang up at once, smacking her cheek against the corner of the desk in the process. "Ouch!" she cried, and bounded back up into the chair. Jesu, but she was determined to kill herself in this place!

"Meghan?" Lyon said as though he didn't recognize her. His brows drew together as he stared.

Meghan tried to appear unaware of his careful scrutiny. "Aye?" she answered, clearing her throat.

"Are . . . are you well?"

"Certainly!" she said brightly, and cast a glance down at the little desk to be certain the telltale powder was gone. She brushed away the last remaining traces and lifted her gaze to the door where he stood. "Why should I no' be?" she asked, and then for good measure, lifted the vial of *médecine* within her hand to show him. She held her breath as he entered the room, closing the door behind him. He faltered in his stride as he approached her, and was frowning still as he sat upon the bed beside the small desk, scrutinizing her.

She lifted the vial once more and said a little nervously, "I—I thought I'd broken it."

He didn't seem to hear her. And he wouldn't stop staring. Meghan's heart thundered in apprehension.

Had she not blended the powders well enough? Was it so obvious what she had done? Did he think her hideous now? And would it matter to him if he thought her less than lovely?

He reached out and fingered the air before her face, almost as though he were afraid to touch her, and Meghan held her breath.

"Christ and bedamned!" he cursed softly.

"What is it?"

He had only just left her.

How could this be?

Lyon's gaze fell to the small vial Meghan held within her hand, and then he lifted his eyes once more to her face, scarcely able to believe the changes that had come over her in so swift a time.

"You have a welt upon your cheek," he told her, forcing himself to touch her at last, uncertain what else to say.

"Oh," she answered, lifting her hand to the flesh that was even now beginning to bruise, "that! I bumped my face upon the desk when I bent tae retrieve the vial."

"I see that," Lyon replied.

God's bloody teeth, it appeared she'd bruised the rest of her face as well!

In fact, she looked much like she'd been beaten to death, buried, and then exhumed. He wanted to ask about the rest of her face, not merely the bruise, but didn't dare. He wanted to ask if it hurt, but couldn't find the words to speak.

His gaze returned to the vial she held.

"You ... uh ... took your *médecine*?" he

asked her, swallowing the knot that rose in his throat, knowing she must have.

It was all his fault.

He had done this to her.

"Aye," she answered, smiling, her eyes even now beginning to glaze over with that bleary-eyed stare the *médecine* seemed to give her—her gaze slightly askew, slightly unfocused.

He reached out to take the vial from her. "I do not think you need that any longer," he said, but she jerked her hand away, placing the vial behind her back, out of his reach.

"Aye," she asserted crossly, "I do!"

"Why?" he demanded, scowling at her.

"It lessens the pain in my arm," she told him. "Is that no' what ye gave it tae me for?" She tilted her head, gazing at him as though to read him.

Lyon had no answer.

Christ.

She turned from him, and he continued to stare at her profile, aghast. And yet, even with her complexion so deteriorated, there was a loveliness to her features that could not be diminished. She reminded him of the *bean sidhe*— the sort of apparition who haunted a man by night, who stood within the shadows of the forest and wailed for his soul.

"I was reading," he heard her say.

Lyon blinked. "My manuscripts?"

"Aye," she answered softly.

He tried to focus upon her words and not

her appearance, but seemed to be failing miserably. What in God's name had he done to her? "And what conclusions have you drawn?" he asked her absently, trying to sound casual.

"Only that these essays ha' a single theme among them."

Her appearance forgotten for the instant in his curiosity, he lifted a brow. "And what might that be?"

"The pursuit o' happiness."

Lyon was struck with wonder at her conclusion. It was, in fact, the driving theme behind his efforts. All of his essays, though disguised behind a thousand other questions, amounted to little more than a simple quest for contentment—that was all. Though he understood what drove him, the answers eluded him still. In her arms he had come closest to experiencing that elusive fulfillment of the soul. And yet . . . now that it was done . . . and he sat before her . . . he felt content no longer.

He felt only discomposed.

Which drove him to wonder . . . was he truly so frivolous that he could love only beauty? Was he so shallow that only beauty could appease him? From past experience, he understood only too well how fleeting that form of pleasure was.

But there was no denying the way he felt this instant as he sat before her.

Confused.

Troubled.

Unfulfilled.

The feeling had begun the instant he'd left her late this afternoon and had spoken to Baldwin, for her brothers had returned once again, demanding to see her. Baldwin had sent them away, per Lyon's instructions, and truth to tell Lyon was beginning to feel like the villain in some satyric play.

She peered up at him, and he focused upon her lovely eyes. The torch flame flared in the silence that fell between them. Its light flickered against her face, flashed within her eyes. He grimaced, for it gave them a slightly demonic gleam.

"What else?" he asked her, glancing away. "What else have you found?"

"That ye are still searching."

She brought her hand from her back and set the vial down upon the desk between them, luring his gaze to it. Lyon resisted the urge to seize it and smash it against the bloody wall, lest it damage her further. He let it be, however, respecting her wishes, though he wanted more than anything to warn her what it was doing to her. And yet, to tell her such a thing he would need to reveal the true reason he had given her the potion to begin with, and the old woman's warning, as well. And how could he say such a thing to her? That he'd thought her insane and meant to cure her? He was certain she would appreciate that just as well!

His lips twisted in self-disgust.

What was he doing to her? Greedy bastard, he was.

"Am I?" he asked her. "Still searching, Meghan?"

She nodded, her eyes fixed upon his face.

"And do you know where I might find it? This happiness." As he sure as hell did not.

"Nay," she answered, and then added, "But I knoo where ye lost it, Piers Montgomerie." It was the first time she'd ever used his given name, and he might have savored the sound of it upon her lips, but sensed a point to her use of it.

Lyon lifted a brow. "You know where I lost it?" he asked her. How could she possibly, when he'd never possessed it at all? He studied her face. What was it she had gleaned from his words? "And where is that, Meghan Brodie?"

She shook her head, and answered simply, "That ye must discern for yerself!" She gazed at him sadly, and in that instant, Lyon knew that she truly did know. How was it that he had searched all these many years, poring over his books, studying them meticulously, and this woman sitting before him could read his manuscripts and discover, in the span of mere days, what he had been searching for?

Was it the potion, he wondered, that gave her such insight? God's bloody truth, perhaps he should take it himself!

"If I tell ye," she continued, shaking her

head, " 'twill be naught more than words tae
ye."

His jaw tautened as he nodded, understanding. Averting his gaze from her face to her
hand once more, he noted it was stained black.
Reaching out to pluck it up, he inspected it
closely. Gasping softly, she jerked it back from
his scrutiny.

"I smeared ink upon myself!" she said,
seeming embarrassed by his study of her hand.
"I hope ye dinna mind, but I scribbled a bit
upon yer papers."

Had she? In his curiosity, he reached to lift
up the manuscript.

Her eyes widened in alarm. "Nay!" she exclaimed. "Dinna!" And she stayed his hand.

He drew his brows together in confusion.

"Later," she begged him, and he was acutely
aware of the delicate way her hand lay upon
his own.

The beat of his heart quickened at the
warmth of her touch.

"Why?" he demanded.

"Because!"

"Because why?" he persisted, and his gaze
was at once drawn to her mouth. Perfectly
formed. Sweet lips that were made for kissing . . .

He could scarcely help but recall the way
they had trembled so sweetly beneath his own.

"Because," she answered, and seemed to
note the direction of his gaze . . . the turn of his

thoughts . . . for her breath caught as he stared. Her tongue darted out to moisten lips gone dry, and they seemed to pinken before his very eyes.

He wanted to feel those lips upon his flesh . . . suckling . . . wanted to know what they felt like wrapped about him in the most intimate way . . .

His heart thundered within his chest.

"Do you not realize," he told her, "what those lips of yours do to a man, Meghan Brodie?"

She didn't respond, merely stared at his own mouth, her breasts lifting with her inhaled breath. Her fingers curled about his hand, and the feel of them made him swallow the knot that formed in his throat.

Warmth spread through his loins, hardening him fully.

Need clawed at him, and he felt a surge of satisfaction in the return of his body's fierce hunger.

"Nay," she answered at last, lifting her chin slightly. "But ye told me once that I would ask . . . Show me," she bade him, her eyes flashing with invitation.

His heart hammering, Lyon stood before her, holding her gaze, his body taut with anticipation as he lifted her hand to the laces of his braies.

Chapter 24

The next morning, the vial was missing from the little desk.

Meghan didn't bother to search for it, since she knew where it had gone. There was little doubt in her mind that Lyon had confiscated it from her. It didn't matter; her arm was better and she could continue the scheme without the potion. She had her powders and that was all that was needed.

She painted her face the instant she awoke, taking the pouch from its hiding place beneath Lyon's bed only long enough to make use of its contents before putting it back. This time, however, rather than simply using the powders Alison had sent, she pulled out the wimple and veil as well; using the little mirror once more, she fastened the headdress as best she was able. She knew he would wonder where she had procured it, but she would simply tell him that she had borrowed it. If he pressed her for a name, she would tell him the first that came to mind. He couldn't possibly remember the name of every one of the wives who had remained upon his land.

When she was done, she sat once more at the little desk, and opened his manuscripts to read . . .

And to wait . . .

There must be a way to reverse the effect of the potion, Lyon had determined. He'd sought out Cameron at first light and sent out a handful of his men to find the midwife who'd tended Meghan.

Cameron, the daft old fool, however, seemed to be leading them upon a merry chase. Either the old man was truly decrepit, or he was purposely keeping them from the old witch. He had quite conveniently forgotten her name, it seemed, though he had remembered it easily enough, he recalled, the night of Meghan's accident. Neither had it seemed he'd had much trouble locating the woman that evening, for she'd come to Meghan quickly enough. And yet now he could scarcely remember the direction of her woodland hut.

Lyon couldn't imagine why he might contrive to keep the old witch from him.

Neither could he help but wonder what Meghan was doing, as he'd left her within his bed looking a bit like a cadaver with her sunken eyes and bruised face. He hadn't dared even to touch her, much less wake her, as she was sleeping so peacefully thanks to the rotten *médecine* she had ingested.

He reined in his mount, growing impatient with the search, and fell back to ride beside Cameron. "Tell me once more, old man. Was this hut upon my own land? Or does it sit upon someone else's?"

Cameron screwed up his face, as though to consider the question, and then peered up at the sun, as though to gauge it. He shook his head. "I dunno," he answered after a moment.

Lyon gritted his teeth to keep from howling in frustration. "Why bloody not?" he demanded. They had long since ridden from any woodlands and now were well into the moorlands. The terrain was hillier here and generously marked with chiseled stones.

The old man shook his head. "I dunno," he said.

Lyon cursed beneath his breath and spurred his mount to where Baldwin rode beside yet another bloody Scotsman he'd managed to inherit. Only this lad was younger and seemed more eager to please.

"Duncan," he called out tersely. "Have you any bloody notion where it is we are, lad?"

Duncan peered about, then turned to him, and nodded. "MacKinnon land," he announced without doubt.

Lyon eyed him incredulously. "MacKinnon! Have we ridden so far?"

"Aye, my laird," Duncan replied.

Christ, but that was all he needed—to deal with Iain MacKinnon just now. He swore an oath beneath his breath, and decided that he was desperate enough to pay MacKinnon a visit anyway. Cameron had been leading them all afternoon to no avail, and they hadn't gotten anywhere but lost.

"Do you know where lies his manor?" Lyon asked Duncan. "Is it near?"

Duncan nodded, and pointed toward a gently sloping, heathered hill in the distance. "Chreagach Mhor," he disclosed. "Over the rise, upon the cliff."

"Lead me there," Lyon commanded the lad.

The youth protested, saying, "But we are only four!"

Lyon narrowed his gaze at the boy. "Do you tell me that MacKinnon will not greet us evenhandedly?"

"Nay, but—"

"Because that is not what I have heard," Lyon assured him. "I understand his position here in these Highlands," he said, "but I have heard that he deals fairly with his neighbors, and what am I but his neighbor?"

"Aye," Duncan agreed. "But ye dinna understand, laird."

"I understand quite well," Lyon said. "You think he will greet me with his blade simply because my blood is English?"

Duncan shook his head. " 'Tis no' his way, no, but ye dinna knoo that his son was stolen

by King David and given to an English laird as
ward. MacKinnon has only just noo returned
from retrieving the boy. He canna be pleased,
and I dinna wish tae face him if he is angry."

"So David has told me," Lyon countered, angered, "and yet MacKinnon has already faced
David squarely. I cannot see that he would accord me any less courtesy when I come in the
name of peace."

"Lyon . . . are you certain you wish to?"
Baldwin asked, frowning.

Lyon was unused to having his authority
questioned.

"I am certain I wish to," he said, his tone
clipped. "Christ, if any of you are man enough
to follow, then do so. If not, then take your
bloody arses back to the manor, pack your belongings, and get the hell out of my sight, as I
do not want or need craven men in my company!" he told them, and then spurred his
mount toward the hillock, leaving them to follow or not at their own discretion.

If they chose not to, however, they had
damned well better not be waiting for him
upon his return!

As well as Lyon knew David, he was surprised to find that his friend had returned to
see Iain MacKinnon. He was not so surprised
when he learned why.

It seemed the MacKinnon was getting married—wedding his English love.

Lyon nearly interrupted the ceremony and was glad he had calmed himself before riding in. As it was, Iain MacKinnon was well aware of his presence, but he seemed to realize at once that Lyon's visit was not one of ill bodings. MacKinnon eyed him, nodded to acknowledge him, but dismissed him as he returned his attention to his bride and exchanged with her his vows. Spotting David within the crowd, Lyon joined him and watched the couple.

"I did not realize," Lyon said, "that I would be intruding."

David turned to him, looking surprised. "Lyon! Neither did I, until the messenger came to invite the Brodies. They, of course, did not come, but I thought it prudent to pay my respects."

Lyon smiled. "Quite benificent of you," he said. "And did he receive you well?"

"Cordially," was David's response. "Cordially, but the wily bastard does not show his appreciation so well. If he found my presence an honor, he has yet to reveal it." Despite his words, he chuckled. "You have to admire a man who will not be cowed. Damn the rotten bastard!"

Lyon chuckled softly.

"It is also what I like about you, Lyon." David smiled at him. "From that day so long ago when we were both naught more than whelps."

Lyon shook his head at the memory, then turned his attention to the wedding couple. The ceremony was over and they were locked within an embrace.

"You were never a man to act against himself," David added.

Lyon looked at his friend and liege in surprise. David couldn't know him that well if he thought so, but Lyon said nothing.

"I am honored, Piers, to have you at my back."

Lyon nodded his thanks. "It is my pleasure to do so," he told David.

"And more," David added, "as my friend. I count myself a fortunate man."

Lyon didn't know what to say. Instead he gazed at the MacKinnon and his bride. "Thank you," he said finally, uncomfortably.

David seemed to understand for he changed the subject at once. "She's a lovely little thing, is she not?"

"That she is," Lyon agreed. "Who is she?"

"Page FitzSimon," David said. "Her father is the man to whom I entrusted Iain's son as ward until Henry could take him, as he was both mine and Henry's vassal." He too watched the couple; they were both smiling and basking in the adoration of their people. "It seems there is no reason to regret my actions, is there? All is well that ends well. Have you ever seen two people more in love?"

Lyon considered that question, and had to ask himself, *What is love?*

What did he feel for Meghan?

Certainly he thought of her every moment of every day—wanted to be with her every instant he could. The very image of her made his heart beat a little faster, and the thought of spending the rest of his life with her made him smile.

And she was bright. The simple fact that she could read had amazed him. She'd read his papers with an open mind, without condemning him for his thoughts—not once had she thrown his words back into his face. Nay, she'd read them with an open heart as well.

And then she had given him everything.

He wanted to take care of her for the rest of her life. He wanted to wake up with her upon a morn and look into her beautiful eyes. He wanted to make love with her, and to laugh with her, and to show her things, to see her suckling his babe at her breast, to see her hold him to her and look down upon him with loving eyes. And he wanted to suckle those breasts, as well, for the rest of his days. He wanted to wake up and lazily draw her into his arms, set his mouth against her bosom and nuzzle gently.

When he thought of her, he felt both a flutter in his heart, as though it sprouted wings to fly, and a glorious warmth that cocooned him unlike anything else he'd known in his life.

For the first time ever, he felt a communion of spirit with another living soul.

So then, was that love?

If so, then he damned well loved Meghan Brodie!

And he wanted to have with her what he saw in the couple making their way through the celebrating crowd. Shouts and laughter surrounded them.

Now MacKinnon and his bride were coming toward him. MacKinnon grabbed his wife by the arm, dragging her after him, and, laughing, she followed.

"If ye return in peace, then welcome!" Iain MacKinnon said to David, eyeing Lyon cautiously.

"That I do!" David assured him. "I came to see with my own eyes that Page FitzSimon is content." He nodded at Page, and she smiled and blushed prettily.

"I am," she told David, and her smile deepened as she tilted a loving glance to her new husband.

Lyon felt a pang of envy at the sight of them together.

So happy.

"Your father will not trouble you here, lass," David swore. "Be well, and be happy!"

"I shall be very well," she answered shyly, and once again smiled up at her husband.

The two of them shared a secret look together—one that was warm and unmistakably hungry, and Lyon's body tensed at the thought of Meghan looking at him in such a way.

A grin spread across Iain MacKinnon's face. He turned to David abruptly, tearing his gaze away from his bride, though clearly with reluctance. "And sae I ha' yer backing in this?" he asked David. "If FitzSimon returns I can be sure tae knoo where ye stand?"

David nodded. "You may at that, MacKinnon. And I can see very well that your bride is happy."

Page blushed even more fiercely, then looked at Lyon, meeting his gaze.

Lyon smiled down at her, thinking her blush as sweet as her smile. He added his own felicitations, and then said, "And you may count upon me as well, as David's position is mine, too."

Iain thrust out a hand in welcome. "Iain MacKinnon, as ye knoo."

"Piers Montgomerie," Lyon said, grasping the other's hand.

"Aye, then!" MacKinnon declared, grinning. "I knew that! Make yerselves welcome!" He turned to Page. "Gentlemen, my wife has made me a verra happy mon!" And then he turned to David and thrust out his hand once more. David grasped it, and MacKinnon said, "We begin anew. While I cannat be happy for the matter o' my son, I ha' gained so much more."

" 'Tis good to know," David said, nodding.

MacKinnon turned to Lyon and smacked

him companionably upon the shoulder. "Eat! Drink! Make merry wi' me and my bride!"

"Da! Da!" came a little voice below. Lyon peered down in time to see a child scurry between his legs.

"Get yerself up from yer knees, Malcom!" Iain demanded of the boy.

"Aye, but Merry is swillin' the ale from the vats as fast as Glenna pours them an' she is gettin' mad, mad, mad!"

Lyon chuckled.

His father did as well. "Is she noo? Well then, ye gae and tell her I am on my way, and find Brock and tell him tae fetch his bluidy dog!"

"I shall go!" Page offered, and made to leave. He dragged her back against him, embracing her.

"Nay," he replied, "ye are comin' wi' me!" He lifted her up into his arms, unconcerned by the presence of their guests.

"All right, Da!" the boy said to his oblivious father, and bolted away.

Page was squealing and laughing. "Jesu, but you *are* a savage Scot!" she declared, and Iain MacKinnon merely chuckled at her accusation.

"Sae ye ha' said, wife!" he told her and kissed her swiftly upon the lips. He started to carry her away, stopping only to turn toward Lyon and David once more. "Stay," he invited them, "and we shall share a toast together for my bride once I've salvaged the ale from that damned greedy dog!"

David laughed, and so too did Lyon.

"We shall," said David. "And we thank you for your hospitality, Iain MacKinnon."

"Aye, well," Iain responded, grinning almost stupidly with his joy, "ye caught me on a guid day, I suppose." And he winked at them and turned away, bearing his giggling wife with him.

Their laughter trailed after them as they disappeared into the crowd.

Meghan had fallen asleep waiting.

She awoke to a dark room: no torchlight, no taper, only the light from the hole in the roof to orient her.

"Meghan!" came a whisper, and she lifted her head from her arm to peer groggily through the shadows, wondering if she were dreaming yet, so confused was she from the *drogue* still coursing within her body.

"Meghan!"

Her eyes focused upon the door, where it seemed the sound emanated.

The door was closed, and she could make out the figure of someone standing before it, arms outstretched as though to bar it.

"Where are ye, Meghan?" the voice said a bit in panic.

She recognized the voice suddenly and bounded up from the chair. "Alison!" she exclaimed. "Here!" Stumbling over herself in her sleepy state, Meghan made her way around the bed. Alison spied her at last and came rushing to her.

"How is yer arm?" Alison asked at once. "And how do ye feel? Did Cameron give ye my message?"

"Weel enough," Meghan assured her. "And I am tired, but weel. Aye, Alison, he did!"

"I had tae set the arm, but ye would ha' been proud o' me, Meghan!" she rushed on to say. "I didna even wince when the bone snapped intae place!"

"I *am* proud o' ye!" Meghan said, and she was certainly. She had been from the instant Cameron had revealed to her what Alison had done. Her dear friend had been brave even to show her face here in Lyon's home. "How did ye get in tonight?" she asked. "And where is Lyon?"

"He's yet tae return," Alison replied hurriedly. "But we must hurry, as I've little notion how much time we ha' before he does. Cameron's wife," she revealed to Meghan. "She let me in. Cameron was supposed tae sneak me in, though he's no' returned as yet either. Iona led me in, instead. She awaits ye in the corridor, even noo, and will take ye tae her brother Angus who will see ye home."

"And what o' ye?" Meghan asked her, suddenly disinclined to go.

"Dinna ye worry aboot me!" Alison assured

her, and reached out to remove the wimple and veil from Meghan's head.

"Ouch!" Meghan cried. "I shall get that! Ye take the sling from my arm, instead!"

Together they worked under cover of darkness, removing veils and exchanging clothing, dressing quickly.

"Oh! and I ha' a bruise upon my cheek," Meghan told her. "Dinna forget tae blacken it well!"

"Never ye mind!" Alison said as she slipped the sling about her arm. "I will! But what shall ye do aboot yer arm," she fretted, "if I am tae wear this?"

"Dinna fash yerself over it," Meghan told her. "My arm will be fine in the short time whilst I find my way home. Oh! The pouch ye sent me is under the bed," she added.

"I came wi' my face already painted," Alison disclosed. "But aye, I will find it as soon as ye gae, and color a bruise upon my cheek at once!"

"Och, Alison!" Meghan said, and peered at her friend through the darkness. "Are ye certain ye wish tae do this?" And she held her breath, part of her hoping the answer would be nay.

"I am sure and certain!" Alison replied. "And now ye'll do me the favor o' hurrying home!" She led Meghan to the door, and opened it without ceremony. "Iona?" she called out.

"I am here!" the woman answered from the corridor. "Hurry noo!"

"Gae," Alison directed Meghan.

Meghan's feet would not move.

She forced herself to walk into the corridor. "Alison," she began, "I dunno . . ."

"Come noo!" Iona commanded her. "We haven't time for farewells!"

"I shall be fine, Meghan!" Alison swore, but she didn't understand! Meghan didn't want to go!

Iona dragged Meghan away, clutching her by her good arm, and led her away down the stairs perforce.

"Do me one favor," Alison called softly after them.

"Anything!" Meghan exclaimed and halted, shrugging free of Iona's grip and turning back up the stairs. "I knew this would frighten ye," she told Alison. "Ye dinna ha' tae do this!"

"I want tae!" Alison asserted. "I simply want ye tae tell yer brother that no' only do I wed him, but I wed him wi' all my heart."

"Colin?" Meghan said in surprise. "You mean Colin?"

"Nay, Meghan Brodie," Alison corrected her. "Leith. Gae and carry him my message, noo, and tell him tae please tell my da where I am."

Meghan stood there upon the steps in stunned disbelief.

"Leith?"

"Aye," Alison answered, and Meghan could spy her brilliant smile even in the darkness.

And this time when Iona dragged her away, she was entirely too dumbfounded to protest.

Chapter 25

Weary to his bones, Lyon climbed the
stairs to his bedchamber, eager to see
Meghan, yet anxious to discover whether she
had worsened during his absence.

While he'd taken the potion from her this
morn, there was no guarantee that what she
had ingested already would not cause further
damage, for she'd been consuming it for days
now.

He only hoped he was not too late.

He'd not found the old witch, and neither
had MacKinnon or any of his kinfolk ever
heard of her. Glenna, of MacKinnon's own
clan, was the only midwife his people knew. It
was as though, given the old witch's sudden
appearance and disappearance that eve, she
was formed of mist and to mist she had returned. They had encountered no woodland
hut, and there was not even a name he had to
go by to search for her.

Carrying a taper before him to light the way,

he entered his chamber, quietly lest he should wake her if she slept. At this late hour, it was entirely likely that she did.

He spied her lithe form upon the bed and went to the bedside, impatient to see her, but she was lying upon her belly, as she was so oft inclined to sleep, and her face was hidden from his view. He couldn't help but note, however, that she was wearing a wimple, and his heart sank to see it. He had not told her of the changes that had come over her face, and so she must have discovered them for herself.

His heart ached for her.

He wondered how she'd learned, and wished he could have been there with her to ease her distress. He should have told her himself, by damn, but he was a craven bastard— and he'd dared to accuse his own men of such a thing!

God's teeth, it was a simple matter to face the enemy with a blade in his hand, but another entirely to look Meghan in the eyes and face his own truth—that he was a greedy bastard who would stop at little to have his own way. He'd fought his battles for his own personal gain—for mere gold, he'd thought, would buy contentment.

But gold, he'd discovered all too soon, was a cold bedfellow.

Disgusted with himself, he turned away from Meghan's sleeping form, and made his way about the bed to the little desk. Setting the

candle down upon it, he sat within his chair to
contemplate the day.

He'd ridden into MacKinnon's home only to
find every damned thing he'd ever wanted
staring him in the face.

Far from discovering a man in mourning or
bitter in his ale, he'd interrupted a wedding
celebration of the sort he could hardly imagine
sharing with Meghan.

Nay, if he were to wed Meghan now, it
would be perforce, and what satisfaction was
he going to gain from that?

Did he truly want her, even unwilling?

Or did he want her smiling beauteously . . .
as MacKinnon's bride had done with him . . .
with such adoration in her eyes to make a
grown man weep.

Lyon had paid his respects and drank a toast
to the new bride and groom, and another, and
another, and all the while his heart had been
heavy with guilt for the woman he had locked
away within his chamber.

He had stolen Meghan and brought her
home perforce—as though she were some
beast without a will of its own.

What honor was there in that?

And he had turned her brothers away when
they had come to see only that she was well.
All they had asked of him was simply to set
eyes upon the sister they adored.

And Lyon had refused them.

Why?

Because he was afraid she would leave him.

He'd heard tell, time and again, at Mac-Kinnon's wedding, how Iain MacKinnon had set out to mend his wife's broken wings, shielding her all along from the knowledge that her father had repudiated her—and then had been willing to let her go when her father had come after her at last. Knowing how much it had meant to her, he had given her a choice. He loved her enough to set her free.

It was a heroic tale, and despite that he and MacKinnon were destined to have differences between them, Lyon had to respect the man for his integrity.

He had much to learn from the man, in truth.

His gaze fell to the manuscript upon his desk, and he flipped absently through the pages, considering his options.

Meghan's neat script caught his immediate attention and he began to read her entries one by one. Her first observation was within the first essay, written cleanly beside the paragraph where he'd first bespoken his love of akadémeia. Beside where he had so carefully explained his reasons for abandoning it—his rationalizations and justifications—was written merely *First instance*.

He lifted a brow.

What that meant, he didn't know.

Drawing the taper closer, he turned the page, reading the places where she had marked *Second instance* and *Third*.

All of them were times in his life when he had expressed some regret, some departure from his convictions.

Turning the pages he found many more, and read them all. Dozens of them! One after another.

He was beginning to see the point.

On the last page, he found her final observation. In her careful script was written: *What profited a man if he shall gain the whole world and lose his own soul?*

He looked up, staring, his heart pounding, at the sight of the woman lying so serenely within his bed.

She was incredible.

Through her eyes, he saw everything so clearly now.

She was bloody brilliant, and he was an arse and an imbecile!

The answer was so obvious, and yet like a blind man he had not seen it when it had been there before his very eyes all along!

All his life, he had been *searching* for something beyond himself when he should have simply *returned* to that place within himself he had abandoned so long ago.

He wasn't going to *find* contentment.

It had been there all along for the taking, and he had simply to accept it. Every time he had compromised himself—every instance he had gone against his own convictions—had taken him yet another turn down a long and winding road toward discontent. And the further down the road he had traveled, the harder he had searched, even going so far as to put his words upon paper to study and mull over. His manuscript had been at times naught more than a journal he'd kept simply to remind himself of every turn he'd made in the proverbial road—because at times it seemed he'd taken so many, he no longer recalled which he'd traveled and which he had not. He had grasped at every prospect for gratification, and explored every inclination in search of it.

And he had ended up empty-handed.

Until now.

Rising from the desk, he abandoned the manuscript and went to sit upon the bed, swallowing hard at what he knew he must do.

And he had to do it now, before he changed his mind.

Because he could not.

This woman was a gift.

His gift.

Lyon no longer knew for certain if there was a God, but if there was, he had seen fit to favor him with this last chance to save himself.

He felt it way down deep in his bones.

In forcing her to wed with him, in keeping her from her brothers, he compromised himself one last time.

And if he forced her to wed with him, she'd suffer the consequences as well as he.

And he would watch her suffer, and slowly die.

He couldn't bear that.

He reached out, wanting to run his fingers through her beautiful hair, but didn't dare. They hovered above her head, as though to caress her, but he was afraid to touch her yet.

He could see her ... see himself years from now ... if he forced her ... She would resent him. And her brothers would too. And by virtue of the fact that he would be her husband, he would be forcing her to choose between them.

He couldn't do it.

Now was the time to let her go.

Now before he planted his child within her belly.

Now before she no longer had a choice.

If she would choose him ... it would have to be of her own free will.

Aye, Meghan Brodie was his gift all right.

And now he was going to give her one in return: her freedom of choice.

He laid his hand upon her head. "Meghan," he whispered and shook her gently. "Meghan!"

She turned to look up at him, sleepily, and his heart jolted.

He had to blink at what he saw.

Christ, though her face was covered with a wimple, he no longer recognized it entirely. Aye, the hair and eyes were the same, but her beautiful eyes crossed as she peered up at him. She didn't seem able to focus, or mayhap it was his imagination, a trick of the candlelight, as he seemed to recall her bruise being upon the other cheek, as well. The swelling had diminished but the bruise had darkened, and the bruises upon the rest of her face had darkened, as well.

He stared at her face, incredulous at the changes that had come over her, disgusted with himself for the way it repelled him.

It was his fault, he reminded himself.

His fault!

"Meghan?" he whispered, his voice uncertain and shaky.

"Aye," she answered softly, almost too softly to be heard, and he shook his head.

"I . . . I . . ." But he could scarcely find his voice to speak. How could he send her away after what he'd done to her?

And then again, how could he not offer her her freedom?

She had the right to live her own life.

"I . . . I've come to a decision," he managed at last.

She cocked her head up at him, looking confused, and Lyon's brow furrowed at the skewed way in which she looked at him. His stomach turned.

"I . . . I've decided to send you home."

Her eyes widened incredulously. "Ye ha'!"

"Aye! But get up! You have to go *now*," he

told her firmly. "This instant, before I change my mind." And he bounded from the bed, intending to fetch Baldwin before he could chance to settle in to sleep. He couldn't take her himself, couldn't look upon her any longer, couldn't look into her eyes, filled as he was with shame.

Never had a walk home through the forest felt so depressive—nay, for this had been Meghan's and Fia's place.

And now, more than ever, she wished Fia were here to keep her company rather than stone-faced Angus. The man had spoken nary a word since they'd left Lyon's manor, and the silence was beginning to grate upon Meghan's nerves.

Neither did she know what she was going to say to her brothers when she faced them once more.

Och, not only had she given her body to their enemy, but she'd given her heart as well!

God's truth, with every step she took, every twig she snapped beneath her feet, even knowing that leaving was the right thing to do, she wanted to turn about and fly back to him.

Was he home yet?

And was he lying now within the bed with a horrified Alison?

Meghan knew how much Alison disliked him. She could scarcely believe her friend was doing this for her, scarcely believe how diffi-

cult it was to take each and every step away
from Montgomerie land. To think, only a short
time ago, she had gone kicking and screeching
in the opposite direction.

So much had happened since then.

It was as though it were a lifetime had
passed since, and Meghan only wanted to lie
once more within Lyon Montgomerie's arms.

There were so many things she hadn't said
to him—she wanted him to know that he was
not so bad, in truth, as he thought himself,
wanted him to know that she admired the way
he had been so brutally honest within his papers.

She wanted him to know . . .

That she was in love with him.

That he had, indeed, managed to steal her
heart.

She wanted him to know that for the first
time in her life she didn't look at herself in the
mirror and loathe the woman she saw. She
wanted him to know that she loved seeing herself through his eyes, and that she loved the
way he held her . . . touched her . . . lay with
her . . . loved her.

Och, but her heart felt near to bursting with
anguish, and with every faltering step she took,
it felt all the more burdened.

Whose life are ye livin' anyhoo, Meghan Brodie?
she heard Fia's voice ask.

It was so real to her in that moment that she

had to peer over her shoulder to be sure it was not Angus who had spoken to her.

Och, but she *was* going mad!

"Did ye say something tae me?" she asked Angus.

Meghan felt more than saw that he shook his head at her in the darkness—and why had she thought so? She had to wonder, even, if the man had a tongue to speak with.

"I didna think sae," she said peevishly, and returned to walking beside him in silence.

They continued onward without another word spoken between them, and Meghan, clutching at her sore arm, began to consider once more what she would say to her sweet brothers.

Would they be disappointed in her?

She knew they would be, because she had let them down.

Well, she just wouldn't tell them everything. In fact, she would tell them naught at all! All they needed know was that she had snuck away from Lyon. If Lyon came after her, she would deal with that then.

And if he did not . . . Well then, she would keep her secret until the day she joined Fia in her grave. Then she would spill her tears upon Fia's shoulders. Fia was the only one who could possibly understand—the only one who ever had.

Meghan was wholly uncertain what to expect when she arrived home, but the very last thing she expected to discover ... was Alison MacLean.

They arrived at the break of the new day, and Meghan froze at the sight of her friend there within the courtyard, escorted safely home by Baldwin and surrounded by her brothers.

And Lyon Montgomerie was nowhere within sight.

Chapter 26

~~~ ⌒ ⌒ ⌒ ~~~

Lyon sat at his bedside desk, poring over the manuscripts by candlelight until the wee hours of the morn, reading Meghan's notes. He sat there, brooding, his head within his hands, watching the candle burn down to its quick.

He couldn't sleep.

Couldn't think.

Why did things still feel so wrong?

He'd done what he'd thought he was supposed to—set her free. He'd taken Mac-Kinnon's example and had accorded her choices. But now he couldn't forget the look in her eyes as he'd bade her good-bye and walked away, leaving her to Baldwin's care with that look of utter confusion upon her face.

And then the unspoken fury in her crossed eyes as she'd realized he was truly setting her free.

Christ, but what had he done to her?

And how could he simply leave her?

He read her notes once more, drinking in her wisdom, hearing her cheeky voice, seeing her smile as he'd peered down into her face, and slammed his fist down upon the desk. Damned if he could just walk away!

So what the devil was he doing sitting here, brooding like a sullen boy?

When in his bloody life had he wanted something and not gone after it?

Never, that he could recall.

Damned if he was going to this time!

He surged upward from the desk, knocking it over, spilling his manuscripts in his haste to go after her.

He *had* done the right thing, he realized—except for the fact that he'd let her go without telling her what was in his heart.

And it was not too bloody late for that!

Meghan could scarcely believe the anger she felt.

"And he woke ye, took one bluidy look at ye, and *sent* ye off?" she repeated once more, enraged by Alison's tale. She was weary from her long walk home, her arm hurt, and her heart ached all the more! "Ye didna ha' tae e'en ask?"

Alison shook her head, and her own eyes were full of fury for Meghan's sake.

"Bluidy Sassenach bastard!" Colin spat, though he did not understand the half of it.

Meghan clutched at her arm, heartbroken.

"Och, Meghan, here ye gae," Alison said, removing the sling from about her own neck. Hanging it about Meghan's, she helped her to place her arm within it.

She felt like weeping.

She felt like screaming.

She merely stood there, allowing Alison to tend her arm, though her heart felt mortally wounded.

So much for her hopes that he would love her for more than her face.

So much for his love.

Then again, he had never claimed to love her, Meghan reminded herself. He had only said he *wanted* her. And that he *wanted* her heart. Those were far different things from vowing his own love, and that he had not.

Foolish girl, she berated herself.

She held back the tears, telling herself that it was better to learn now, rather than later.

Alison reached out to embrace her. "Noo, noo," she crooned, "dinna cry, Meghan!"

Meghan gulped back a sob, unable to restrain it, and returned Alison's embrace with her good arm.

"Och, but ye look horrid!" Alison said, breaking into tears. "I've never seen ye look sae bad!"

Meghan didn't know whether to laugh or cry. "Ye look horrid, too!" she cried, unable to hold back her sobs any longer. "And ye put yer bruise on the wrong cheek!"

Colin and Leith and Gavin all exchanged awkward glances with each other.

"Daff women," Colin said, shaking his head. "All right noo, Alison. Enough! Let someone else hug her too!" And he moved in to hug Meghan as Alison released her.

She wept upon Colin's shoulder, and then Leith's, and then Gavin's.

"Welcome home, Meghan," Gavin said softly. "We've missed ye, lass!"

"Enough tae spare me yer sermons?" Meghan asked through her tears.

Gavin chuckled. "Weel, that I dunno. We shall see, I suppose."

Meghan choked upon her laughter. " 'Tis guid tae be home," she told him.

" 'Tis guid tae ha' ye home!" Leith said. "Ye're a sight for sore eyes, tae be sure!"

"I am sae sorry!" she said. "I should never ha' risked myself sae."

" 'Tis no' as though ye did sae apurpose, Meghan," Leith replied.

"It's my fault," Colin interjected. "I should never ha' let yet gae alone tae meet Alison."

"How can ye say such a thing, Colin?" she asked him. "It was hardly the first time I'd gone intae those woods alone. What will ye do, silly mon? Escort me everywhere I gae for the rest of our bluidy lives?"

Colin frowned, at a loss for words, and she went on.

"I dinna think sae! I can just imagine what

yer women would say then, ye silly fool."

"Aye," Gavin put in. "Precisely what they should be saying anyway—nay!" He spoke with such heartfelt conviction that Meghan felt at home immediately. One thing everyone could count upon was Gavin's piety in the face of anything at all. He was unswerving in his faith.

Colin cast Gavin a pained glance, and Meghan laughed, telling him, "Dinna say such a thing, Gavin. He will die elsewise."

Leith and Colin both chuckled and so too did Alison.

"And Meghan," Leith continued, "I've something tae tell ye . . ."

Meghan looked up at her eldest brother to see that he had moved behind Alison, and she suddenly recalled her friend's message.

"Oh! And I ye!" she exclaimed. "Alison asked me tae tell ye, Leith, that no' only does she wed ye, but she weds ye wi' all her heart!"

Leith peered down at Alison in surprise. "Is this true?" he asked her, his hands going to her shoulders. He turned her to face him.

Alison smiled shyly up at him, and Meghan was so happy for the two of them—so happy she could cry! With a heartbroken sob, she cast herself between them. Alison took her once more into her arms.

"Bluidy, rotten, heart-stealing, lying, conniving Sassenach wretch!" Meghan cried out. "I'm sae happy for ye, Alison!"

"Och, noo!" Alison said, patting Meghan's back, soothing her. "I knoo ye are, Meghan! Just think . . . we're going tae be sisters noo, in truth!" she said cheerily.

"I'm *sae* happy!" Meghan exclaimed, and wept as though her heart would rent in twain.

"Alison," Colin said, his tone contrite. Alison turned to look at him, continuing to pat Meghan's back. "Thank ye for risking yerself for Meghan," he said. "That was a brave thing for ye tae do, lass. We owe ye a lot for it."

Alison smiled brightly at him. "Ye owe me naught for that, Colin Mac Brodie! But thank ye anyhoo!"

"Och, noo who could that be?" Leith said suddenly.

Meghan was so busy weeping, burying her face against Alison's shoulder, that she didn't see the approaching riders, nor did she hear them, until Colin exploded with anger.

"Gaddamn him!" her brother said.

"How dare he show his face here!" Leith said angrily. "English bastard!"

"It's bluidy Montgomerie!" Gavin said.

Meghan froze.

She peered up to see Lyon and his men approaching quickly.

Seated high atop his destrier, with his golden hair flowing behind him, he rode toward them, his look wrathful and full of purpose.

"Och, God!" Meghan exclaimed, coming to

life as her brothers drew their swords and went to greet him. She seized Alison by the arm. "I canna face him, Alison. Come wi' me!"

And she dragged Alison toward the chapel.

Chapter 27

He didn't bother to deal with her brothers.

Meghan knew he must have spied her, for the rumbling of hooves reverberated throughout the sanctuary as he reined in before the chapel doors. His voice was an echo within the stone building as he commanded his men to remain and guard the door.

Meghan heard her brothers' furious voices beyond the chapel doors. Threats passed between the men, and she prayed they'd not come to arms.

"I merely wish to speak with her," Lyon assured her angry brothers. "And I shall go once I have said my piece."

Meghan scarcely had time to return the sling to Alison and to replace her veil. No sooner had she hid herself behind a pew when Lyon came bursting into the chapel.

Meghan gasped at the sight of him and lay down on the floor upon her belly in a desperate attempt to conceal herself from his view.

She couldn't face him just now! Couldn't look into his eyes!

And she bloody well didn't care what he had to say—didn't wish to hear a word of it!

"Meghan!" His voice thundered within the tiny chapel. It bounced off the walls and beat against her heart. Her heart racing madly, she shimmied beneath the pew, desperate to conceal herself from his eyes.

Watching breathlessly as he approached Alison, his stride full of purpose and his expression stern with determination, she shuddered at the sight of him. He wore the same tunic and braies he'd worn yesterday, with the plaid belted at his waist, and his eyes seemed to glitter like the blue of a hot flame.

Och, but he was beautiful—beautiful but treacherous to her defenseless heart, for her arms cried out to hold him still, despite his falseness.

"Meghan," he said with feeling, taking Alison by the shoulders and turning her about to face him.

The breath left her lungs as Alison cried out softly. Meghan felt ashamed for putting her friend once more in such an untenable position. And yet she just wasn't brave enough to confront him herself.

He fell to his knees before Alison, and Meghan blinked in surprise as he took her gently by the hand.

"I read your notes upon my papers," he disclosed, "and sent you away because I thought it was the right thing to do. Forgive me, Meghan!"

Alison remained silent, and Meghan bit her lower lip to keep from crying out that he was a lowly bastard, and that she would never forgive him—not ever!

Did he want her absolution now for being such a shallow-minded knave?

"You see," he continued, "you were right! I *have* been searching all my life for something I should have discovered within my own self long ago. And it took you, Meghan Brodie, to open my eyes!"

And a fine way he had of showing his appreciation, Meghan thought.

"Can you ever forgive me?" he entreated.

Never!

Alison stood frozen, staring down at him, and Meghan knew she was afraid to speak. Not Meghan! If she were standing there before him, she thought she would rear back and slap his much-too-bonnie face!

"Meghan," he said, staring up at Alison's veiled face. He shook his head. "All those years I searched for contentment in the arms of so many women . . ."

Meghan felt nigh to bursting with outrage at that.

How dare he remind her of such a thing just now!

How dare he rub salt into her wounds!

"And I never found it," he confessed. "Not until you," he swore, and Meghan blinked in confusion.

Me? she thought, and mouthed the word, stunned by his revelation.

Me?

"Aye," he answered, as though she'd spoken the question aloud. "Not until you!" he repeated, and then said, "Do not look so surprised, my love."

My love?

Shock reverberated through her as surely as his voice echoed within the church walls. Meghan's heart pummeled her ribs as she lay there upon the cold wood floor, listening to his confession.

"I love you, Meghan Brodie," he declared fiercely. "I love you from the very depths of my soul!"

Meghan's heart tripped a painful beat. Tears welled in her eyes, and a sob caught in her throat.

"Ye do?" she thought she'd asked, but it was Alison's voice that echoed through the chapel and not hers. She couldn't have spoken in that instant had she tried.

"Aye!" he answered with feeling. "I do not give a bloody damn what you look like! You could have warts upon your eyelids and hair upon your chin! You are my precious gift," he told her. "And your heart is more precious to me than gold! And your smile," he continued, "makes my heart sing. And your words . . . I wait with bated breath but to hear them. And your eyes . . . I would give the sparkle from every jewel I own simply to see its glitter for even a single day more! And your wisdom . . . I love you, Meghan Brodie! And if you will have me, I would be honored to have you for my wife. And I swear that I will love and adore you until the day I last close my eyes!"

Meghan's heart blossomed with joy. Tears slid unchecked down her cheeks. She could scarcely believe her ears.

She held her breath, watching Alison and him together. The sight of him kneeling before her, pouring out his heart to her, was the most romantic thing she had ever beheld in all her life. It was the sort of thing troubadours sang of and bards wove their tales over. And his words were all for her—and she was hiding under a bloody rotten pew! *Och!* she thought. *Say something, Alison!*

Tell him I love him too!

His blood pumping like fire through his veins, Lyon held his breath and waited for Meghan to respond. But she simply stood there, staring down at him as though he were a viper curled before her feet.

And then he happened to note the hand he held within his own, and his brows drew together in confusion. It was her left hand, not her right he held. And yet she had injured her left arm. How could it be that he was holding it now?

He peered up into her face.

Her crossed eyes gazed down at him in confusion and in fear. And his frown deepened as he noted once more that her bruise was on her left cheek and not the right. Where had it been last night when he'd sent her away? He'd been so weary and so preoccupied with his guilty conscience that he hadn't taken the time to consider what it meant. But now that he did, he was more than certain she had injured her right cheek, and not her left . . .

And then his gaze fell once more to the hand he held, for he knew without a bloody doubt that it was her left hand she had injured and that was precisely the hand which he held within his own just now.

Something was definitely not right here.

He released her hand and stood, his body taut with growing suspicion, and stared into her face, his anger mounting.

The silence within the chapel was a roar in his ears.

His heart sank as he studied her eyes . . . They were familiar to him, certain enough, but though they were the same color, they were *not* Meghan Brodie's eyes.

Bloody hell!

He ripped off the veil and was at first startled at the face that peered back at him.

And then his face hardened with fury.

"I see I have been played for a fool," he said tautly, and nothing more.

Meghan thought she would weep at the look upon his face as he turned to go.

Tears coursing down her cheeks, she tried to crawl out from under the pew, but with her injured arm she was not fast enough.

"Nay!" she cried out. "Wait!"

He stopped and turned to face her, but didn't see her, and Meghan waved from under the pew.

"Wait!" she exclaimed, wriggling as fast as she could out from under her wooden prison.

He saw her at last, and his expression was wholly unreadable for an instant as he stared down at her. Meghan stilled, her heart thumping wildly. She held her breath, lest he spit down upon the floor in disgust and leave her before she could chance to speak her mind.

"I do love ye!" she cried out. "I do!" And she muttered an oath in sheer frustration. "But I am stuck beneath this bluidy pew! Help me oot!"

"You do?" he asked, and came to her at once.

"I do!" she swore, and was vaguely aware that Alison stole away, leaving them alone to speak.

"Christ, woman, what the devil are you doing beneath there?"

"Och! Ye daff mon!" she said. "I was hiding, o' course!"

He dragged her out and took her into his arms, kissing her lips fiercely.

"Ah, Meghan," he said. "Come home with me, my love?"

Meghan wrapped her good arm about his neck. "Aye," she answered. "I want tae gae!"

That was all Lyon needed to hear.

He lifted her up into his arms and carried her out of the chapel, commanding his men to get out of his way.

Her brothers all shouted warnings, fought to reach her, swords drawn.

"Let her gae!" Leith demanded of him.

"Not a bloody chance!" Lyon refused them.

"Bastard!" Colin shouted, and Meghan laughed.

" 'Tis all right!" she told them, announcing to one and all, " 'Cause I'm going tae wed the bluidy bastard, after all!"

Her brothers fell silent. They stared at one another in shock.

Lyon chuckled at her choice of words, but didn't feel the least bit offended by them, and this time, as he stole his wife away from her brothers, she filled his ears with laughter and his heart with joy.

"Ah, Meghan!" he whispered. "You're going to make me a very happy man!" David had not lied to him after all, it occurred to him as he looked back at the chapel, remembering the childhood promise. He'd found happiness and then had it all but handed to him upon a silver plate.

"As ye will me," Meghan assured him. "As ye already ha'."

And so he had.

And so she did.

Avon Romantic Treasures

*Unforgettable, enthralling love stories,
sparkling with passion and adventure
from Romance's bestselling authors*

LADY OF WINTER *by Emma Merritt*
77985-4/$5.99 US/$7.99 Can

SILVER MOON SONG *by Genell Dellin*
78602-8/$5.99 US/$7.99 Can

FIRE HAWK'S BRIDE *by Judith E. French*
78745-8/$5.99 US/$7.99 Can

WANTED ACROSS TIME *by Eugenia Riley*
78909-4/$5.99 US/$7.99 Can

EVERYTHING AND THE MOON *by Julia Quinn*
78933-7/$5.99 US/$7.99 Can

BEAST *by Judith Ivory*
78644-3/$5.99 US/$7.99 Can

HIS FORBIDDEN TOUCH *by Shelley Thacker*
78120-4/$5.99 US/$7.99 Can

LYON'S GIFT *by Tanya Anne Crosby*
78571-4/$5.99 US/$7.99 Can

Buy these books at your local bookstore or use this coupon for ordering:

Mail to: Avon Books, Dept BP, Box 767, Rte 2, Dresden, TN 38225   F
Please send me the book(s) I have checked above.
❑ My check or money order—no cash or CODs please—for $_____ is enclosed (please
add $1.50 per order to cover postage and handling—Canadian residents add 7% GST).
❑ Charge my VISA/MC Acct#_____Exp Date_____
Minimum credit card order is two books or $7.50 (please add postage and handling
charge of $1.50 per order—Canadian residents add 7% GST). For faster service, call
1-800-762-0779. Prices and numbers are subject to change without notice. Please allow six to
eight weeks for delivery.

Name_____
Address_____
City_____State/Zip_____
Telephone No._____   RT 0397

Avon Romances—
the best in exceptional authors and unforgettable novels!

Discover Contemporary Romances at Their Sizzling Hot Best from Avon Books

RYAN'S RETURN   *by Barbara Freethy*
78531-5/$5.99 US/$7.99 Can

CATCH ME IF YOU CAN   *by Jillian Karr*
77876-9/$5.99 US/$7.99 Can

WINNING WAYS   *by Barbara Boswell*
72743-9/$5.99 US/$7.99 Can

CARRIED AWAY   *by Sue Civil-Brown*
72774-9/$5.99 US/$7.99 Can

LOVE IN A SMALL TOWN   *by Curtiss Ann Matlock*
78107-7/$5.99 US/$7.99 Can

HEAVEN KNOWS BEST   *by Nikki Holiday*
78797-0/$5.99 US/$7.99 Can

FOREVER ENCHANTED   *by Maggie Shayne*
78746-6/$5.99 US/$7.99 Can